RAVEN

GHOST MOUNTAIN WOLF SHIFTERS BOOK 4

AUDREY FAYE

FALLON

My bird squawks as her feathers catch on the tight squeeze. It's a deeply felt protest, but a silent one. She's smart enough not to protest audibly when there's a polar bear snoring in the next room.

At least I hope he's in the next room. I didn't have time to do proper reconnaissance this trip. Reilly needs me for a video shoot and Dorie wants to bring the school kids to one of my secret streams to collect pretty rocks and the business of being a three-week-old baby pack is generally taking over my life.

Which I can't complain about, because Brandy's nightmares stopped two days after we got our new tents and moved the nightly sleeping pile into one of them. She might have lived in the forest for the last six years, but something inside her is still comforted by the trappings of home and den, even if the actual den is full of things she can't handle anymore.

I shake my head. Wrong word. Things she can't handle *yet*. The baby packs are temporary. Stepping stones to help wolves make their way back to home and den and the unified sense of pack that they all need to feel whole. We're one of the healthier baby packs. Less broken. Readying to be an example and live in the light.

Some of us, anyhow.

I frown into the dark. I need to focus. Getting my ass caught by a polar bear while sneaking into his den won't help Brandy's nightmares at all.

I hop across a small, dusty stretch of gravel to the opening that will take me out of this rough passageway through six feet of rock. The rocks scratch uncomfortably against my tightly wrapped wings. I apologize to my bird for all the yummy food I've been eating lately. I'm not a cookie fiend like the rest of my baby pack, but I've got a deep weakness for Shelley's roasted-nut mixes, the spicier the better.

My bird says a lot of unfriendly things inside my head that basically boil down to ravens shouldn't like wasabi and they don't belong in stupid holes in stupid rocks, either. Which is all true, but this particular hole is the only way into Ivan's den.

I heave a very quiet sigh of relief as my tail feathers exit the jagged triangular crevice without getting snagged on anything else. My bird is unreasonably proud of them, and she's already cranky because rocks are cold and the caves I had to fly through to get to this sad excuse for a way in were even colder, and it's supposed to be freaking summer up here. The very end of it, which is why I'm here. I need to get this job done before the seasons turn. Even if I could convince my bird to freeze, black ravens do not belong anywhere near snow-covered landscapes, even in the dead of night.

Not when we're actively pissing off polar bears, anyhow.

Ivan is still snoring, but he won't necessarily stay that way. I do not want him to wake up. I saw him when he came to pick up Eamon. It's not the cute, cuddly bears who volunteer to be parole officers for the bad guys of the shifter world.

My bird shivers, and it's not with fear. When we flew up here, I made sure we kept far away from the ramshackle shed where Eamon is supposedly holed up. She hates every bone of his body, and I don't trust her not to do something really dumb.

She caws wryly.

Fine. Something dumber than breaking into a polar bear's den.

She subsides back into the fulsome silence that's mostly been my companion on this journey.

I angle my beak and straighten a ruffled feather. It's not the breaking and entering that's making her crazy. It's the fact that we're returning a shiny to the polar bear. Three of them, in fact.

Sadly for her, she has to share a brain with a human who has ethics that don't always play nice with raven instincts. Former street kids don't have a whole lot of moral constants, but not stealing from friends is one of them, and the very scary man making sure Eamon never hurts my pack again absolutely qualifies. Which means he's getting his shinies back and my raven is just going to have to deal.

I hop off the high bookcase I entered on and shift as I fall, hoping Ivan hasn't changed his furniture setup since the last time I was here. Relief streams through me, quick and bright, as my feet land on a rug thick enough to muffle the sounds of a rhino landing.

My bird frets. There's nothing like standing on a thick pelt of fur to remind her that we're invading the den of an apex predator.

I sigh. Ivan probably wouldn't eat me. Hopefully he still has indigestion from eating Eamon's tail.

My bird informs me that it was his daughter who ate the evil wolf's tail.

I don't argue. Unlike me, she never forgets anything. I do tell her to focus and remember something useful, like where Ivan kept all his tripping hazards. The inside of a granite cave is freaking dark, and smart thieves try to avoid faceplanting in the middle of a job. Then again, a smart thief would just leave the damn shinies on top of the bookshelf and hope Ivan finds them someday and blames vodka-induced stupidity for misplacing them, or something.

Except I don't think Ivan actually drinks all that much vodka. He just collects it. Every kind in the world that has a bear on its label, or anything that looks like food. Which is a disturbingly wide swath of the animal kingdom, including artistic renditions of several of my wild relations.

My feet find the edge of the rug, which is menacing in both its width and depth. I brush my toes in a delicate fan, seeking the direction of the cracks in the wide-plank floors. I've got an infallible sense of direction outside, and I think I know the way to the middle of his living room, but when the world grants you big lines in the floor to double-check your instincts, a smart raven uses them.

The lines verify what I already knew. I step onto the wood floor with both feet and hold my breath. Fortunately, it doesn't register my presence. Early fall is a good season for that. Spring makes everything creak more, and bears have an inordinate fondness for things made of wood.

I take three steps forward and two left, finding the curving wall that should get me to where I'm headed. My fingers skim a painting that wasn't there the last time I visited, which ratchets my focus higher, fast. Bears don't tend to change things quickly, especially one as arrogant and sure of himself as Ivan, but all it takes is one change I don't notice to turn me into a bear snack.

A cold draft from the far side of the room slides over my skin. I try not to shiver. My human feels particularly vulnerable creeping around naked, but it's a long flight to get here, and I couldn't carry clothes and the clunky, heavy coins. Since the point of this little excursion was to get the coins to this particular stretch of frozen tundra, that means I get to sneak around a bear's den in my birthday suit.

I reach for the pouch hanging over my breastbone. It holds the coins, carefully padded with moss so they don't clink. They're shinier than when I stole them four years ago, which isn't my fault. The collector I sold them to polished them, which is a sin second only to melting them down. A fact I tried to point out when I bought them back, hoping it might make the price look less like highway robbery, but it didn't get me far.

My bird squawks. She had to give up a lot of pretties to get the coins back.

I sigh. It was more complicated than a straight trade, but she doesn't understand online selling, thank goodness. And it was the right thing to do. Ivan is protecting my pack in a way that he probably doesn't even fully understand because he's never been small and scared and weak. But I do.

I tiptoe another two steps in the dark.

Almost there.

HAYDEN

Bears.

I know Reilly's just a small one, relatively speaking, but they always seem to take up more space in a pack than they actually occupy. I look over at the green-eyed wolf who's helping me sort school supplies, and shake my head. "Is there anything Reilly isn't getting for his birthday?"

Lissa scans the huddled conversations happening in three different corners of the den and laughs. "It's a good excuse to spoil everyone a little."

The grocery list Shelley made for his birthday feast could spoil a small country for a year. "Ebony said every baby pack is sending at least one member."

The gladness hits Lissa's eyes with a force that still makes my heart stutter. "I know."

I scowl for form. "Even the cats are coming." A small contingent, which apparently took a minor act of God, Reese pulling alpha rank, and Sierra and Sienna promising to deliver a birthday video which has reportedly taken on the scale of a Bollywood dance production.

Lissa leans in and rubs her cheek against mine. "He's a really well-loved bear."

My wolf wants to lay his head in her lap and never leave. Something he tries on a regular basis, because she knows how to find that itchy spot behind his left ear better than anyone. He's never pleased to discover that there's actual work to be done. Especially when it involves incomprehensible things like sorting through writing implements and rulers and five kinds of paper.

I pull another package out of the box that Rio somehow managed to wedge in his truck along with half a continent's worth of groceries. "They didn't make pink pencils when I was a kid."

"Face it, you're getting old." Kel drops down beside us and hands Lissa a crinkled sheet of paper. "I vetoed all party ideas involving explosives. For the rest, you're on your own."

She laughs and nuzzles his cheek, too, an easy affection his wolf soaks up like water. "Big, tough beta."

He snorts. "They want to do a honey taste test. Blindfolded."

They both look at me, like I somehow turned into an alpha who would ruin good, innocent fun.

I shrug. "We can rig up a shower outside the kitchen to hose people down." The stream is getting cold, which doesn't bother bears or most wolves, but cats are more finicky creatures, especially if they have honey in their fur, and so is our resident raven.

Who I haven't seen for a couple of days. My wolf tilts his head, scenting. "Have either of you seen Fallon recently?"

They both pick up on the shiver that runs through my fur. It happens fairly regularly these days, some kind of unreliable but fairly sensitive pack radar, and one of the stranger side effects of Kennedy's gravity beams.

Lissa frowns. "Not since Saturday, but her pack is in far orbit."

That hasn't stopped them from sending frequent emissaries, but maybe that's easing off now that we have the baby packs mostly stocked up. Or she's gone on a flyabout. Which isn't unusual for a raven, especially one who knows all the secret places for finding some of our suddenly popular trade goods. Her baby pack has spent the last couple of weeks making shifters all over the continent drool. Pretty rocks, semiprecious stones, healer teas, and a handful of fossils that made a coyote pack in Manitoba nearly lose their minds.

Kel lays a hand on my arm. "Want me to go check on her?"

Nobody trusts gut instincts more than he does, but this one is hazy enough that I don't think it's worth pulling him away from his other work. "No. You can keep sorting birthday logistics." Reilly's birthday has somehow sprawled over several days and several locations, and I'm probably not in the loop on all of them.

Kel mostly manages to hide a grimace.

Lissa laughs. "It will be over in a few days."

He snorts. "There's Jade after that, and then Kelsey and Stinky in November, and that's not even looking at the adults."

She nuzzles his wolf again. "The adults just get a special dinner, and most of us combine ours together. We only make a big deal for the pups."

Shelley's chart has at least two special dinners a month, and she wouldn't budge a millimeter on feeding them to every shifter in our pack. Which means I delivered soufflés and strawberries out to the far orbits just a few days ago. Dorie wouldn't tell us how old she is, but she put in her dinner order like a boss.

She also announced that her baby pack is moving inside the old inner perimeter. They'll stay in their tents still, but with school starting, she wants the youngsters to be able to roam freely back and forth between her base camp and the den.

Which is a nice, reasonable excuse to move a bunch of knitters and teenagers one large step closer to home. They aren't all sitting easy with that, but Dorie runs her baby pack with a combination of gruff love and snark that only a cat could pull off, and the wolves of the den are doing everything they can to assist her. That assistance mostly seems to involve cookies, pranks, and naked toddlers who never know where they left their clothes. My wolf is really glad perimeter security isn't his job.

Lissa pulls out a box of pens and sets them neatly next to the pink pencils. They're lime green. Reilly will love them.

I look up as the bear in question runs over, the pack sat phone in his hand. He slides to a stop, a little breathless. "It's a raven named Martha. She was looking for Ebony, but I can't find her and this sounds kind of important."

I reach for the phone and catch my first glimpse of the older woman on the other end of the video call. She's got a wry look in her eyes, and she's casting a fond glance Reilly's way. "You did well, young man, thank you. And you're exactly right. I'm calling on an important matter, but not a worrisome one."

Reilly breathes out a sigh of relief and charges off again, a bear with responsibilities.

The raven on my screen chuckles. "I look forward to meeting your youngsters. I'm Martha Lee, beta over here in Desolation Inlet. I know your Myrna from way back."

"I'm Hayden Scott, which I suspect you already know."

She nods slightly, and the warmth stays in her eyes. "I do. Your pack speaks well of you."

I grin. "I bribe them well."

She laughs, a bright sound that reminds me of my grandmother. "You've a knack for bribing birds as well. We got our first delivery of trade goods from your pack. You've made some ravens very happy."

Some wolves, too. I can't keep up with all the things we're apparently using for barter. I only know the tendrils of quiet, astonished pleasure it's extending into even the farthest reaches of our pack. "Good. How can I help you? I presume that if you were looking for Ebony, this is an official call."

A nod. "It is. My alpha would like to bring a small group for a visit."

It's not a surprising request. The cat alpha has already brokered informal introductions, and more connections are springing up every day. "We would welcome that."

"Excellent. I hear that you have a birthday party happening this week, so perhaps we can set something up for after that."

Like all good betas, she clearly has her ear to the ground. And no problem with serious pack business taking a backseat to stoking a bear cub's joy. Which means we're going to get along just fine.

Lissa slides in under my arm and smiles at the woman on the screen. "The game you sent for Reilly is wonderful. Myrna showed me how to play it last night."

I saw the game—a board with two rows of shallow holes, pretty stones, and enough strategy to have Lissa's eyes crossing. "I didn't realize that came from your flock. Thank you."

Martha laughs. "It breaks my brain, but Myrna was quite good at it once upon a time, and we thought your young bear might like it." A pause. "Perhaps your raven as well. We're eager to meet her."

There are layers in her words. Welcome. Dismay. Regret. My wolf cocks his head.

"We were more insular eight years ago," she says quietly. "We didn't know she had joined your pack. Perhaps if we had known, we might have helped."

The niggling connected to Fallon twinges again. Inviting the ravens to visit is a good, solid step. But I'm also going to send an emissary out to the far orbits to pay her a visit. Just in case those niggles are connected to something bigger.

IVAN

I stare at the three coins on my coffee table.

They're shiny. Some heathen has polished them, cleaning off six hundred years of history like so much dust. My bear would roar for that alone. It wasn't valuable dust, but it was mine. It was story. It was history.

I move closer. They are the same three that were taken, not some shiny imposters. I can see the nick in the first, put there by Johanna's cub.

Some history isn't so easily polished away.

My bear reaches out, oddly tentative. They are coins of little value. Pennies of a bygone age, worth perhaps a three or four hundred dollars each in an honest market, less in a dishonest one. But they were my first. The beginnings of my collection, and it left a hole when they were gone.

I pick up the first of the coins, brushing my thumb over the roughly textured bear on its surface. It's a placid black bear, the first of our cousins to willingly share their land with humans and the first to suffer for it.

The middle coin is the one that shows most clearly how humans see us. Growling monsters of big teeth and bigger claws. As it should be. We are predators. Fear is a tool, just like any other.

It is the last coin, however, that I felt the lack of most. I pick her up carefully, with appropriate reverence. She's not a bear of tooth and claw, or one of quiet eyes. She is somehow both of those and everything more, regal and fierce and demanding the respect of all who gaze upon her.

She has always had mine.

I lay the three coins across my palm. I seek, on my best days, to be all of them. Much of the time I fail, but there is worthy endeavor merely in the seeking.

My bear mutters.

I chuckle into the quiet of my den. I know better than to philosophize before consuming the gallon of coffee it takes to put him in a good mood. And the coffee will be necessary. There are many unanswered questions to think on.

Starting with why my den smells faintly of bird.

2

BEN

I squint up at the sky for the third time in as many minutes and sigh when there are no dots of black in the unrelenting blue.

An elbow digs into my side, none too gently. "She'll be back soon enough. Enjoy the sunshine while we have it. Winter's coming."

Brown hates all the seasons equally, and his black bear meets them all with the same equanimity. My wolf tries, but his mate makes that more difficult. Fallon isn't fond of the cold, and she's even less fond of the snow that makes her stand out like a sore thumb. The hazards of deciding to love a wolf who lives three hours inland from the nearest shifter ravens.

I grab my wolf before he gets all melancholy about that. Moving here cost her more than I ever would have dreamed, but she refuses to allow me to wallow over her sacrifices, and Brown will be more than happy to enforce the no-wallowing rule in her absence. For good reason—Brandy's wolf gets less stable when I brood.

I look over at our two fancy new canvas tents, set up on boards neatly hewn by Eliza's chainsaw and hammered into platforms by Brown and Mikayla and Hoot. It didn't take them much more than a couple of hours to entirely reshape our little corner of the world, and while my wolf thinks it's strange not to feel the earth below him as he sleeps, even he can appreciate the warmth the platforms will bring in winter.

And the ease they bring my big sister. Brandy is napping in one right now, her tail hanging out the unzipped opening.

Brown scowls at a wolf who's wide awake. "Don't you be burning my lunch."

Mikayla glances up from her careful focus on the contents of her frying pan and grins. "I burned Ben's, not yours."

I snort. I'll eat anything and they all know it, but the chances that she's burned anyone's lunch are vanishingly small. She was a mediocre cook just like the rest of us when meals were made from whatever we could scrounge, but she took one look at the new groceries that started arriving at our new base camp three weeks back and marched herself to the den to get lessons.

Which means we're probably getting something fancy and delicious for lunch. I try not to drool. We have work to do first, and I have a mate I need to wish all the way home.

My wolf sighs. He had no idea choosing a mate with wings would be this complicated.

I try not to laugh at him. Fallon didn't give him enough time to do the choosing. She took one look at us as she flew overhead and decided we were shiny and that was the end of that. Which I've had so very many days to regret, but never on my own behalf. She loves me with a fierceness that has no end, even when I might wish otherwise.

"You're sagging."

I look down at the board in my hands. It's still right on the mark Brown made with a carpenter's pencil that's older than I am. "Nope. Right place."

"Don't tell me how to build, dammit. Snick it up a bit or this thing will leak worse than a new mama's tits."

I shake my head wryly. Bringing Brown into this century is a work in progress. I also snick the board up a little. He's never wrong about what's needed to build something strong and true. Which is a skill that didn't get much use over the last six years. We were trying too hard to stay hidden. "You sure this is a good idea?"

He snorts. "Wrinkles said it to get it done and Hoot agreed. I just take orders, same as you."

I hide a grin. Wrinkles isn't a particularly bossy wolf, but her human more than makes up for her animal, and she's been on a rampage since the baby packs got formed. A really good one. Her latest brainwave is a cooking shack, something that will be a distant cousin to a wood-fired oven and take a lot less fuel to keep us fed. It will also keep the cooks and whatever we forage in the woods dry.

Brown's job is to build it so that it doesn't leak. Mine is to be extra hands. Nobody gives me a hammer on purpose.

I hold the board in place while he backs up and grunts. "You spending the night or heading back to yours?" Their base camp is a couple of miles away. Just the two of them, because Brown is a cranky bastard who can't hang around anyone for long, and Wrinkles somehow manages to put up with him. But anyone with half a brain could see Kennedy's writing on the wall. Brown is going to have to work darn hard if he intends to stay a recluse.

He shrugs. "We'll see what's for dinner. My bear has a hankering for some good grub."

I don't miss Mikayla's quick smile. There will be something good for dinner. I lift the next board into place, or as close as I dare without Brown's prior approval. "Mik, want us to catch some fish to go with whatever you're making?"

She shakes her head. "I helped Shelley make a marinade for that beef you traded for. She wants more, by the way. And she says you're a bad man for not telling her your source."

My trading partners aren't as eclectic as Brown's or as flaming dangerous as Fallon's, but they make hermits look positively chatty. The small human pack that herds cows in the deep woods, along with growing some interesting plant life, appreciates me warning off some of the local wildlife that eats their crops, but that only earns me about three words most visits. And payment from their garden or fields or chicken coop. It's one of the alternative ways to hunt that my wolf worked out when his new mate turned green every time he chased a deer.

The beef will be a nice treat. It wasn't a smell we risked very often these last years.

I smile at Mikayla. I wasn't sure about Kennedy assigning one of Dorie's young adults to our baby pack, but she's less shy about connecting with the den than the rest of us, she's good for Brandy and incredibly useful around camp, and she can go toe to toe with Brown any day of the week. "We keep our sources secret, you know that." She might be new to our trading gig, but she's catching on fast.

She snorts. "You're a strange, paranoid man, Benjamin Dunn." She opens up one of the large, bear-proof canisters that Brown has deemed adequate for food storage, and consults the contents of our larder. "You want rice with the beef, or potatoes?"

I'm never ready. They're such simple sentences, and always, they come out of nowhere and plant a fist in my gut. I close my eyes, trying to get a grip. It's good that we have food in abundance now. Eventually I'll forget how often I watched packmates with hungry eyes, wishing furiously that I could offer them something decent to eat. Or how often Fallon took stupid risks so that we could.

Brown leans into my shoulder and covers the show of

support by growling at the board I'm holding. "You build like a guy I used to work with. He downed half a bottle of whiskey before work every day."

Mikayla giggles. "Okay, rice it is. I'm also making spicy green beans, and if you complain, I'll feed your share of the beef to Hoot when she stops by."

That last is directed at Brown, who managed to avoid all green vegetables for the last six years and is not pleased that he can't insist on saving them for the pups anymore. I move the board a little so that he's got something else to distract him, and wink at Mik. "Growing wolves need to eat." Hoot might not be very big, but she eats like a giant.

Brown hammers extra loudly and ignores us.

The red-gold tail that was hanging out of the tent door vanishes, and Brandy's head appears a moment later. She blinks sleepily until her eyes clear. "Hey. How long did I sleep? Is Fallon back yet?"

I answer the last question first. "No. She'll be back soon."

My older sister's brow creases. "She should be back by now."

I walk over to the tent and sit down on the edge of the platform. Brandy slides into a flannel shirt, which makes my heart glad. Her anxiety is easier to manage in wolf form, but no one should have to retreat to their fur just to stay sane. "Want to help Brown build the cook shack?"

She shoots me a wry grin. "Why, did he fire you?"

He snorts. "I was just getting around to it. Get over

here. I could use an extra set of hands that knows up from down."

Brandy's eyes haze in that way they do when she's measuring her internal fortitude. I wait patiently. We're pack. We want what she can comfortably give and not a damn drop more. "Nope. I'm going to eat whatever smells so ridiculously good, and then I'm taking Mikayla gold-hunting. It's time she started pulling her weight around here."

Mikayla does nothing but pull her weight, but her eyes light up. "Gold? Really?"

It's a really thoughtful thing for Brandy to do, and a great idea. We scrupulously avoided conspicuous trade goods during Samuel's reign of terror, but now they're in hot demand on ShifterNet, and Brandy is excellent at finding the mountain rivulets that toss out rare metals. She'll enjoy sharing some of her knowledge, and Mikayla's easy, cheerful company will help keep Brandy steady while they hunt.

Freedom, in so many small, precious varieties.

I shake my head at Brown so that I don't get pulled into brooding about wolves we can't set free. "Ravens, all of them."

Brandy snickers. "Just because Brown thinks gold is a useless metal doesn't mean it's true."

He grunts, but I can see his eyes. He's enjoying light, happy Brandy just as much as I am. "Darn useless, it is. Too damn soft to be good for anything."

She comes over and wraps her arm around his waist.

"Wrinkles might like something made from the gold. Or Reilly. Most bears like pretty things."

Another grunt. "Wrinkles is all the pretty I need."

Both women melt where they stand. I roll my eyes, because someone has to keep this from turning into a disaster. "You're such a romantic, Brown."

He shoots me the kind of glare you never want to see from a black bear holding a hammer.

I grin. "You can give me lessons later. Fallon might appreciate me upping my game."

He snorts. "She's gone over you. Has been forever. Flowery words won't change that."

She still deserves them. I look up at the sky again, and this time, my heart finally spies what it's been seeking all morning.

My mate is coming home.

FALLON

I can see them, their heads tilted up, watching me ride the friendly thermals that are carrying me back to camp. It's been an easy flight, with fair skies and warm winds and no clunky coins to throw my raven off kilter—but their faces do. I'm used to sneaking in at night, picking a different flight path each time, landing miles from where my mate is and waiting for him to find me so we don't lead harm to our door.

Before Ben, it was friends waiting and grimy streets, but the sneaking was the same.

Flying right into camp in broad daylight to a warm welcome and what looks like a platter of sandwiches and apple slices makes the discomfort that's been growing in me for three weeks throb. My pack is walking out of the shadows so freaking fast, and I have no idea how to live in the light.

My raven caws happily, ignoring my muttering. She likes apples.

Mikayla tips back her head and howls a welcome. Another one comes from off to my left. Wrinkles, picking rocks, most likely. Her favorite stream for pretty stones is over that way, and she's got a big new order to fill. No trace of Reuben, but we're still trying to convince him that he's ours.

I drop out of my thermal and let the cooler air carry me into the trees. Out of sight of my baby pack, but that won't stop Ben. His wolf has no trouble tracking my scent, even when it's several hundred feet over his head. Which doesn't conform to any of the known laws of science, but it's been one of our core truths ever since the day I flew over an unfamiliar ridge and my heart tumbled out of my ribs and landed on an unsuspecting wolf.

He isn't unsuspecting this time. I shift as I fall the last few feet, letting him catch me in warm, strong arms. I wrap mine around his neck. "Hey, beautiful. What brings you to my forest?"

He chuckles. "Are you going to keep stealing my line forever?"

It was his line—the first thing he ever said to me, and the first inkling I had that maybe my wayward heart wasn't a complete idiot. "Probably."

He nuzzles my cheek, which my bird has learned to interpret as affection, even if it ruffles her feathers. "Everything go all right?"

I nod and cuddle into his shoulder. I know that he needs it. He didn't want me to do this job. It was too scattered. Too rushed. Not enough planning.

Which is all truth, but I did it anyhow. I'd been going slowly, thinking I had time, but then things changed so fast. One day we were quiet, nearly invisible cogs in the shadow pack's machinery. The ones who knew people and could always find something to trade for a little food. The next day we were a baby pack with regular grocery deliveries and den responsibilities and people dropping by every darn hour of the day.

I have no idea how to have a life with grocery deliveries in it. But I'm trying to deal, because the day it happened, every last wolf in my baby pack steadied.

Ben strokes my hair. "Shh. You're thinking way too hard."

He knows I'm having trouble coping. I'm trying hard not to lay that on him, because he's already got so much to carry, and he's never held it against me that I have no idea how to be a normal shifter. "I'm good. I made it in and back out with no troubles."

He exhales by my ear, soft and fierce. He hates it when I do this, and he hates it even more that I wouldn't just put the shiny coins in a box and mail them to Ivan.

But he trusts me to know what I need, even when it makes his wolf crazy.

That's the best kind of love there is, right there.

I slide into the leggings and sweater he brought for me. Nobody else is wearing their woolies yet, but my bird gets cold easily, and she just spent fourteen hours flying over semi-frozen tundra. I snuggle into the oversized sweater. It smells like him, which doesn't matter a fig to my raven, but my human likes it, and it matters deeply to my mate.

He wraps his arms around me and the bulky sweater, his kisses gentle on my forehead. "I picked up a couple more things for you to sell when I was in town."

He's got better skills at a garage sale than any raven. I meet his soft kisses with some of my own, knowing he's offering more than trade goods. He's sacrificing his own peace so that I can find mine. "Thanks. How's Brandy?" It's hard for her when any of us are gone.

He smiles, his hands kneading the spots between my shoulder blades that get tense after a long stretch of flying. "Joking around with Brown and requesting potatoes for dinner."

The happiness in his eyes is so freaking good to see. I kiss him like I mean it, which I do. He tastes like sun tea and cookies, which isn't exactly a hardship. I lean into him a little more, grinning as his hands slide up under my sweater. Our new tents are great for lots of things, but this part of who we are has always happened in the woods.

"Cut that out, you two." Wrinkles walks out of the

trees. "We've got youngsters around now. You'll give them ideas."

Wrinkles and Brown can handle that job all by themselves. I grin at her and keep my arms wrapped around my sexy guy. "Don't you have rocks to collect or something?"

"Done." She pats the leather pouch at her hip. "Found a couple of nice agates for that cat down in Oregon, and some boring gray rocks that should have pretty insides if I can convince Brown to crack them open for me."

Wrinkles could convince a cactus to buy sand. And she's never wrong about rocks with pretty insides.

She walks over and kisses each of our cheeks in turn. "The agates are for that secret fund of yours that you don't want to tell anyone about."

I glare at the guy who's still trying to cop a feel under my sweater.

He shrugs, entirely unrepentant. "Wasn't me."

Wrinkles cackles. "It wasn't, and don't you go hunting down my source. I don't know what you need cold, hard cash for, but I've always got a spare rock or two when you need one."

She gives them over whether they're spare or not. Wrinkles has odd notions of who's pack sometimes, but she's as loyal to her chosen ones as the moon is to the sun. I reach out an arm and pull her in to our cuddle. "It's done now. It was something I needed to take care of myself." She won't like that explanation, but she's mated to a man who lives it.

She snorts. "You've been drinking too much of Brown's whiskey if you think I'm going to let that slide."

None of us has touched a drop. It's the first bottle he's had in six years, and it's a really small one. The walk to believing we can have luxuries now is going to be harder for him than most. "I made a mistake and I needed to fix it."

Ben growls, which is as pushy as his wolf ever gets. "It wasn't a mistake."

That's an argument neither of us will ever win. I lean my forehead against his. Sometimes, it's not about being right—it's about being whole.

Wrinkles pats my back and steps away briskly. "You do what you need to do. If you ever need rocks or smoked fish or gold nuggets, your baby pack has your back. Even the cranky ones who aren't sure they belong yet."

I snort. Reuben spied me as I took off northward, so he'll likely show up sometime in the next day or two, demanding to know what the hell I was doing flying into bear country. Hopefully, he'll do it quietly.

Wrinkles reaches down to pluck a mushroom and adds it to the gathering bag over her other shoulder. It looks almost as full as her rock pouch. She never takes more than the land can easily give, but she's been harvesting far and wide these last few weeks.

I smile, remembering the moment she realized just how much the shifters of Whistler Pack were willing to pay for a handful of dried mushrooms.

I wrap my arm around Ben's waist as we follow her back to camp. One job done. Now to figure out the next one. I might not know how to live in the light, but I will do everything in my power to help the wolves I love to get there.

Even if I'm way more skeptical than the wolves of the den that it will actually work.

3

FALLON

Ben adds more kindling to the base he's laying for the cooking fire, weaving small twigs into the nest of dry moss and birch bark he pulled out of his pocket. We probably won't light it for a couple of hours yet, but setting it up has become one of his afternoon rituals. A reminder, Benjamin Dunn–style, that we're still going to be here when the sun sets.

Brandy looks up from the cheerful yellow scarf she's knitting, which I imagine she'll wrap around Brown's neck at some point. "Are you sure we can't eat that beef now, Mik? My wolf is starving."

My raven tries not to gag. Raw meat is disgusting, no matter how much marinade it's hiding under.

I shake my head. She's such a strange bird. Fond of earthworms and slugs like some darn robin, and turning her nose up at the fancy stuff. She'll like it just fine once it's cooked, but Brandy is practically drooling, and Ben too, even if he drools more quietly.

Mikayla snickers. "There are spicy nuts if you're hungry, or some leftover pan bread from lunch."

I already had some of that. It was delish. Some parts of our new camp life are definitely good, and readily available leftovers are high on that list. "I ate most of the bread, sorry."

Brandy rolls her eyes at me. "Brat."

Ben, his back to his big sister, takes a slow, quiet breath and lets it go again. Every small step Brandy takes means so very much to him—and always, he sees how many are left to go. For her, and for the missing sister who hasn't been able to sit near anyone or make a small joke or knit a scarf for almost five years.

I reach out and run my fingers through his hair. It's getting long and messy, just the way I like it, and it helps pull him back into this moment. The first lesson of the streets—worrying about all the other moments makes it too hard to get through this one.

Except this one is really good. Which messes with every rule I've got.

I smirk at Brandy, who didn't miss her brother's exhale or my fingers reaching out to soothe him. "I can fry you up some earthworms."

She makes a face. "No, thanks. They taste like dirt."

I wash the dirt off. Usually. "Picky wolf."

She snorts. "Right. Says the bird who is always too hot, or too cold, or can't sleep because there's a lump under her somewhere."

That lump is usually a wolf paw. They always put me in the middle of the pile to keep me warm. "You are kind of lumpy."

Mikayla shakes her head. "Ben, make them stop."

She's new to our squabbling, but it didn't take her more than a couple of hours to figure out why we do it.

He looks over his shoulder at her and grins. "But they like it so much."

Mikayla rolls her eyes right on cue, but he speaks absolute truth and we all know it. When I first showed up eight years ago, all prickly feathers and big eyes and clutching Ben's hand, Brandy was the first one to figure out that I had no idea what to do with his family's open, exuberant welcome. So she shoulder-bumped me into her kid sister Rennie and told me I smelled awfully funny for a wolf.

Friendship by insult, I understood just fine. And it gave me the foothold I needed to hesitantly, awkwardly begin to find a place in their welcome.

These days, it gives her a foothold in something resembling peace. I let my eyes drift to her knitting. She does a lot of it, but some days, her fingers clutch the yarn like it's some kind of lifeline. This doesn't seem to be one of those days. I'm glad. "That scarf looks big enough for Wrinkles and Brown to wear at the same time."

She laughs. "It's not a scarf. A bunch of us are knitting stripes. Myrna's assembling them into blankets that we can sell on ShifterNet."

I eye the waterfall of yellow with new eyes. "That's really smart." My inner trader approves, and so does my bird. She's flown over lone wolves sitting under trees with knitting needles in their hands. A connection to pack, even in their solitude. Knitting something that gets attached to the work of other packmates and used to feed the pups—even better.

Brandy smiles softly. "I hope some of them come tomorrow."

So much yearning. I look down at my hands. I know how to do insults. I've never known how to do the other stuff. But I'll be out in the woods tomorrow, trying my very best to deliver on her wish.

RIO

It's been three weeks, and I'm still reminded every day just how damn brilliant Kennedy's instincts are. Fallon doesn't want to be the leader of this baby pack, but she so obviously is. Even when it's making her squirm like hell.

I clear my throat, which is plenty to have all eyes snapping in my direction.

Fallon bounces to her feet, clearly grateful for the interruption. She walks over to me, setting aside whatever was making her uncomfortable so she can get between me and the nerves that just hit some of the others around the unlit fire.

Nerves that vanish as my companion slides down off my back.

Fallon's mate swoops Kelsey up first, planting kisses

on her cheeks and tickling her with his scruff. He grins at her as she giggles like a loon. "We weren't expecting you until tomorrow, cutie."

She licks his nose. "I came to sleep with you."

Ben doesn't even hesitate, smart man. "Awesome. You can sleep next to Brandy. She snores."

His big sister reaches in, snuggling against Kelsey's soft cheek. "Silly guy. He thinks I'm going to share you."

Kelsey licks her nose, too.

A raven exhales beside me and keeps her words quiet enough to hide under the giggles. "Thank you for bringing her."

I snort. "She brought me." She finished her lunch, stacked her plate, and announced that the two of us were headed out to Fallon's camp. Now I know why. Always, Kelsey goes where the flowers are blooming. I've never seen Brandy looking this relaxed and happy.

She sits down beside Mikayla with Kelsey snuggled on her lap.

I smile wryly. I thought maybe we were coming out to help stabilize preparations for the knitting circle tomorrow, but it doesn't surprise my wolf at all that Kelsey has a deeper agenda. I don't know nearly enough about what happened to the family that was once at the center of this pack—but the four-year-old wolf who was born into it after it shattered has a sentinel ready to do her bidding for as long as it takes.

Brandy looks up and meets my eyes. There's worry in hers.

Crap. I'm too used to the den, where they've gotten

used to my strange ways. There, I can lurk and ponder and they just giggle and feed me gummy bears. I slide the bag Kelsey carefully packed before we left off my shoulder and offer it to Fallon. "Banana muffins, straight off the cooling rack."

Mikayla makes happy noises by the fire, but she doesn't leave Brandy's side.

Fallon dives into the bag and extracts three muffins. She tosses them one at a time to Brandy, who fields like someone I need on my team the next time we play our pack's mangled version of baseball. Then she reaches in for two more and offers me one.

I shake my head. "I already ate so many that Shelley chased me out of the kitchen. These are for you."

Her laugh is bright and easy. "Eat another one or your wolf will just drool all over my feathers."

Embarrassing, but true. And it makes the trio by the fire pit giggle, which was probably Fallon's intention. I take the muffin, which is still warm, thanks to Shelley's fancy new insulated bags. My wolf approves. There are a lot of forces at work in our pack these days, but none of them are doing as much heavy lifting as Shelley Martins's baked goods.

Fallon pops the half-muffin she just bit off into her cheek like a squirrel. "You're supposed to eat them, not stare at them and compose poetry."

I grin—she's not far from wrong.

Ben walks over, chuckling, and pokes her cheek. "You're not supposed to store them for winter, either."

She mumbles something that mostly gets muffled by what she's eating. It doesn't sound overly complimentary.

Her mate laughs and sniffs the other half of her muffin. "My wolf still doesn't think he wants to eat bananas."

Fallon grins at me. "More for us."

I bump my shoulder into hers. She might be a raven, but I've been around her enough to know that she speaks fluent wolf. "He'll come around."

She snickers. "Myrna says the same thing about you and zucchini."

Smart raven. Every time she teases me, Brandy gets a little easier with me being here, and so does the quiet wolf lurking in the woods. "Never. Have you seen those things? They double in size overnight. Ghost found one in the garden yesterday that was almost as big as Braden."

Ben shakes his head, amused. "Mikayla made pan-fried zukes with melted cheese last night. They were really good."

Fallon wrinkles her nose, about to protest—and then a wall of caution slams into her eyes.

I sigh internally. My sentinel is well aware she was outside our territory last night, and he hopes she knows what the hell she's doing up in polar bear country, but she's clearly not anywhere near to trusting him with that information. Which is fine. I know how to wait, and how to be companionably annoying while I do it. I look over at Mikayla, who's had more time around my big, bad wolf than the rest of her baby pack. "If I stay for dinner, you won't try to hide green stuff on my plate, right?"

She grins at me. "No promises."

I put on my best sulky-wolf face. "Fine. I'll go see if Brown will feed me. He won't try to poison me with stealth vegetables."

Brandy snickers. "He's eating whatever Mikayla is cooking."

Excellent. That means Kennedy's not-so-secret plan to lure a hermit bear out of his chosen solitude is working just fine. "In that case, I'll be brave and eat my dinner and hope not to die, and then I'll head back to the den."

Kelsey sits up straight in Brandy's arms and shakes her head.

I raise an eyebrow. We chatted about this on the way out. Most of the baby packs aren't ready for a big black wolf in their sleeping pile yet.

The sweetest four-year-old on the planet raises her own eyebrows right back.

My wolf blinks.

Brandy looks down at her niece and over at me. She clears her throat carefully. "You could stay. There are two tents. We have plenty of room."

I look at her quietly. Listening. Waiting. Letting her get a read on whether she made that offer for the right reasons and whether she wants to keep holding it out there. I'm fine with it being an aspiration for another day.

When she finally smiles, it's a little shaky, but it's real. "Yes. You should stay. We even have some marsh-mallows we could roast, I think."

Wow. When the wounded ones of this pack decide to take charge of their own healing, they can be really fierce about it. I grin. "I don't know what stories the den has been telling you about me, but I am actually capable of going a whole night without sugar."

She laughs. "The marshmallows will make up for the spicy green beans Mikayla is going to make you eat."

I groan and look at the former sentry who is apparently remaking herself into an excellent chef. "You shouldn't do that. Those will make me fart."

She snorts. "Then you can sleep with Brown."

"That's my job," says a very amused wolf as she walks out of the trees. Wrinkles strolls over and kisses my forehead. Then she turns and catches the small girl running to greet her. "Hello, sweetness. Did you come to make Brown less growly?"

Kelsey beams at her. "Bears are supposed to growl."

Wrinkles chuckles. "He's just down by the river. You can go surprise him if you want."

"I'm not down by the river, woman." Brown drops his bucket to the ground by the half-built cooking shed. "A man can't do anything in peace around here anymore."

My wolf snorts as three people start genially insulting him and a small girl runs over to give him a hug. This baby pack might be a motley assortment of personalities, but apparently they've figured out how to handle each other just fine. Which is a handy cover story for the fierce work of helping each other heal that they're also doing.

I smile, well pleased at what I can see, and more than a little amused. I thought that maybe Kelsey brought me out here because there was sentinel work to do.

I suspect she just brought me along to carry the muffins.

FALLON

I back up slowly, into the dim of the half-finished cook shack, delighting in the easy happiness on Ben's face and wishing that I better understood how to stand there beside him.

I've never been a loner. I've spent my whole life hanging out with others, but I've done it in the shadows. Closets first, and dingy staircases. Then dirty doorways, and alleys, and under the occasional bridge when my bird couldn't handle the unending concrete anymore.

Ben's family tried to offer me something different, but my first two years here, I was still jumping at all the weird noises in the woods—and then Samuel took over and I got thrown back into living in the shadows again, trying to survive the bad things that went bump in the night.

Trying to help what was left of the family I loved survive them, too.

I look around at the neat piles of boards and Brown's carefully stashed tools, seeking something to do. Brandy and Ben will both pick up on it if I get morbid, and so will the ray of sunshine who just came to visit. Dunn psychics, all of them.

The tense feeling in my shoulders eases when I spy Wrinkles's gathering bag. I can unload that. I'm not a great cook and I don't know much about most domestic stuff, but I can be trusted to bundle herbs and hang them under cover.

"Need help?"

I squint at the face that's invaded my shadows. "No, I'm good. Just getting stuff out of the way before the knitting invasion lands."

Rio chuckles. "Can I hide in here and pretend to look useful, then? Brandy is still getting used to my wolf, and I want her to be able to really enjoy her time with Kelsey."

I probably shouldn't peck his eyes out for being a good guy. I jam one of the solar lights into his hands. They're run by some kind of magic my raven can't seem to figure out. "See if you can make this work so that we don't accidentally mix up the edible greens with the healer ingredients." They don't really divide up that neatly, but there are some I'm only willing to consume if there are death threats involved.

Which Wrinkles is quite capable of handing out if you don't drink her teas when she catches you sneezing.

Rio deftly snaps the base of the light into place and adjusts it to a dim glow.

I stare at it, astonished. "I didn't know it could do that."

He chuckles. "Shelley likes them on high beam, so maybe she didn't show Mikayla how the settings work."

Mikayla knows how to be in bright light. I'm the one who doesn't. I've been okay these past few weeks, but we've been quiet. Muted. I'm just starting to realize how fast we might turn into something really different. Six years in the shadows is a long time, but it's really different from spending a lifetime there.

I get my hands moving. I'm not a moody raven, but nobody who could hear the inside of my head today would know that.

Rio picks up a ball of string and starts cutting off lengths to wrap around the stems of the broad leaves I'm bundling. They look oddly like nettles, except I thought those grew in the spring. I shrug and keep picking them out of the rest of what she gathered. Wrinkles will know what they are, and the rest of us are smart enough not to eat greens we can't identify. "Have the den knitters figured out who's coming first, yet?"

Rio snorts. "No. There might be fistfights."

I grin. Myrna is probably starting all of them. She's fierce. "It's the kickoff to Reilly's birthday week. Nobody wants to miss it." Hoot and Ghost and Kennedy have had to do a *lot* of explaining on why we need the knitting circle to be small and mellow. It was insanely brave of Brandy to volunteer to host any kind of group gathering. It needs to stay a size she can cope with, and some of the wolves she's hoping might come, too.

Which means that the knitters will be coming in shifts, and most of the dominants and a raven who can't knit will be finding ourselves something else to do tomorrow.

I wrap off the nettle bundle and set it on the rough board I'm using as a table. I know what I'm going to be doing, even if I haven't mostly admitted it even to myself yet. I look over at Kelsey, who's back in Brandy's lap. And at the unblinking joy in the eyes of my mate, who's watching her.

Yup. I know exactly what I'm going to be doing.

Rio leans against me gently.

I sigh. Darn sentinel who doesn't know how to keep his nose out of anything. "Ben is so stinking happy that she's here."

A long pause. "His bond with her runs deep."

Pushy wolf. Also an exquisitely careful one, but I can't tell him anything. It's not my story to tell. I remember it all, though. The start of the bond between a good man and his tiny niece is one of my most anguished and cherished memories.

It was the first time he saw her. She was this tiny little baby, wrapped in a soft blanket and staring out at the world with big, brown eyes. Bailey was holding her, every line of her body a study in fierce, rending grief. Ben took one look at the baby and let that same grief rend him— and then he did what he's always done better than anyone I know. He took Kelsey out of Bailey's quaking arms and kissed her forehead and sang her a lullaby.

He chose to love her.

Even when his voice cracked on every note.

4

KEL

My wolf whines as I pull up at the base of a tree and shift. That was a nice run, but it wasn't nearly long enough.

I tell him to suck it up, and turn to help the yellow-gold wolf who's wearing two shoulder bags so full of yarn that he looks like a mutant camel. And this is just the extra the den sent in case we run out. Which I suspect has something to do with a Whistler Pack polar bear who doesn't comprehend just how little storage space we have at the moment, but he's not my problem. Not today, at least.

"Thanks." Hayden shakes as he shifts, his wolf trying to fix his disordered fur even as it disappears. "Put all this yarn to good use, would you? If it comes back to the den, someone will probably try to make me learn how to knit again."

I toss him a canteen and snort. "Knitting lessons are wasted on you."

He makes a face. "This is one of the very few days in my life when I actually wish they'd stuck."

There's almost a whine in there. I lean against his shoulder. "You couldn't have come, anyhow. Your wolf is too bossy."

He jams his fists into the pockets of his shorts. "I know."

Nothing is harder for Hayden Scott than knowing someone is ten minutes from home and there's not a damn thing he can do to get them all the way there—and he volunteered for those shoes today. Most people only saw Reilly walk over to the knitters on the riverbank and ask for a knitting circle as part of his birthday revelry. A few know how long Reilly studied them before he walked over. As far as I know, only two of us saw Hayden give a bear cub the respectful nod that got him onto his feet.

Ghost Mountain's alpha absolutely engineered this, and he understands its value at least as well as the bear cub who asked for it and the brave wolf who found her voice long enough to volunteer to host it—but today is still going to drive him nuts. "Lissa will be here. If any of the ghost wolves show up, she won't let them get away."

His lips quirk. "She is kind of fast."

She can outrun every wolf in this pack—and she'll know whether that's the right thing to do or not. Unlike those of us who still don't understand all the ways in which this pack is fractured. Which means we need to be fucking careful. Something I'm probably going to need to remind myself of about a thousand times today, seeing as how I'm the only brawler who got himself a seat at the knitting circle.

I hoist the two bags. Hayden is going to have to fight his demons without my help. I have my own to deal with, and the long list of suspicions Rio handed me besides. He thinks there's shit brewing.

I push off Hayden's shoulder. "Go make sure nobody at the den escapes." Myrna and Shelley put everyone to work this morning, including a big contingent from the baby packs. They'll spend the day getting ready for the huge party that might render a cute bear deaf for his eleventh birthday.

He shoots me a wry look. "You don't think that Myrna's frying pan is a big enough threat?"

I snort. She's perfectly capable of leading the breakout. She won't, though. Not until it's her turn to come out here. She set up the shifts of knitters, and there's no chance they're random. Reilly just wanted a quieter gathering for some of the wolves who won't be able to handle the exuberant party at the den. Our pack elder isn't herding anything nearly that simple.

A raven caws overhead and angles down in our direction.

Hayden nods. "That's my cue. Don't forget to take pictures for Ronan."

I roll my eyes. I'm under strict orders to take photos all damn day. If I don't, the den might riot and a polar bear might cry. "Has he got shit under control up there?" A northern shifter pack's den just fell into a sinkhole of melting permafrost, which means Ronan's not actually going to make it to Reilly's birthday party. Our juvenile bear took the news a lot more stoically than the grown-up one on his way to the Arctic.

Hayden shrugs. "I asked. He growled."

That makes him Adrianna's problem. Hopefully not literally—she's supposed to be at the big party tomorrow night, along with a couple of surprises Reilly doesn't know about yet.

The raven buzzes us, making clear shooing motions with her wings.

Hayden snorts and shifts.

Fallon waits until it's clear he's headed back to the den, and lands beside me. I keep my eyes averted until she's dressed. Wolves and cats and bears could care less about being naked, but ravens and hawks are trickier, and I haven't spent nearly enough time out in the far orbits to have a read on this one yet.

She lays a hand on my arm, reminding me that she speaks perfectly good wolf. "You're early."

I give her a quick scan. A lot more than her baby pack will be out here today, but they're likely taking cues from their leader. She doesn't blink, which tweaks my wolf's curiosity. She's less cautious out here. More sure of herself. "Is it safe to join you, or should I make myself busy checking the perimeter?"

She shakes her head. "Perimeter's fine. Some of Dorie's crew are already on their way, and Mikayla made pancakes."

That would explain all the flour and eggs Brown

uneremoniously swiped from the pantry yesterday. "Reilly's probably going to be early, too. He could hardly contain himself this morning." And he missed his sleeping buddy. Kelsey usually curls up right next to his bear.

Fallon takes one of the sacks of yarn off my shoulder and starts walking in the direction of her base camp. "We're ready. Kelsey woke us up singing at the crack of dawn."

I fall into step beside her. There's more to that story than she's saying, but I don't ask. Today has all kinds of quietly ticking explosives. Trauma under pressure is never predictable, and whatever Kelsey was giving voice to, it was almost certainly necessary and good. "Anything in particular you'd like me to keep an eye out for?"

Fallon just looks at me, her eyebrows cocked.

I know that look. I'm usually the one wearing it. She's street, unless I miss my guess, and street's not so different from being a soldier. "You're the leader of your baby pack for a reason." One that maybe has some trickiness I need to keep an eye on. Soldiers are good at leading their people home. They aren't necessarily so good at reintegrating themselves.

She snorts. "Because Kennedy made me?"

I shoot her the look she just gave me.

Her lips quirk.

I wait.

Her eyes shutter. "Don't push."

I'm not. Yet. But I will be paying much closer attention. "On you or your packmates?"

47

She grunts. "Either."

My wolf takes that under advisement. She's easier out here, more sure of herself. I was like that, once. It took a hell of a push to get me to come home.

BEN

"You cannot possibly eat any more pancakes." I grin at the small girl in my lap who should be twice as big as she is from this breakfast alone.

"Growing pups need to eat." Brown flips her another slice of bacon from over where he's washing dishes.

Kelsey nibbles on the crispy parts she likes best, which is why all the bacon is half-burnt this morning. "Myrna says that Reilly is going to grow lots now that he's eleven. Jade thinks he might get as big as an elephant."

Jade's a cutie, but I don't think she has any idea how big elephants are. "He's already pretty big. Way bigger than Brown."

Brown snorts. "He's not nearly as mean, though."

I make funny faces at my niece. "I don't think that's a contest Reilly wants to win."

She shakes her head solemnly. "He's my sweet bear."

Wrinkles chuckles from where she's arranging snacks on plates. "Mikayla put lots of honey on everything to help keep him sweet."

Kelsey slides off my lap and walks over to the low table, her eyes scanning the snacks like a general who knows her troops very well and wants to make sure they will be properly fed. When she gets to the end, she holds her arms up to Mikayla.

The young woman who got tossed into the deep end of our baby pack scoops her up, eyes puzzled. "What is it, sweetie? Do you think we need something else?"

I hope not. Mik made every single thing she knows how to make, and she did it all with nothing more than bags of ingredients from the den and buckets of fish from Brown and Shelley's recipes written down on scraps of paper.

Kelsey shakes her head and reaches up a small hand to pat Mikayla's cheek. "You love Reilly."

Mikayla blinks fast. "Yeah, I do. He's a really awesome bear."

"You made all his favorite things."

A stray tear manages to escape. "I tried. I also made the melon balls you like, and the baby cheese balls."

I look at Brown, who carried many bags of ingredients from the den. At Wrinkles, who's been Mik's quiet assistant for days. At Brandy, who's grinning and trying not to cry, because she really likes baby cheese balls, too. At Fallon, walking in from the trees with Kel, a puzzled look on her face and love in her eyes.

Damn.

I've been trying so hard not to be too invested in this day—to let it be what it needs to be and not hope too hard and just support the people I love on the crooked paths they need to walk to wherever they need to go.

I've apparently been left in the dust.

FALLON

He looks so adorably befuddled, and I don't know why. I walk over to Ben and wrap my arms around him and hold him and his wolf tight, because that's all he's ever asked of me. "You look like someone tried to make you eat a bacon-and-zucchini sandwich."

He pushes back far enough to scowl. "That's a thing?"

Mikayla giggles behind me. "It could be."

Brown growls. Wrinkles says something that makes Kelsey and Brandy laugh. I ignore all of them because I can feel the turbulence inside my mate. "What's up?"

He chuckles and tips his forehead against mine. "You mean besides a dozen people with pointy sticks coming to visit?"

He knits just fine, and he'll be doing it all day, sitting somewhere innocuous and giving his sister someone to lean on if she needs it. I frown. I expected her to be pacing this morning, or holding one of the worry carvings Brown makes for her to rub, or drinking tea from the ugly blue mug she bought with her share of the bank-robbery money. "Brandy seems pretty chill."

He smiles, his eyes lighting up with simple happiness. "She is."

That doesn't always happen when she challenges herself. Dominant wolves don't tend to play nice when their humans have anxiety issues. "Kelsey's helping, I bet."

"Mikayla, too."

Her cheerful, unflappable snark is the elixir we didn't know we needed. One that just might give this day the alchemy it needs to work. There's a birthday bear on his way, the sun is shining, and there's enough food to feed an army. Which is good. I think there might be an army coming. A really well-behaved one, in shifts, but still.

Ben exhales quietly by my ear.

I sigh. I'm not good with feelings, at least the part that requires talking about them, but he's clearly having some, and there are rules to this mate deal. I rub my cheek against his in case he needs to talk wolf.

He chuckles. "I'm fine. Lots of stuff swirling, but it doesn't get to land today."

That's not how swirling stuff tends to work in my experience, but some parts of his life have been way more normal than mine. "Let me know if you need a sharp beak to peck at anything."

He grins and pulls me in a little snugger, his eyes heating up with something that has nothing to do with sharp beaks.

Oh, no. Not a chance. "There are a hundred shifters heading our way right now. We are not messing around in the woods."

He gives me the wolf version of puppy-dog eyes. In his defense, they usually work. However, I'm not kidding about all the people in our woods. "Rain check?"

He groans. "It's not going to rain for weeks. You know that, right?"

I grin. "Knit me something sexy and maybe it will rain tonight."

He huffs out a laugh. "One knee-length sweater, coming right up."

My raven sighs happily. There's her sweet, strong, sexy wolf.

KEL

I sit down beside Brown, because apparently I'm a useless beta who got here early enough that he might as well help with the dishes. "Got a towel?"

He tosses me a rag that's as decrepit as his t-shirt. "Knock yourself out."

I lift a plate out of the pot he's using as a makeshift sink, and start drying it. "Reilly hasn't let go of that carving you made him."

Brown makes noises that sound like he's got an engine in his throat. One that needs tuning.

I hide a grin. Embarrassing bears is one of my favorite pastimes. "You knitting today?"

He shoots me a look that would strip skin if I were in the mood to let it. "Do I look like I know what to do with a couple of pointy sticks and sheep fur?"

Smartass. "They're just tools, and you seem pretty good with those."

He slams a mug down in the pot sink hard enough to make the entire thing shake. "Wrinkles showed me how to do the bear-track stitch. She said I have to stay and represent."

I hide another grin. Wrinkles has been picking up some interesting slang from the ShifterNet forums. "Anything I should know about so that I'm not an asshole today?"

He shoots me another look, this one several degrees nicer than the last one. "Mikayla made all the food and she's worried that it maybe isn't spicy enough, Reuben is lurking in the woods and wants someone to chase his ass in here, and Wrinkles is nervous about the gift she made for Reilly."

When the man decides to be a source, he's a hell of an informant. "What did she make him?"

He rolls his eyes and slams another mug into the drying pot.

My wolf snorts. One informant, closed for business. Fair enough. I also have eyes, and I plan to use them.

I cast a quick look around, but nothing's changed. Kelsey is still doling out her special brand of medicine to the two women cuddling her, Wrinkles is watching me and smiling faintly, and Fallon is steadying her mate with every breath the two of them take.

A baby pack on their feet, facing forward, and impressively ready to go.

Which is right about when shit usually hits the fan. I pick up a mug and start drying it. That's why I'm here. Until then, I can do dishes.

5

LISSA

I look over at Ravi, who's got his guitar case slung over one shoulder, and shake my head. "We should have run a few loops around Ghost Mountain on our way here."

He chuckles and looks over at where Jade and Cori are running circles around an exuberant bear. "They'll calm down when we get there. I think."

I snort. "That's in about two minutes."

He grins. "In that case, we're doomed."

I laugh. It will be fine. My wolf flatly refuses to harbor any doubts about this day. Pack will gather and pack will drink in the joy of a bear who is being celebrated for all of who he is, and the happy energy of a little girl and her mama aren't going to do a moment of harm to any of that.

Cori scoops up her wriggling, naked daughter and pours her into a bright purple sundress. Jade picked it out at the thrift store herself, special for Reilly's birthday. It matches the shirt she picked for him.

Reilly walks over, wearing it proudly, and takes her hand. "Ready?"

Cori slides her arm around Ravi's waist as their girl proudly leads the birthday bear toward the first of his celebrations.

My wolf sulks. She misses her sexy wolf and her pup.

I shake my head at her. Robbie is off running in the woods with Bailey, and Hayden is in charge of getting the treasure hunt ready. They'll both be happy as clams.

She wrinkles her nose. Clams don't have fur.

I giggle, which everyone ignores, because there's a small girl walking toward us holding a flower, and a row of people following her. They're all smiling except Brown, and even he looks a lot less growly than usual.

Kelsey stops and beams up at the boy who has become her soft place to land.

He squats down and takes the flower, very gently. "Is this for me?"

Silly bear.

Kelsey reaches her fingers out to touch the big, glittery purple heart on the front of his shirt.

He grins. "Maybe it will fit you next."

She tilts her head. "Stinky first. Then Robbie. Then me."

If they know she wants it, it just might survive the antics of three wild boys.

Kelsey takes the birthday boy's other hand and,

together with Jade, tugs him toward the very fancy setup that awaits us, clearly expecting us all to follow.

I shake my head at Brandy and Wrinkles. "It looks amazing. How did you get your camp this organized?"

Wrinkles snorts. "First time it's looked like this. Usually we're a disaster waiting to happen."

Brandy grins. "Says the woman who considers a stray fork a disaster."

Wrinkles elbows her, only half in jest. "Do you have any idea how much damage a fork can do after a bear steps on it?"

Fallon rolls her eyes. "That would be the bear doing the damage, not the fork."

Jade and Kelsey both look up at Reilly and giggle. He looks at Brown, who growls. And just like that, we've arrived, shepherded in by a baby pack who have obviously figured out how they're going to roll with an invasion.

I make a wry face at Kel. We clearly made a lot of really useless plans.

He smiles faintly and keeps stirring what looks like a jug of lemonade.

I look around. They've cleared the tents off their two sleeping platforms and laid out pillows and big baskets of yarn, and there's a low table bearing an astonishing array of food and what looks like five different kinds of tea. "Wow."

"This is amazing." Reilly surveys his kingdom for the day, his voice a little breathless.

"We wanted to do right by your birthday, young

man." Wrinkles gives him an enormous hug. "Come sit right over here. We've got honey tea and honey cookies and honey berry bars and some sandwiches in case you don't want to eat honey all day long."

Two pups and a bear cub make an abrupt turn toward the food.

I grin at Mikayla, who I actually know the best of this baby pack. The rest of them were our traders, living on the edges of our territory and doing the vital bartering and bargaining that kept our pack alive. "I have orders from Shelley to get your recipe for those berry bars. The ones you sent vanished in about three minutes."

Mikayla's cheeks flush with pleasure. "I just mixed up some stuff and squished it together."

"That's how I make my best music." Ravi wraps her up in a hug that includes Wrinkles and Kelsey.

"Don't you be stealing all my hugs," says a voice from the trees.

I look up and grin at Dorie, who is naked as a jaybird above my head. There are two other jaybirds in the same tree, calling out greetings as they pull on clothes and drop bags down into cooperative arms.

Brandy looks up, her hands on her hips. "Seriously, can't you arrive on the ground like normal people?"

Hoot lands beside her with the catlike grace Dorie teaches all her charges. "That's no fun, and besides, you have some of the best walking trees in the territory."

Brandy gives her niece a fierce hug that belies the scolding. "You know you're a wolf, not a squirrel, right?"

Oh, it's good to see her this full of cheerful sarcasm. It

used to be a way of life for most of the Dunn cousins. Before.

I give Hoot a hug and move back to make room for the rest of the tree dwellers to descend. Dorie lands first and immediately smacks a big kiss on Cori's cheek. "Hello, lovely. Let me steal your girl. I promise to give her back by sundown."

Wrinkles snorts. "No being a greedy cat."

They're both going to have to arm-wrestle Brown, who's currently dangling Jade upside down over a plate of cookies.

Ravi and Cori just look at each other and grin.

I snort. They'll learn. No good naps ever come after pups have been hung upside down.

I patiently hold the bag Dorie tossed down to me and cast a careful look around. Brandy was the wolf we were expecting might need some support, but she's in the thick of the happy noise. That doesn't mean everyone is rolling with our arrival, however. If I've learned anything these past few months, it's that the tides of trauma and grief are unpredictable—and happiness can sometimes make them shift in an instant.

Fallon is hanging out on the periphery in a way that catches my wolf's attention, but her mate is beside her, and there is no one steadier than Ben. Just behind them, though, Kel is walking out of the trees with a disgruntled-looking guy half a step ahead of him.

Reilly lights up. "Reuben!"

Reuben crashes to a halt, staring at the crowd.

Kel slings an arm around his shoulders, one that I

suspect is as much about containment as support. Which rapidly gets an assist as a cheerful Jade, well used to helping corral wolves who might want to make a run for it, dashes over and wraps her arms around his knees.

She beams up at a man she hardly knows. "My knit a hat."

He blinks down at her.

Jade pats his belly. "My need help."

I snicker at Ravi. "Reuben hasn't got a chance."

Cori cuddles into his side. "That's our girl."

The happiness that zooms between them puts a big grin on Glow's face as she steps out of the shadows. Moon Girl is following her, still in her fur. Elijah isn't quite making it out of the trees, but he's already got knitting in his hands and Brown closing in on him with a look of profound relief in his eyes.

My wolf wriggles happily.

The gang, at least the starter version, is all here.

FALLON

I'm glad someone knows how to run one of these things. My version of a get-together involves setting lookouts and moving garbage dumpsters around to provide better sight lines. This looks a lot more like what used to happen at the den before evil arrived. I used to hide myself in the shadows on the edges then, too.

"Want some?" Kel leans against the tree beside me and holds out a plate.

I take something that looks like an orange snowman. "Aren't you supposed to be knitting?"

He just shrugs and chooses a bar from his plate.

I look over at the sleeping platforms. So far, Elijah and Brandy are the only ones with knitting needles in their hands. Cori is peering into a big basket of yarn with Mikayla and Wrinkles and Glow and Dorie and Katrina, which means they won't agree on an answer until at least tomorrow. Brown is wrapping a skein of something into a ball, with Reilly chattering at his side. Ravi is set up with his guitar on the stump that Brown usually uses for carving, with Moon Girl curled up in the wood shavings at his feet. Ben is chatting with Lissa and Hoot and adding more food to their plates than they can probably eat in a week. Reuben has Kelsey in his lap, which is kind of funny, because he was obviously trying to escape before she sat on him.

"Finished counting?" Kel looks amused.

I scowl and bite the head off the orange snowman. It tastes like melon, but with cream-cheese brains in the middle. Which are surprisingly good. "My raven likes to know where everyone's at."

"My wolf, too."

He didn't come over here to feed me melon brains. He's got an agenda. I'm not sure what it is, though. Doesn't feel like a turf thing, and he's not leaning on me, at least not yet. Not even sniffing, really. But he's still got my feathers in a twist.

Ben looks over my way and smiles. Jade is showing him two balls of pretty yellow yarn, and he looks so damn happy.

I sigh. I'll let my feathers get twisted plenty if it lets my mate have this kind of moment.

Kel nods his chin vaguely up and left. "That high ridge over there has a pretty good view of your camp."

I scowl at him again. I watch from up there all the time, but there's no way he should know that.

His lips quirk. "Your raven is going to make me work for this."

Yes, she is. "Work for what?"

He snorts. "I spotted a wolf up there while I was chasing down Reuben. Older, I think. Light gray, might favor his right hip."

My raven goes very, very still. "That's a lot to notice."

He's not taking his eyes off my bird, which makes him smarter than most wolves. "This is your show. If you want me to go chase him down here, I can do that. If you want me to pretend I didn't see him, I can do that, too."

I think he actually means it. "You know that I'm only the leader of this baby pack because Hoot refused to pick someone else, right?"

He just keeps watching me.

Crap. If it's the wolf I think it is, I need to stop playing head games with my beta. Without actually telling him what's going on, because smart ravens don't open up five cans of worms at the same time.

My bird squawks. She would never eat worms from a can.

I roll my eyes and catch Hoot's attention with one of the old signals.

Her eyes widen a little. She extracts herself from the knitting huddle and materializes at my shoulder, scanning the guy beside me and then meeting my eyes. Her wolf has always known how to deal with my bird. "You can trust Kel. Or you can trust me and know that I trust him."

Kel says nothing.

She grins at him. "If you mess up, she'll peck your eyes out while you sleep."

He smiles faintly.

I sigh and nod at the sleeping platform. "Go knit and don't ask questions. I need to talk to Hoot."

He doesn't say a word. He just heads over to the basket beside Elijah and picks out a ball of lime-green yarn.

Hoot snorts. "He's got eyes. You know that, right?"

I do. "You said you trust him."

She looks at me, serious and careful and ready. "What do you need me to do?"

I need her to help me aim a ray of sunshine into the shadows. And then I need to get the heck out of here before I get sunburn.

KEL

This pack has so fucking many leaders who can't see their own damn selves in the mirror. One of them is currently taking to the sky, her bird shedding more than her clothes on the way out. She was easy and steady all morning— until the horde arrived and her small camp in the woods started to resemble a baby version of the den. A raven who feels like an outsider, even though she just neatly herded her baby pack through an intricate dance and all of them moved their feet simply because she asked.

I sigh. I know just how hard it is to look into that particular mirror.

Which means I need to chat with a raven, but it's going to have to wait until she's exercised her wings some, and there's plenty going on down here on the ground in the meantime. I glance at the simple hat I started an hour ago. It's starting to look like something that might fit Hayden's head, which will amuse me if nothing else. I shouldn't be the only one who has to go blind from the glare of my own clothes.

Kelsey comes over with a cheese ball and I open my mouth like an obedient baby bird. "Thanks, cutie."

She smiles. "Fallon went to see who's in the woods."

In the woods and up on the ridges, but I'll be damned if I'm going to let a four-year-old worry about that kind of pack business today. Her giggles are doing plenty to attract whoever might be inching in this direction. "Probably a whole bunch of wild bears. I bet they can smell all the honey."

The delighted grin she shoots in Reilly's direction lights up every knitter in the vicinity. Which is a lot of faces. Three new wolves have joined us. A couple have found quiet spots in the nearby shade, and Moon Girl is up in a tree with Katrina, but all the rest are sitting where Hoot and Fallon put them.

Which is an interesting configuration, to say the least.

I let my eyes follow the path of the small girl who has carefully kept her movements within a few feet of the larger of the two sleeping platforms, and wonder just how much she knows. My wolf is kicking himself that he doesn't know every square inch of what can be seen from that ridge, but he suspects Kelsey does.

Fallon certainly did, and she made darn sure that whoever is up there has something to watch. Something that clearly involves Ben and Brandy and, if I don't miss my guess, Hoot as well. Which means the Dunn clan is bigger than I thought it was, and I'd lay bets it extends to a gray wolf with a hell of a limp, too.

I look up into several sets of cautious eyes.

Damn. I haven't asked a single question, but there are plenty of smart wolves here who know I have eyes in my head, and I'm using them way too loudly. Which is a mistake. This isn't a day for solving pack problems—it's a day for celebrating what has lived through them. I stick my needles into my ball of yarn and roll to my feet. "Have we eaten all the cookies, yet?"

Wrinkles smirks. She's about as easy to fool as Myrna, but she's clearly fine with helping me extract myself from a hole I shouldn't have fallen down in the first place. "Those are for people who are knitting blanket squares."

I hold up my lime-green circle, which is admittedly

not square. "It's a hat. How can those not count for cookies?"

She grins at me. "I don't make the rules. Talk to Reilly."

He looks completely horrified for the half a second it takes him to realize that she's joking. "You could have a berry bar. They're really good."

I snort. "So I heard."

His eyes widen. "They're all gone?"

Mikayla jumps up. "Seriously? I made two whole trays of them."

Giggles pour out of the tree overhead.

She looks up. "Dorie Eleanor Aboye, you're supposed to share those."

Dorie's head pokes out of the leaves, the branch she's balancing on barely big enough to hold a squirrel. "I am."

Mikayla makes a valiant effort to hide her grin. "With people who can't climb trees."

Dorie snorts. "Don't you use that tone on me, young lady."

Hoot laughs and tosses a pinecone at the head in the tree. "She learned it from you."

A second pinecone actually hits Dorie. She glares at me.

I grin. This pack does not lack for troublesome elders. "Nice toss there, Reilly."

He shoots me an astonished look. "It wasn't me."

I carefully don't look at Brandy's pink cheeks, but it doesn't take long for Ben to elbow her, happiness dancing in his eyes. "This is supposed to be a quiet, well-behaved knitting circle, Brandy Dunn. I can't believe you did that."

Jade toddles over, a pinecone clutched in each hand. "My help."

Ben elbows his big sister again. "See? Look what you started."

I inch backward on the sleeping platform. Healing trauma is sometimes a very crooked path—and if we're going to have a pinecone fight, I'm woefully under-armed.

6

FALLON

The knitting circle was supposed to be over by now. It's not even close. I stare at the clearing in the forest that was once my nice, neat base camp. "What happened? It looks like a pinecone factory exploded."

"Those would be called trees, sweetie." Ben, who looks far more disheveled than knitting should have ever made him, kisses my cheek, grinning like a loon. "Brandy started a fight."

I blink.

Reilly giggles. "It was great. Dorie and Glow and Katrina were up in the tree, so they had a height advantage, but they ran out of ammunition, and Moon Girl and Kel led a sneak attack from the woods, and Mikayla laughed so hard that she fell over in a plate of cheese balls."

My raven shakes her head, trying to dislodge the cloud she just flew through. "What?"

Eliza, who wasn't here earlier, grins. "We arrived just in time to watch Jade lick cheese balls off Mikayla's cheeks."

Our resident chef shakes her head wryly. "At least it wasn't a food fight."

Myrna snorts. "You think we would waste anything this good?" She holds up one of the honey cakes that are the closest Mikayla could come to something Brown once tasted at a country fair.

A quiet face I hardly recognize smiles and ducks her chin. "Those are really good."

I stare. I haven't seen Moon Girl out of her fur in years.

Reilly leans against her gently. "I bet if I asked really nicely, Mikayla would show us how to make them. Since it's my birthday week and all."

Wrinkles grins. "I could go raid Brown's secret honey stash."

Dorie sticks her head out of some high branches. "I'll help."

Brandy snickers. "You don't even like honey."

Dorie grins. "Nope. But I like messing with Brown."

Cats like messing with everyone. I look around for Brown, because he should be growling by now, and find him sitting with his carving knife, a small hunk of wood, and a couple of knitters companionably leaning against his log.

"That would be the introvert corner," says Ben quietly.

I scan the rest of our camp, more slowly this time. There are new faces—and a lot of old ones. Which is crazy. I was in the sky for at least three hours. "Has anyone left?"

He shakes his head slowly. "No."

That isn't how we planned this. Wolves were supposed to wander in and slip away, easy visits with no expectations. Ten minutes. An hour. A chance to spend a little bit of time in a small, mellow celebration. This is almost two dozen people and more time than some of these shifters have spent with this many packmates in years.

Rowdy packmates, apparently. "How's Brandy?"

Light concern hits Ben's eyes. "Close to done. So are some of the others. Kel's been helping to hold things steady, and so has Kelsey, but there are a few who need to escape." He shrugs sadly. "It's just that it's been a really great day, and nobody wants to let it go."

Of course they don't. I take his hand and rub his knuckles against my cheek. The knitting circle was a carefully calibrated call to pack, one that would gently reel people in and just as gently let them go again. An impromptu game with teams and silliness and exuberance is more like a truck full of catnip. One that somehow plowed into a whole bunch of shifters who are nowhere near catnip-ready.

Which means today was a miracle, and now we need to get people out of here. Fortunately, three hours in the sky wasn't entirely a waste of time. I turn in Ben's arms to face the pinecone wasteland that was once my base camp. "I could use some help, if some of you are willing."

Curious heads turn in my direction.

"There are some knitters in the woods. I'm thinking that they might appreciate some snacks."

Reilly's eyes light up—and then shadow with worry. "Maybe we were too noisy for them to make it all the way here."

An eleven-year-old bear just spent his day generating so much happiness that no one can figure out how to leave. He doesn't get to feel guilty. Not if I can help it. "I think you did just right." I smile at Moon Girl, who is sitting right beside him. In her human skin. Eating apple slices.

She swallows loudly enough for me to hear, but she also nudges his shoulder.

Reilly's eyes soften. "We had a lot of fun. Maybe the knitters in the woods would like to hear about the pinecone fight."

My raven always forgets that, for wolves, stories are shiny things. "That's a great idea. A teaser so that they'll be looking forward to the next *GhostPack News*."

He grins. "It's going to be really big."

Big newspaper editions, we can handle. It's big days that are a challenge. I look over at Mikayla and Elijah, who are already bundling small packages of snacks, and the handful of wolves easing in their direction.

Then I wince, because I can also see the ones who aren't ready to go. One of them is a wolf who still shakes when she sees a man in human form, and today she apparently led an attack from the woods with one. I shake my head. We've tried all kinds of ways to help Moon Girl stay human for more than a few minutes alone in the forest. Nobody ever considered starting a fight where paws can't throw the weapon of choice.

My raven hops from one foot to the other, radiating her distress. Brandy matters and Moon Girl matters and Reilly matters and I'm not used to navigating packs this big. There isn't one right answer for everyone, but I can see the exhaustion hitting Brandy's eyes. Whatever her wolf might want, her human is done.

I grasp at the only straw I can come up with on short notice and hope Brown will forgive me eventually. "Since the secret honey stash is over at Wrinkles and Brown's camp, maybe the honey-cakes lesson can happen over there."

Ben smiles, relief and gratitude in his eyes. "That's a great idea. Less sticky dishes for me to wash."

Wrinkles nods, her eyes twinkling. "Done."

Dorie swings out of her tree. Mikayla picks up an enormous mixing bowl. Reilly says something to Moon Girl, and she shyly joins him in the group readying to head to the other base camp.

Ravi takes his guitar over to where Brown and the silent knitters are sitting.

Brown snorts. "I'm staying here."

The two knitters flanking him nod silently.

That works. His cantankerous, solid presence will help ground Brandy's wolf, and it means Wrinkles and

Mikayla can go make honey cakes, and the wolves who need to leave can carry snacks and messages out into the woods, and this day can bring itself to a safe landing in several separate pieces that won't cause each other to crash.

Myrna gives Eliza a gentle push toward Wrinkles. "I'll stay to help with dishes here." She looks around and shakes her head. "And pinecone retrieval."

Cori smiles. "If someone takes Jade to the cooking lesson, I can help with cleanup here."

Dorie snorts and holds out her arms for the bright-eyed pup. "You thought we were letting you keep her?"

I exhale a very quiet sigh of relief. There are a lot of people here who are really good at herding wolves. Almost there.

I catch Ben's quiet, wistful glance at the rowdy honey-cakes crew. My raven nearly pecks my eyes out from the inside. I lean in, nuzzling his cheek. "Go. We're fine here."

He shakes his head. "She's had such a good day. I want it to stay that way."

Two wolves move themselves into position, one at Brandy's side, the other in her lap. Hoot yawns, and Kelsey shifts into a small red wolf and curls up with her chin on Brandy's knee. I snort. "I think that just got covered. I can fetch you in thirty seconds if something goes wrong. Go."

He huffs out a laugh. "You're not that fast."

Troublesome man. "Bring me back some honey cakes."

He leans his forehead against mine. "Are you sure about this?"

Yes. I'm in wild doubt about a lot of things, but Benjamin Dunn's right to have a life isn't one of them. "You're walking ten minutes through the woods so that you can wash all of Brown's dirty dishes. I'm sure."

He kisses me long enough to have Dorie and Wrinkles making entirely inappropriate commentary for pup ears, or it would be if this wasn't a wolf pack. I push off his chest, drinking in one long last gulp of the happiness in his eyes. "Go. I need to tell Glow and Reuben where to find the knitters in the woods."

Curiosity hits his eyes—and that damned sense of responsibility.

I pull out a look that used to work in back alleys. "Bring me back honey cakes, or there will be no more kissing, mister."

He kisses me again, just to prove that he can.

KEL

Reilly slams his hands over his eyes and sets off a wave of laughter that infects even the silent knitters. I shake my head. Goofy bear. One who has surfed the complicated waters of this week with grace and sensitivity and impeccable eleven-year-old timing.

Dorie and Wrinkles start herding their crew off into the woods, including a couple of wolves who are very surprised to find themselves in that group. I grin as Mikayla sticks out her tongue at a straggling Ben and neatly teases him into catching up.

The noise quotient goes down considerably as they make their way into the forest. I bend over and start picking up pinecones, listening to what's left and waiting for better clues on how to be useful.

Brandy is already in her fur, with Hoot and Kelsey leaning against her in human form and telling a story that involves Braden and a mysteriously vanishing bottle of ketchup. I hide a grin. It's a good story, and Hoot has meticulous instincts for how to apply the tales of the den out here in the woods.

Myrna and Cori are stacking dishes, and Elijah is using a pine bough as a surprisingly effective broom. I study him for a moment, my wolf's ears perking up as he leans against Myrna in the easy motion of lifelong friends. He's an older wolf who lives in the outermost reaches of our territory. I had him figured for a loner, but he's been here for hours and his movements are still relaxed and easy.

I don't have time to consider that for long, though. Invisible radar tickles the back of my neck and tugs my gaze elsewhere. Fallon has a small group gathered over by the tall tree that Dorie used as an excellent aerial attack zone. They're mostly the wolves I expected to leave hours ago—and they're all settling now that the chaos has departed and they have a job to do.

Which are just two of the darn smart moves Fallon pulled out of her back pocket without even trying hard.

My wolf tries to slink closer.

I roll my eyes. He knows the rules. We don't spy on packmates unless they deserve it. We can watch, though. I don't know much about the wolves Fallon is talking to. Reuben is in her baby pack, but he's a dotted line. A gravity beam, but a tenuous one. He's a submissive wolf, about my age, and he's got the feel of a man comfortable in the woods on his own—and of one who has something that keeps dragging him out of them.

I hide a grin. There was a second dotted line to him on Kennedy's whiteboard, and the other end connected to one of the most fiery, opinionated, ferociously independent wolves in this pack. Cheri has a weakness for Shelley's baking, so we see her at the den fairly often, but even Hayden hasn't been able to slow her down when she decides to roll right back out again.

I chuckle quietly. If there's a mate wind blowing there, I suspect that Reuben lives in interesting times.

The other two are sentries. Katrina is chatty and I'm surprised she's not off making honey cakes. Glow is a teenager I know far too little about, given how many hours she's spent in a tree on my turf. But as I look at them standing next to Fallon, I see a pattern. One I missed.

All of them know the shadows. Maybe not street, but something similar.

I frown. There are a lot of young wolves in this pack who adore Dorie and don't seem to have biological parents. Most have been a part of this pack for as long as they can remember, but not all. I scowl as I assemble the pieces.

The trauma in this pack didn't all come from Samuel's reign—and neither did its fierce survival skills.

I shake my head as I study the four of them. The ingrained caution is obvious now that I'm looking for it—and so is the orientation of their bodies toward Fallon as she gives them rough coordinates for the lone knitters in the woods. The shadow dwellers, assembling themselves to serve.

My wolf tries to slink in again. They need a liaison. An orbital communications guy.

I snort. Even my wolf has turned into a geek. And he knows better. You don't liaise with the shadows by walking up and asking for the job. Especially when I think it's already been taken.

A few moments ago, Lissa very quietly slipped off into the woods—and she's not headed back to the den.

7

FALLON

Yesterday was the carnival. Today is dealing with the toddlers who ate way too much cotton candy and didn't get a nap. I glare at Brown as he growls at me for the fourth time in two minutes. "Chill. Coffee doesn't do its thing any faster because you're being an annoying bear."

Wrinkles bumps into him almost hard enough to knock him over. Bear love. "Somebody slept on too many pinecones last night."

We picked up a ton of them, but the leftovers seem to have bred in the dark. "I told him to use the sleeping platform." Darn bear who insists on sleeping on the ground.

Wrinkles silently squats and presses down on the handle of the glass container that makes us coffee.

I sigh. "Sorry. I should know better than to try to speak in complete sentences before I've had at least two cups." First-world problems. I managed six years without coffee just fine, but Shelley keeps us well supplied now, and my bird thinks it's liquid gold. Which is really high praise from a raven.

Ben grunts as he drops off an armload of firewood, which is as close as he ever gets to a temper tantrum. He came back late in the night with Mikayla, both of them tipsy on pack shenanigans and honey cakes and tales of Brown defending his honey stash against all comers. This morning, he's as grumpy as I've ever seen him.

A wolf who once used to live at the center. Who thrived there.

I stare at the coffee and will it to be ready faster.

Brandy's tail disappears out of the doorway of the tent she's sharing with Mikayla and Hoot, and her tousled head puts in an appearance a few moments later. "Ugh. How is it morning already?"

This, I know how to fix. "You slept for eleventy billion hours, lazypants."

She glares at me.

My raven squawks, very sure it's a bad idea to poke at cranky wolves. I already know that. I also know that these ones need all the help I can give them to land on their feet, because today is going to be hard.

It's the day they all have to slide back into the shadows.

I sigh. I've had a few sunshine days in my life, on the streets and before. Days that made me forget who I was and what my life was like and gave me a real taste of something so good that when it slipped away again, every part of me wept.

Which we somehow have to navigate while a whole bunch of wolves head into the big party at the den tonight. Until this morning, I didn't think anyone in my baby pack would really care. We live out here in the shadows and like it, and we go visit the den for a few hours if we need a dose of sunshine and crowds and chocolate.

Which was all fine and good until a pinecone fight crashed into our camp and reminded us of just how much is still missing.

And why.

For a lot of the wolves I love, yesterday was their first big taste of sunshine in six years—and a sharp, potent reminder of who they once were. For me, it was a reminder that I've never been comfortable in the light.

Freaking knitting circle.

I drop a fork loudly enough to hopefully wake up Hoot, because I need reinforcements. There's a groan from somewhere inside the tent, but it doesn't result in any additional bleary eyes peering out the door.

Wrinkles puts a steaming mug of coffee in my hands. I shoot her a look of gratitude. She's awfully quiet this morning, but she's coping better than most of us. More practice, I guess. Even before, Brown mostly couldn't handle living at the den. She knows what it is to step into the center of pack and then have to step out again.

I inhale deeply and try to let the smell of caffeine soothe me.

I know what the problem of today will be. I just don't know how to make it hurt any less.

LISSA

I smile as I come around the bend of the small stream that flows through Bailey's camp. My son is about as muddy as a pup can be, and he's not the only one. Stinky could probably create a whole new boy from all the mud he's wearing, and Mellie looks more like a roly-poly hedgehog than a wolf.

I make my way over to Bailey, who's sitting safely out of mud-slinging distance, and grin. "Looks like they've had fun."

She snorts. "Mom started it. She just left to see if she can manage to get the mud out of her fur before tonight."

The pups pulled Tara back from the edge when Samuel killed her mate, and she's never forgotten it. Always, she's found ways to protect their right to be pups. "Is she coming back to clean up these three?" The showers at the den are cranky at best, and my son howls if I try to make him use them.

Bailey chuckles. "Rio dropped by and told me about the treasure hunt. You might as well just let them stay dirty."

I shake my head. That didn't sound like it involved mud when I left this morning, but Miriam has plans, and Hayden is really easy to lead astray when it's making one of his wolves happy. "Can I send him to the first day of school as a muddy wolf, too?"

That's happening the morning after the big party,

because our bear cub said so and because we were collectively dumb enough to agree with him.

Bailey rolls her eyes. "It's not school. Once we have a building, it will be school, and someone else will be teaching."

I grin cheerfully. That's Hayden's battle to fight. I won mine. All the members of the pack who are even close to school age are coming out here the day after the big party, and they're expecting a lesson. Which Bailey will provide because she can't help herself, no matter what lines she might be trying to draw inside her head. "What topic are you going to pick?"

The juveniles and teenagers have been making a list of things they want to learn about in the pack's online classroom. I don't think Bailey knows that they can see how often she drops by to check on it. The hazards of an eleven-year-old bear who figured out how to make himself the classroom administrator.

It's had some other interesting side effects, too. Last I checked, Rio and Myrna were both on the student list. Third and seventh grades, respectively.

Co-signed by their alpha.

I lean into my best friend's shoulder. "A lot of the teenagers are feeling insecure about how behind they are." Which is part of why we have a sentinel in third grade, but he can only fix so much. "And some of Dorie's crew were behind before they got here."

Bailey makes a face. "I'm not the teacher."

She needs to be. Because it's what she was born to do, and because it's going to take something that big to hold her steady, given what's coming. I wrap my arm around her and tug on her scraggly braid. It's only a little muddy, which seems strangely defiant of the laws of mud physics. "There were wolves watching the knitting circle yesterday."

Her body goes instantly still. "Who?"

I didn't go look, even though my wolf loves the high ridges. "I'm not sure. But Kelsey kept herself in view, and Hoot."

A long silence. "Grandpa Cleve?"

He's actually her uncle, and he's the most likely possibility, but he's not the only Dunn ghost in the forest. "They're feeling the call of pack, B."

Bailey exhales a ragged breath, one drenched in fear and grief and guilt.

I let my head rest on her shoulder. "Hayden needs to know." Kel, too, but once the veil of secrecy is lifted, he'll be able to find out all of the things he's carefully not let himself learn. Rio, too. He's sniffing things out in his own way, but his sentinel is in handcuffs.

We're going to need him free, really soon. All of them. "They can't do this blind. They need to know where to help, and where and why they can't, and there's no way they can figure that out until they know what happened."

Resistance billows out of Bailey and her wolf.

I let her feel the certainty in mine. The love. The absolute trust in a yellow-gold wolf who knows what it is to have his family shattered—and the love and trust I have for my best friend.

Bailey's head tips against mine, and I feel the tears, hot and wet, on my shoulder. "I don't know if I can get the words out, Liss."

I know that, too. I wrap my arms tight around her, offering the only thing I've ever really had to give, and hoping that it will eventually be enough. "You don't have to. You just have to give me permission to have them said. I'll have Myrna talk to him."

A shaky exhale of surprise. "Not you?"

I don't know if I could get them out, either. "She's our pack historian." She can start the story where it needs to start. All the way back at the beginning.

Bailey stays where she is for a very long time. When she finally sits up, I can feel the gathering of her wolf, of the dominant who needs to find her feet again. But her shoulder stays against mine as we watch three ridiculously muddy pups add just enough water from the stream that they don't crack.

I close my eyes.

The six years under Samuel, we were so very short of water.

BEN

The repetitive *thunk*ing in the woods isn't my first clue about where to find my mate, but it's the easiest to track.

I approach upwind, which won't matter to her raven, but my wolf has some manners he's never been able to ditch. She's in the shadows, and so is the tree she's aiming at. Not with pinecones. Nothing that wimpy for my feathered menace. She's throwing stones, palm-sized ones that would make a dent in most trees but are just bouncing off the one she picked.

Fallon always knows how to find the survivors.

I watch as she retrieves her weapons and goes back to her throwing spot. She's been angry since the day she fell out of the sky and dented the hell out of my easy, comfortable, unimaginative life. Which is a really good thing. I don't know if I would have survived what came two years later if she hadn't toughened me up some, first.

She didn't mean to do the toughening. That's just what happens when you love grit and steel.

I make some intentional noise as I walk over to where she's standing. She doesn't acknowledge me, but I've never seen anyone sneak up on her. I stand beside her, admiring her aim and trying not to think too hard about why she has it. Her early years didn't come with pretty accessories like baseball camp.

"Your brain is too noisy."

My lips quirk. "You could just ask nicely what I'm thinking."

She grins and fires another rock at the tree. "What would be the fun in that?"

Some days, Fallon is just funny. Other days, it serves as her quills. I reach out and gently squeeze her shoulder, looking for the woman under the porcupine. "Talk to me."

She growls, which is a behavior she picked up from

our wolves in a nanosecond, and hurls her last rock. "This sucks."

She has the most finely honed sense of justice of anyone I've ever known—and the most pithy ways of expressing it. "What part, exactly?"

"All of it." She throws up her arms. "Every person in this pack has gone through so much crap, and while we were in the middle of it, the answers were the same for everyone. Food, warmth, love, and don't die."

Fallon's hierarchy of needs. She was unrelentingly fierce in making sure we got all of them. "We still need those things."

Her raven caws, a sound that rings bell-deep inside me. "But they mean different things, now. It's so complicated."

My heart aches. Freedom is complicated, and she's never had it.

"How does everyone get what they want?" She stomps off to retrieve her stones. "I can't believe I'm even asking that, because I grew up knowing that nobody gets what they want, but all this birthday crap is messing with me."

My wolf honors her waterfall of words as the wild trust they are. I lean in and kiss the back of her head as she turns to throw her rocks again. "Hope isn't a dirty word, beautiful."

Thunk. "Says you."

My throat constricts. She's spent the last six years demanding that I believe in something she thinks is a fairy tale. Which is an act of love so enormous, I've never been able to fully wrap my arms around it.

Another rock hits the tree. I shake my head, cautiously amused. "We could have used you in the pinecone fight. It sucked not to have air cover."

Her lips twist into a reluctant smile. "Never pick a fight with someone who's got the high ground."

I'm next to useless as a fighter. That kind, anyhow. "Hoot said that Dad was maybe up on the ridge yesterday."

Fallon's face closes down. She turns to me, sorrow and guilt in her eyes. "I'm sorry. I should have told you."

I reach out and stroke her hair, as gently as I can. Her raven hasn't ever had any defenses against soft. "I knew, love. As soon as Hoot started moving us around."

Her cheek presses against my hand. "Is that why Brandy's tent is set up to face that way?"

I shrug helplessly. "Yes. I think I've seen him up there a couple of times. I didn't want to get anyone's hopes up, though."

She nods quietly.

I sigh. She's right. It's so complicated. "I hope it was him. I hope he heard Kelsey laughing, and saw Brandy throwing pinecones like a maniac."

A small, heartfelt smile. "She was happy?"

I wrap my arms around the woman who has always seen my shiny things. "She wasn't thinking. She wasn't being careful. She was just being goofy, exchanging fake hand signals with Hoot, and tickling Reilly to throw off his aim, and lifting Kelsey up so she could tie Dorie's tail to a tree branch with a big orange ribbon."

Which helped our team immensely—laughing cats have terrible aim.

Fallon's forehead tips into mine, her smile a lot bigger this time. "The sister you remember."

She always gets it. She can't always say it, but she always understands. "Yes."

A long, slow exhale. "Today is going to be hard for her."

For all of us. Those of us who would have been at the den party, once—and a beautiful raven who's never truly believed that she belongs there.

She strokes my shoulders, soothing me, bird-style. "You could go tonight."

Not a chance. I had my fun yesterday, and today I've got a sister who will resolutely try to glue herself back together without any help, a bear who needs to be in a far better mood by sundown or his mate will duct-tape him to a tree, and a couple of baby packmates who need to believe that the world won't end if they go to the den and have some fun. "I'm staying. You could go, though. You could make sure Mikayla and Wrinkles get there, and you could steal Brown some more honey. We did a lot of damage to his stash last night."

She raises an eyebrow. "I'm a retired thief, remember?"

She's never been a thief, not in any of the ways she thinks. "Fine. Take them some pretty rocks and bring back honey." It will get her as far as Shelley's kitchen pantry, and I trust the smart wolves of the den to figure out how to keep her there for a little while.

Fallon's eyebrows aren't done with me. "I can see what you're trying to do. You know that, right?"

I grin. "Is it working?"

She looks at me for a long time. "I might fly around for a while."

My wolf scowls. He made a promise eight years ago, and he was making progress until Samuel showed up. Now we have a good alpha, and it's way past time for his mate to feel like she belongs. Which can't happen if she's up in the sky.

I scratch behind his ears. She'll come down eventually. She always does. "Promise me you'll at least stop by the den?"

Her snort sounds exactly like Brown's. "Pushy wolf."

I wasn't. Not until a raven fell into my arms.

8

HAYDEN

I grab Kennedy before she lands face-first in the fire pit. Which nearly dumps us both in there as Ghost, hot on her heels, crashes into us.

They grin at me as they right themselves. Kennedy unbends her sword, which has lost most of its tinfoil covering. "I don't suppose you know which way Myrna went? Or Lissa?"

I know exactly where they both are, but if I tell the marauding invaders, there will be spinach in my cookies for weeks. "How did this treasure hunt get pirates, exactly?"

Ghost laughs and catches Braden as he tries to make the exact same leap over the fire pit as she did. "Argh, matey! We need to find ourselves some gold and silver."

Reilly giggles as he runs by with a map covered in big, red Xs. I'm pretty sure it's a spare one for Whistler territory that Rio dug out of the bottom of his backpack, but lack of accuracy has never stopped any self-respecting treasure hunter. Ebony rolls the one eye that isn't under a pirate patch and chases after him, hampered substantially by the toddler attached to her leg. Mellie loved the three-legged race so much that she's refusing to let anyone untie them.

Shelley walks over, looking pleasantly exhausted and stupendously pleased with herself. As she should. She laid out a birthday feast for the ages. I wrap an arm around her, because my wolf needs to hold on to someone and everyone else is running around hunting chocolate doubloons. Or those have been found and eaten and they're just hunting empty air. I don't think anyone cares. I glance up at the darkening sky. "Think anyone's planning on sleeping tonight?"

She chuckles. "This was your idea, Alpha."

I snort. The part of this that was my idea got trampled into dust days ago. "Really? And who made the pirate patches?"

She shoots me a prim look, but her shoulders are shaking with silent laughter. "That was Myrna."

Myrna can't sew any better than I can, and I happen to know that the sewing machine is currently hiding in the back corner of the pantry. Which means if Shelley wasn't the enabler of pirates, she knows who is. "And the tinfoil swords?"

Her eyes shine. "That was Kenny."

Damn, I missed that one. I saw him earlier, though, patiently teaching Stinky and Robbie the fine art of trying to run with two of their legs tied together. "So I guess you didn't make sure a half-dozen wolves from the satellite packs got turned into photographers for the night." All the ones who were looking uncomfortable and smelling furry when they arrived.

She snickers. "Don't you know anything that's going on in your pack?"

Not even close. I know all about the treasure who runs my kitchen, though. I squeeze her shoulders again. "You're a devious and sneaky wolf, Shelley Martins."

She pats my arm, glowing with quiet pleasure she probably thinks I can't see. "It takes one to know one."

There are nights she still cries in her sleep—and then there are nights like this. I keep my arm around her, because this much happiness in my pack makes me dizzy. I also scan the den again, because just like the woman who was once mated to evil, this pack still has swirling undercurrents that can suck a wolf under without notice. It isn't my shift on lifeguard duty, but it will be, soon.

Shelley leans into my ribs. "How many are out there?"

Of course she knows. "I'm not sure. At least a few."

She exhales quietly. "I saw Kel picking up some of the care packages."

It isn't his shift on lifeguard duty, either, but that never stops him. He has help tonight, though. The big black wolf of death, and some volunteers that Kel quietly noted and said nothing about. I cast a glance up at the sky. Fallon landed earlier and told us where to find a couple of stragglers who were having trouble crossing the old inner perimeter.

Which worries my wolf. He can't use his teeth and claws on invisible lines.

"Don't." A brisk nudge from the wolf beside me. "The problems will still be there tomorrow, and the joy might not be." Shelley puts a battered tinfoil sword in my hand. "Go chase some pirates."

I shake my head, my wolf thoroughly amused by his feisty packmate. "Doesn't a sword *make* me a pirate?"

She chuckles and pushes me toward the other side of the river, where a pitched battle appears to be in progress. "I guess you'll find out."

I grin. Story of my life.

FALLON

My bird complains as I bank toward the den again. She doesn't like being up this high or out this late. The moon's too bright. Dark birds are too easily seen.

I tell her to hush. The moon is helping me keep an eye on the woods below. The den is wild tonight, but the forest around it isn't much quieter. There are wolves slinking around all over the place, some coming and some going and some stuck in between the two.

I swing toward the sector Kel asked me to cover next. I didn't expect to be part of anything this organized, but he's had me doing flyovers, finding the stuck wolves and passing their coordinates to someone who can help get them moving again. Glow is out here, and so is Reuben, and a huge black shadow that Bailey told me to go fetch when Moon Girl started to shake.

Rio got her to the den with some gummy bears, a toy sword, and a patently false story about Shelley needing help defending the kitchen from cookie pirates.

My raven kind of wanted the sword. It was really shiny.

I see a couple of faces and skim through pine branches until I can get a better look, but it's just Hoot and Adelina. On their way out to Dorie's camp, probably. Hoot's been escorting a lot of the wolves as they leave. Helping them carry their care packages and separate gently and go when they need to go.

This pack might make mistakes once, but they rarely make them twice.

I guess we learned that the hard way.

I see a pale face pressed against a tree and bank sharply. My raven squawks. Urban jungles are a lot more predictable and well lit. I soothe her as best as I can and try to avoid running into any stealth branches. I saw Rio not too far away. I'll go tell him where to find the tree-hugger.

Or not. I spy Teesha, incoming under my flight path, her loping stride as fast as any wolf. That works. Most of the ghosts who are making their way in tonight are from her baby pack. The ones with broken wolves and humans who still want to belong. I dive low enough to make sure she sees me, in case she wants a messenger, and when that gets no reaction, I aim skyward again.

Once I clear the zombie pine boughs trying to eat me in the dark, I start an easy, soaring spiral outward from the den. It takes me a while to work out as far as the outer orbits, and when I get there, I'm not the only one on duty. I see Kel up on a ridge, and a red wolf down by the river vanishes into the shadows when I get close. Bailey, maybe, but a lot of the Dunns share her coloring, and they're hard to tell apart in the dark.

I frown. If it's her, she's not supposed to be out here. She's supposed to be hunting for treasure.

My raven smirks. Silly wolves, hunting for shinies that aren't real.

I shake my head. Silly bird, flying in the dark when she could be eating tasty food and listening to good music and keeping the promise her mate wasn't brave enough to ask her to make. I won't ever really know how to be part of a big, boisterous, normal, wholesome pack, but he deserves for me to try.

I sigh and wing down over a rock outcropping that's casting eerie shadows under the light of the moon. It's a place some of the lone wolves sometimes gather in the afternoon sunshine. One in particular that I'm seeking.

Nothing moves as I fly over, and I contemplate heading denward again. I've flown enough acrobatics in the trees that my shoulders are tired. I can go help Teesha herd any last tree-huggers, report in so that Kel doesn't send out a search party for a concussed raven, and maybe make a quick stop at the kitchen to see if any cookies survived the pirates.

One of the shadows at the far end of the rocks develops a tail.

I pivot sharply. The tail vanishes, but I know what rock it's under. I land in haste, which ends up a whole lot less impressive than I intended when one of my legs misses my pants. I hop around like an idiot and keep my eyes pinned on the only shadows down here dark enough to hide a wolf.

Nothing furry emerges, but this isn't my first time visiting this particular ghost. Visits he doesn't always tolerate, but that's fine. He's earned the right to be cranky.

I unbutton the pocket on my cargo pants and pull out the sat phone that caused the problem with my landing. The mesh bag that lets me land in my pants isn't designed to carry all the extra things my bird tries to shove into it. "I've got pictures. Of yesterday."

I hold up the phone and open the photo app. I have no idea if this will work, but I learned on the street—doubts are something you let shake you after. "This one's pretty funny. Brandy faceplanted into some cheese balls, which are really delicious, by the way."

My bird protests. The light from the screen is killing her night vision dead.

She's just mad she didn't get any cheese balls. "Here's another one with Jade licking her off. She's Ravi's pup. A total cutie. All innocent green eyes until she steals your bacon."

There's a sound behind me, so faint I barely hear it.

I remember when Cleve took me out into the forest and tried to teach me how to walk quietly. I was a lost cause, but he was so kind to the awkward raven who had never been in the woods.

I take a seat on the ground and scroll to another photo, holding the phone out at wolf height. "This one is Ben sneaking up on Dorie with a pinecone slingshot he improvised. Which apparently didn't work very well until Brown improved the design."

My heart squeezes. That's my guy, happy to use his incompetence to entice others to come closer. Somehow, they never figure it out.

"Here's Kelsey, howling a fight song she made up." My raven likes that one. Wild pup. Fierce pup.

I don't know if her grandpa even knows her name. Nobody knows how much human is left inside Cleve's wolf.

The next photo is what I saw in real life when I got back to camp the second time. "This is Hoot and Brandy and Kelsey, all taking a nap." The photographer had a sense of humor and included the pinecones that someone piled up beside them in case they needed ammunition when they woke.

That pile is still there.

Warm breath skims over my shoulder.

My raven wants to hit me over the head and knock me unconscious so she can drag me the heck out of here, but I don't move anything except my thumb. "That's Ben, trying to pretend like he didn't eat the last honey cakes this morning. He hid them under some of Wrinkles's teas, so they smelled like dirty socks, but he looked pretty happy when he ate them."

A crackle beside me and a human hand comes into view.

I don't breathe.

I can't.

The hand makes a jerky, frustrated gesture.

I scroll backward through the photos. Slowly. Keeping my eyes very carefully averted from the man crouching beside me.

He says nothing.

That's not a problem.

I speak silence just fine.

9

FALLON

Life, back to normal.

Mostly. We still have a pinecone cairn in the middle of our camp and our kitchen stores are running perilously low, but other than that, this almost feels like a regular day. The kind that landed after hell lost a dominance fight and we got issued a base camp, anyhow.

Brown pounds in a nail on the wall of the cooking shack that's going up at light speed, probably because Ben isn't helping. Wrinkles looks up from where she's carefully brushing dirt off some wild onions, and smiles at me. "Want some tea?"

I make a face. "I feel fine."

She chuckles. "This is mint and chamomile. As far as I know, it won't cure anything."

That doesn't sound bad, actually. I've already had

two cups of coffee, and holding a warm mug in my hands is my new favorite way to do nothing on a crisp morning.

My bird mutters. She thinks we should fly south for the winter.

I hide a grin. She so easily forgets what winters up here are like. This is practically still summer.

Ben's shoulder bumps companionably against mine. "You're in a good mood."

I snort. "I'm not freezing. Yet."

He laughs. "Wrinkles is making me a brand-new sweater, so you'll be plenty warm."

I glare at him, but it's hard to mean it. "I don't steal all your sweaters."

He raises a skeptical eyebrow.

Fine. "I give them back. Sometimes."

He takes my hand in his and rubs his thumb over my palm. My heart jerks. It looks so very much like the hand from last night. The one that reached out a single finger to touch the screen of my phone and stroke a pup's face.

A hand I don't want to talk about, because today desperately needs to be a normal day.

Ben kisses my knuckles. He can always tell when I'm tangled. "Kel called. He's heading into town to pick up some packages if you want to tag along. Apparently the bears sent something for Reilly."

That could be anything from a box to a small country. "I don't have any finished auctions that need to ship, but I could hit up the thrift stores." I try to shift my brain back to the business of helping to keep my pack financially viable. I usually just fly into town when I need concrete under my feet, but a ride might be nice. "What are you doing today?"

The kisses are working their way up my arm. "I thought I might head to the school lesson with Mikayla."

"Yes." A head descends between us. "You should do that. Eliza and Cori are coming here and I'm going to be mending all day. You both suck with a needle and thread, so shoo. Go someplace else."

I rub my cheek against Brandy's bossy wolf. It's really good to see her out and about and saying smart things. If Ben goes with Mikayla, maybe she won't feel so silly about wanting to go to school. We all saw the yearning in her eyes when lessons hit the list of birthday-week activities.

Which my raven doesn't understand at all, but she hated what little school she had to endure. She likes to be on top of buildings, not inside them.

Wrinkles sets a mug of steaming tea in my hands. "I think Shelley's paints for the raven mural have arrived, too. She's trying hard not to be excited about them. I think she's a little worried that she's forgotten how to paint."

At least she learned in the first place. "Sounds like Kel could use the help."

I get a look from my mate that says this conversation isn't over, but I can feel his wolf yearning for the same easy day that I am. It's a walk we've learned together, these past six years. The days can't all be hard. You can't let them be. Sometimes you have to ignore the shit that's lurking and just breathe.

Or drive into town with a taciturn wolf and help him sling packages around. "Do we need anything from the den or town?"

Wrinkles drops a couple of small hunks of wood on her tea-brewing fire. "Already sent Shelley a list. It will be ready for Ben and Mikayla to pick up on their way back from school. Or you can. Or Brown can do a run."

"We've got it." My mate squeezes my shoulder. "You should go. Kel wanted to get an early start."

I snicker. Kel can be evil that way. Wolves, especially young ones, do not do early mornings. The hazards of being creatures of the moon, I guess. "I'll finish my tea and go find him."

Ben drops a smacking kiss on my forehead. "Have fun."

I lean into him. Always, he lets me go to soar the skies and walk the concrete. And always, I come back to him.

When I come back this time, I need to tell him about the hand in the dark.

RIO

I grin into the morning silence. The wise women of the den spread Reilly's birthday gifts out over several days, and today's was a stack of small paper squares in every color of the rainbow.

Which Ebony apparently knows how to fold into something resembling a bear when she does it, and a bunny or a dragon or a flower or a mushy cloud when the rest of us try. That hasn't dampened anyone's enthusiasm, however.

Kennedy holds up her final product, which is bright and cheerful and totally mangled. "This looks just like you, Riles."

He glances up from his careful folding and laughs. "I don't have three ears."

She rotates her creation contemplatively. "I think that's a tail. Or maybe a nose."

My wolf snickers.

I tell him to concentrate on the paper we're still trying to get past the first two folds. Sentinels are really good at a lot of strange things, but origami clearly isn't one of them.

A small head ducks under my arm and climbs into my lap. Kelsey takes the bright blue paper out of my fingers and exchanges it for a very pink folded flower. "Fallon is coming. She's going to pick up Shelley's paints with Kel."

I actually knew that, but I'm a little surprised she does. "How is Shelley feeling about that?"

"Happy-scared, like when she sings with Ravi." She neatly fixes the fold that I didn't do right.

I grin. I suspect my bear is about to become a flower instead. "Does she need someone to hang out with her?"

A head shake that's mostly focused on a new fold. "Kenny brought her a flower growing in a pot this morning. It was happy-scared, too, but I sang it a song."

Sentinels occasionally develop big egos. I'm never

going to have that problem. I can't even keep up with a four-year-old. "Taking care of all the important stuff before I finished my coffee, huh?"

Ebony walks by us, looks down at the paper in Kelsey's hand, and snickers.

I roll my eyes. Troublesome betas. This one held things down at the den last night while Kel and I did our thing in the woods, and could maybe use an escape for a while. "Fallon and Kel are headed into town, if you want to go."

She looks at me blandly. "And miss school?"

Oops. I forgot about that, which is an issue, since I'm supposed to be in third grade with Stinky. "Right. That."

Kelsey giggles. I suspect she's going to end up in third grade, too. Reilly's been spreading the kind of school propaganda that has even most of the skeptical teenagers in the woods signed up, and Kelsey is a way easier sell than Adelina or Katrina.

Although I don't think Dorie plans to give any of them a choice. She's a very fierce cat when she wants to be. One who used to leave for a few days every so often and come back with a stray. Which means my wolf will happily be her minion any day of the week.

Even if that involves sitting through a repeat of third grade.

Hopefully, there won't be any paper-folding involved.

Kelsey and Ebony look up at the horizon in unison. The ex-soldier looks down at the pack psychic and grins.

"Come help me show Ghost how to fold a flower, sweet pea. Rio needs to go chat with Fallon."

Rio didn't know that, but he's a biddable wolf. I kiss the top of Kelsey's head and roll us both up to our feet.

Then I head to the river to find a pretty rock for a raven.

FALLON

It's weirdly quiet. I wing into the den, my eyes peeled for signs of impending doom, but all I see is a dozen shifters of various sizes lazing in a sunny spot by the river.

I land and slide into leggings, and then pull on a woolly sweater that was hell to fly with, but totally worth it. I pop my head through the neck and barely miss the incoming bear paws.

Reilly wraps his arms around me, tight enough to have my bird squawking.

He lets me go instantly, his face rueful. "Sorry about that. I haven't wrestled with Hayden yet this morning, and I guess my bear isn't as calm as I thought he was."

What a crappy thing for an eleven-year-old kid to have to worry about. I ruffle his hair. "It's not a problem. You just surprised me, that's all. Birds are tough, and I like your hugs."

He smiles and gives me a much gentler one. "Thank you for your story. It made me feel really special."

I blink.

He holds up the book in his hands, the one I helped Myrna assemble at a website I found online. A very special edition of *GhostPack News*, full of stories about Reilly and every precious picture we could find.

My offering was a couple of paragraphs about his first board book, one that I found for a nickel at a garage sale and he didn't put down for weeks. "You loved that book. I can probably still recite every word of it in my sleep."

Layla lifts up her head from whatever she's doing and laughs. "Me, too."

Reilly giggles. "It was about snowflakes, right? They were all white except for one that was orange when he was sad and green when he was happy and purple when he felt loved."

Guh. I pull him in for the kind of hug his bear deserves. "I always thought orange got a bad rap in that book."

He grins. "We have orange origami paper if you want to learn how to fold something."

I grab my raven's claws before she derails my plans for the morning. "Maybe when I get back. I need to go find Kel. I'm heading into town with him."

"He's in the kitchen, stealing cookies." Reilly heads back over to what I can now see is a lesson in folding small, bright squares of paper. Which isn't anything my raven can possibly do with good manners, so I wave at the few heads that look up long enough to see if I'm an invader. Then I head to the kitchen.

I detour around the big sunning rock and spy Moon Girl lying in its shadows. She's not alone. Eliza is there with her knitting, and Ravi, playing his guitar. But Moon Girl is struggling, all the same. In her fur, and shaking, and fighting a pitched battle with what lives inside her.

I frown as some of the lack of ease I felt last night finally finds its words. Moon Girl wants to be here, and she deeply wants the wolves of her baby pack to believe they can get here, too. But I can see her visceral reaction —the knowing deep in her bones that her head can't talk her through. Just like the pale face hugging the tree last night. This den, this place, this few hundred square meters of territory, is a really hard place for them to be.

It doesn't feel safe. It doesn't feel like the center, the heart of pack, that their wolves need.

That's not true for everyone. Hoot is over there reading to Robbie, and she looks happy and easy and like she belongs here. But there are a lot of ghosts in the woods who have even more reason to hate these few hundred square meters than Moon Girl.

I wrap my arms around my ribs. I know the pack is working really hard to change that, to make the den a place of safety and home and welcome. I'm just not sure there's any way to talk to Moon Girl's bones.

"I see it, too."

My raven nearly streaks into the sky. I glare at the big guy who just materialized beside me. "Quit scaring people."

Rio chuckles and runs his fingers over my shoulders, neatly unruffling my invisible feathers.

My bird cocks her head. He's never done that before.

He smiles a little. "Whistler Pack has plenty of

ravens. I know you handle being treated like a wolf just fine, and if you prefer that, my big furry dude would be happy to oblige."

Goofball. One who has just mellowed out my bird with a few strokes of his fingers. Maybe there are some ways to talk to bones. I look over at Moon Girl. "It's really hard for her to be here."

He nods. "It was like that for Ravi, too. Still is, some days. For some of the wolves of this pack, this is the den they defended. For others, it's not nearly so straightforward."

I'm pretty sure a lot of that is still on the list of things we aren't talking about, but anybody with half a brain could figure it out just looking at Moon Girl's trembling.

"It's not always like that when she's here," he says quietly. "Today has hit her hard."

I think about the shaking hand in the dark. Some days do that. "Yeah."

He wraps an arm around my shoulders. "She's my job today. Kel is waiting for you by the truck."

My raven doesn't want to go. Moon Girl used to help me dig for earthworms.

Fingers tap quietly on the back of my hand.

I look down. "Is that some kind of weird sentinel woo?"

He chuckles. "Nope. A raven told me that it's how they tell their chicks it's safe to come out of the egg or leave the nest."

There is so much I don't know about being a raven.

I'm probably a better wolf, but I'm no match for Rio,

and I'm definitely not the right shifter to help anyone figure out how to be at the den. Which means my butt needs to load into a truck and help cart packages around while he does the hard stuff. I turn to go. "She likes the orange gummy bears best."

His lips quirk. "What makes you think I have any of those?"

My bird rolls her eyes. "Braden likes the yellow ones, and Lissa and Jade like the green ones that match their eyes, and you eat the heads off of yours to make Reilly laugh."

He gapes at me.

I walk away, grinning.

I see things, too.

10

KEL

I slam the door of Rio's truck and wince at the reverberations it sets off inside my wolf. He's been jumpy all morning. Which might be an actual issue, or just way too much birthday cake.

The raven who rode with me in absolute silence glances over, her eyes wary.

So much for having a casual conversation on the way to pick up a few things from town. My beta skills need a tune-up. "I'm good. My wolf's a little out of sorts."

She huffs out a laugh. "Is that what you call it?"

Smartass. One whose baby pack has settled on a kind of camaraderie that would fit in fine with every group of soldiers I've ever known. Feel deeply and cover it with snark. So I grin. "What do you call it?"

Her lips quirk. "Are we grabbing packages first, or

can I hit the thrift store and meet you at the post office in a bit?"

My wolf is having one of those days where leaving anyone prowling around on their own recognizance is likely to make him crazy. Which isn't reasonable, but sometimes his paranoid furry ass is right. "Let's grab the deliveries first and see if the bears have left us room to load up anything else."

"Our gift will not take up much room."

My wolf jolts to attention. Bear. Polar bear, to be precise, coming up on our six. He's doing his best to blend in, but that's not easy when you're three hundred pounds of casually strolling malevolence. The sidewalk around him is eerily clear of traffic.

I hold out a hand. "Ivan."

He takes it respectfully. "Sergeant."

I snort. "Not for twenty years."

His black eyes glint with amusement.

I shoot a quick look over at Fallon. She's standing by the truck, her hip cocked, a look of bland disinterest on her face.

Which, since she's not a flaming idiot, is an impressive bit of theater. Polar bears trigger every primitive alarm of every shifter I know. My wolf calls this particular bear a friend, and he's still convinced this would be an excellent time to haul ass out of here.

I adjust my stance enough to pull the scary apex predator's attention my way. "I thought you were sending us a package for Reilly."

He reaches a hand into his pocket and pulls out a

thumb drive that's nowhere near as big as his thumb. "I felt a desire for a road trip."

There are no roads between here and where he came from. I eye the thumb drive cautiously. Plenty of bear ideas look innocent enough at first glance. "Do I want to know what's on that?"

He stares at me, unblinking.

I can play that game. I stare back, ignoring my wolf's sizable protests.

Ivan's lips finally quirk. "We talked to the young cats who run the online naturalist website. The ones who have been featuring Reilly of late."

I hide a deeply sincere grimace. The world isn't ready for Sierra and Sienna to know a polar bear. Especially this one.

Ivan looks almost bashful. "They instructed us in the proper collection of raw video footage of wild bears."

Oh, man. Reilly is going to turn into a giant puddle of bear water.

Ivan pats the thumb drive carefully. "There are several hours of polar bear juveniles, one hour of a grizzly bear family, and some footage of a young Russian sand bear."

As far as I know, those don't live in Canada. I try not to grin at the idea of a whole bunch of Inuvik polar bears swarming the planet, trying to film their wild cousins. "That can't have been easy to get."

Ivan looks a little disgruntled. "They assured us this would be adequate for a first delivery. The sand bear was more of a challenge than we expected. But we will learn.

We will send more video each month. Reilly will narrate."

My wolf pulls his head out of his ass. "Will narrate what?"

A raised eyebrow that sends my wolf right back into hiding again. "The new video channel for bears."

I stare. "You're giving him a video channel for his birthday?"

Ivan shrugs, like this is obvious.

I definitely didn't drink enough coffee this morning. I try to come up with some kind of appropriate response, but all words fail me.

Ivan decides that I've taken up enough of his time with my questionable intelligence and smiles at Fallon in the way of terrifying apex predators when they're trying not to be scary. "I know young Reilly prefers bright colors. Perhaps you can help me pick out a gift bag that would be suitable from one of the stores here in town. We do not have such things in my territory."

Everything inside Fallon jerks to red alert long before he's done speaking.

Fuck. I whip out Ivan's most important credential. "This is the bear who's acting as Eamon's parole officer."

A subterranean growl. "She knows who I am."

FALLON

I've faced down predators before. I've never looked into eyes like this.

I try to find words. Ones that will somehow get me out of here, because I was hoping he might just ignore me and now he's not and I have a sudden, desperate need to visit Argentina. Now. Before my bird turns to stone and never flies again.

Except I'm pretty sure the very scary bear isn't going to let me walk away.

He also hasn't eaten me. Yet.

I try to find some of my wits, because this is so much worse than being caught naked in his den with his coins in my hand. He wasn't at all surprised to find me here with Kel, and that means Ivan knows about my pack.

In the streets that shaped me, there is no greater sin.

He holds up his hands, very slowly, the thumb drive hidden in one enormous fist. "I apologize. I've distressed you, and that's not my intention."

I have no idea what his intentions are, but I know how I need to play this. Protect and sever. Absolve my pack of all guilt. "I acted alone. You need to know that."

Surprise lands in his eyes, and something that looks strangely like respect. "Impressive."

I swallow. "When you were assigned as Eamon's parole officer, I tried to make it right. I know the coins aren't in the same condition as when I took them. I'm sorry."

Kel's hand lands on my shoulder. "What the fuck is going on here?"

He's not talking to me. He's talking to the scary bear.

Ivan smiles again and it's the most frightening thing I've ever seen. "It is Fallon's story to tell. Perhaps you will allow me to buy us all lunch while she tells it."

Hell, no. If I'm going to be a polar bear snack, he doesn't get to eat me as a chaser to a cheeseburger. "I can make it short. I'm a thief. A good one. I used to steal when I lived on the street." My bird is pecking a hole through my skull, but Ivan probably doesn't care if his snack is a little dented. "I did it to survive, and to help my friends, and I don't apologize for it."

I don't look at Kel. I've seen the disappointment that sneaks into people's eyes. They don't get it. They never do.

Ivan nods fractionally. "As you shouldn't."

It takes a moment for his words to land. "What?"

He smiles again. It's no less scary the third time. "You think like a polar bear. Now tell me why you stole from one."

My bird gibbers. I grab her tail feathers. I have to stay. Protect and sever. "I went straight when I mated with Ben. I didn't want to bring any trouble to his family, and they gave me so much. There wouldn't have been any point."

Ivan nods like that makes complete sense. "You had no need. To steal under such circumstances would have been inconsistent with your values."

I stare at him again. If you take away most of the fancy words, he's speaking street. "Something like that, yeah."

He just looks at me, a hunter with eternal patience.

My bird sways. I stuff her in a dark corner and tell her not to puke. "When the assholes took over our pack, it got bad. They used all the money for beer and didn't bother to feed the women and pups. We all tried to help. I bought things in town, from garage sales, mostly, and used the computer at the library to sell them online."

They're both watching me now, two utterly silent predators.

I swallow. "Sometimes Eamon and his lieutenants would tighten up the south and west perimeters." I don't tell them why. I saw them catch Gideon's family when they were trying to sneak out.

"The ways into town," says Kel, very quietly.

I nod. "When we got really short of food, I went north. One of the rogue cats let me use his sat phone so I could keep selling things online." I force my eyes to meet violent black ones. "I stole from your bears and sold what I took and used the money to buy food for my pack."

There is nothing but the sound of Kel's quietly indrawn breath.

My raven rises up, fierce and strong and proud, the street in me snapping into place. "I won't apologize for that, either. Except for your coins. I don't steal from friends. If I'd known you were going to become a friend to our pack, I wouldn't have taken them."

The polar bear opens his mouth. Closes it.

Opens it again.

Then he explodes into endless, deafening noise that reverberates through every feather of my bird and reduces my human to quivering slime.

It takes an eternity to realize that he's laughing.

KEL

Fucking bear.

I pull my shit together, because Fallon clearly believes that I would let her swing in the wind alone, and if Ivan keeps laughing at this volume, he's going to render the entire town unconscious.

I try one of the hand signals that I learned from a long-distant mutual acquaintance.

Ivan pulls himself abruptly together. Then he drops a hand on Fallon's shoulder, which takes whatever is left of her courage and turns it to dust. "I have some questions."

If they aren't nice ones, we're going to see just how well my nerve blocks work on a polar bear.

He doesn't take his eyes off Fallon. "Tell me why you took those coins in particular."

Her eyes stare, uncomprehending.

A lightbulb somewhere in my brain starts to glow dimly. "Because they're light enough to fly with, I assume. And worth something."

Ivan is still hunting his prey. "They're three of the least valuable coins in my collection."

"I know." Fallon's throat sounds like it just got run over by a tank, but she gets the words out. "I only wanted enough money to feed the pups, and I only took from bears who I thought could afford the loss."

"The coins have sentimental value."

Her eyes close. "I'm sorry."

"I do not seek your apology. Only that you answer my questions." He shakes her in a way that I suspect he intends to be gentle. "Their value to me is in their history, and now that history has a new chapter. One of loss and homecoming and service to those who suffered and fought valiantly."

Fucking bear. He needs to speak English, not Russian poetry. I open my mouth to try to translate, and get a look that sends my wolf scurrying.

Ivan drops to one knee in front of her. "You only made one mistake, my ferocious friend. And for that, you must make me a promise."

Bloody overdramatic polar bear. I keep that thought to myself, however. I don't know how civilian life has landed for this particular bear, but laughing at him probably isn't the appropriate response. Especially when Fallon is going to blow over in the next stiff breeze.

I lean against her, buttressing her from the side. She doesn't even notice.

Ivan takes her limp hand in his, his eyes nearly level with hers. "Next time you have need of assistance for any reason, you will not fly into my territory and sneak into my den and leave no trace."

My wolf's eyes widen. Polar bears are the best hunters on the planet. Fallon isn't just a thief—she's a *really* good one.

He lifts up her hand and pats it with his free one. "Next time, bright Fallon, you will come to my door and tell me you are in need of assistance, and every bear in the Inuvik territory will be yours to command."

Fucking hell.

He just offered her an army—and she's still not breathing. I lean into her a little harder. I have no idea how to speak raven when she's this far gone, so I'm going with wolf. I raise an eyebrow at the big man on his knees who needs to dial down the intensity about ten notches before she vaporizes. "How do you know it was her?"

His eyes gleam with amusement. "Polar bears are excellent trackers."

I snort. "And full of shit."

His eyes narrow.

Oops. This polar bear hasn't spent as much time with goofy wolves as his cousin Ronan. "So you drove down all this way, following your nose?"

A small, very Russian shrug. "There was a faint scent when she returned the coins. One I did not need to track. I recognized it from the day I came to your territory to supervise the transport of Eamon Martins."

I don't know if it's the name that shakes Fallon, or the realization that she made a mistake. I only know that she starts trembling beside me—and smelling of bird.

I turn my back on the polar bear, because it's not him she's scared of anymore. I know that as deeply as I know anything. He just yanked her out of the shadows and ripped one of the central truths of her life in two.

Always, the fiercest battles are the ones within.

I face her, one person who has hyperventilated in that awful, naked place to another. "Breathe. In. Out."

She stares, uncomprehending.

Hands reach around me and compress her ribs. "Like this, *myshka*."

The sound that comes out of Fallon is more squawk than breath, but it works. She gulps air in when Ivan lets go and squawks it out again on the next compression. By the third one, she's glaring at him.

He lets go of her and grins. "Your beta is a fool. No one should turn their back on a polar bear. However, he is also your friend, so I won't eat him today."

She almost grins back—and then she looks at me, and all the light in her dims.

Fuck. Whiplash days need to come with some warning. I look at her and keep my back to the obnoxious bear. "Don't. I don't have Rio's fancy words, or Hayden's, but don't you dare believe your pack will think less of you for this." I can't give her back her shadows, but I can damn well tell her the truth about the light. This part of it, at least.

A subterranean growl starts up at my back.

I throw up an annoyed hand. "Cut it out, Ivan. You can't threaten to eat me more than once a day. New rule."

The next sound out of him is a reasonably well-behaved snort.

One down, one to go. She doesn't plan to make it remotely easy on me, which is fine. My wolf doesn't trust easy either.

I know what's hit her. There are some universal truths about making your way out of the shadows. One is that you do most of it a slow, painful step at a time.

Another is that sometimes a polar bear or a really annoying ten-year-old wolf will yank the map out of your hands, shred it, and give you a new one. Which feels approximately like setting yourself on fire. "You were feeding the pups. You were providing for pack when the wolves who should have been doing it had utterly failed you. You're a fucking hero, Fallon."

Ivan growls companionably.

Fallon pales, but she apparently learns fast. "Cut it out, Ivan."

I chuckle, which sends my wolf into conniptions. He's already seriously unimpressed with me for ignoring the apex predator at my back. "Reilly is an unusually polite bear."

She snorts. "Brown isn't."

Brown is a cute ball of fluff compared to the man behind me. "Ivan is going to go home and tell this story over copious glasses of vodka all winter. You've made his year. You and I are going to go home and tell this story and you're going to have to work really hard if you don't want to be Reilly's next headline."

Resignation lands in her eyes.

Fuck. She's never been in the center. She truly has no idea what's waiting for her there. "He'll be writing the story of your bravery, Fallon."

Fifty shades of confusion land on her face. "I'm a *thief*."

I could spend the next decade trying to convince her otherwise and lose. Instead, I grin and yank her a little further into the light. "Yup. But you're our thief."

11

FALLON

I feel like I'm flying upside down, like all the laws of gravity just changed and nobody bothered to tell me how the new ones work.

Well, Kel tried, but my raven stopped believing him ten kilometers outside of town.

I walk the last short stretch into camp, timid and wary and a whole bunch of other things I hate dragging in here with me. And still feeling oddly light. I try to tell myself that's just some kind of weird aftereffect from an encounter with a polar bear.

Which I forget about really fast the moment I see Ben's face.

I walk over, sit down next to him, and glare at the woman facing him. I have no idea what bomb Bailey has dropped on my camp, but this was supposed to be a normal day. My baby pack needed one.

Her lips twitch.

I keep glaring. "I just dealt with a polar bear, so whatever you're stirring up needs to go away and come back next week."

Ben freezes beside me.

Crap. Having a pissing contest with Bailey might make my raven feel better, but it was entirely the wrong way to deliver that kind of news to my mate. I turn and face him, lifting his hands to my cheeks. "I'm fine. It was a really weird meeting and I'm still not sure what happened, but he didn't eat me and he didn't eat Kel and he delivered a really sweet birthday present for Reilly."

Ben stares at me for a long time, reading all the places inside me that sometimes don't know how to talk. Finally, his thumb brushes my cheek. "Start at the beginning and add in a few more details, please."

"No way." Brandy sits down behind him and puts her chin on his shoulder. "Start at the end. What did the bears send for Reilly?"

I take a good long look at my mate before I decide to answer her. He sometimes has places that can't find their words, either. "Raw video footage so they can do a bear channel on FollowTheCats." Which our baby pack helps out with a lot, so I'm not surprised when Mikayla and Wrinkles start whooping.

Brown growls. "No playing with wild bears."

I grin as everyone throws pinecones at him. There aren't a lot of wild bears on our territory, but Wrinkles could probably find them. She's got a good bear nose. "That's the point of the gift. The bears will get the footage, and then Reilly and his team can do the voiceovers and editing and all that."

My raven tilts her head. She likes editing. It's fun to take long, boring videos and make them shiny.

Brown grumbles, but looks reasonably mollified. "That is acceptable."

I add in the bit that Kel figured out as we were driving back. "They didn't send any black bear footage, though." And Brown, for all his complaining, has figured out the digital video recorders faster than anyone.

Mikayla's eyes light up. She sits down next to Brown and bumps against him companionably. "Want to go hunt some bears?"

He rolls his eyes. "Take Reilly. Wild black bears won't mess with a grizzly."

She pouts. "He just laughs when I tease him. You're way more fun."

Brown growls on cue, which makes everyone laugh, including Bailey. My bird takes her first really deep breath since the polar bear squeezed her ribs. Some of my safe, warm shadows are right where I left them.

Ben leans forward and nuzzles his cheek against mine. "Now that Mikayla is satisfied, tell me the part about why you were talking to a polar bear in the first place."

He's trying to hide the concern in his eyes, and he's asking a really careful question instead of the one he really wants to ask, because he's always believed that my secrets are mine to keep. But I thought about this a lot on the way back. What I did isn't going to stay a secret—and

I don't want my baby pack slimed by what I chose to do. "He's one of the bears I stole from. I made a mistake and he tracked me."

Shock flares in Ben's eyes—and blazing fear.

I grab for him, because clearly he forgot the part where I said I'm fine and I didn't get eaten. I'm not the only one grabbing. My baby pack is exploding. Wrinkles tackles a furry Brown from across the fire pit. Brandy stays human, but she's bristling and streaming wolf dominance thick enough that I can smell it, and shaking off Mikayla's attempts to calm her down.

Ben winces. "Get a grip, sis. You're strangling my wolf."

That works. Sort of. Brandy sits back down, and Brown shifts back into wiry old guy and starts pulling on his torn pants, but both of them are still riled. Mikayla and Wrinkles take deep, relieved breaths, and Bailey looks ready to murder me where I sit.

Crap. I really need to learn how to drop bombs more gently. "It was back when Eamon was running the blockade on the perimeter. Nobody in, nobody out, and we were running really low on food."

My raven figured she could get by him, but she never wanted to know what he would do to a pup if she messed up.

Wrinkles nods slowly. "I remember. You came up with money when we were at our wits' end. More than once."

I don't want to do this. Kel spent a whole hour telling

me that nobody would care, but I can feel the truth in my guts. I still don't believe him.

Protect and sever. "I stole stuff in town sometimes, too. I mostly lived on the streets before I came here. It's what I knew how to do to survive, so when things got bad, it was my best way to help. When I had a little money, I bought things at garage sales and sold them online for profit. When we were out of money, I stole."

Wrinkles opens her mouth and closes it again.

I can't look at them anymore. I find Ben's eyes. He's never, not once, ever looked at me with judgment. "When the blockade was fiercest, right after they caught Gideon's family, I went the only direction that they weren't patrolling. I went north."

"Into polar bear country?" Mikayla's words are an incredulous whisper.

I have no idea how to explain something that I've always known in my bones. Safety is a luxury. A privilege. "They had things worth stealing."

Brown sounds like Wrinkles is strangling him.

"I only did it a few times. I'm a good thief, and I was careful." I stare into the eyes of my mate. Every time I left, they were full of worry and guilt and gulping fear. And every time I came home again, they were full of love. "It was still a huge risk, so I only did it when the pups were getting hungry and we'd already done everything else we could."

I can't look—but I listen.

My camp is absolutely silent.

My raven shrinks. Kel was wrong.

"Thank you." Wrinkles's words are a bare whisper.

My head snaps up.

"You stole." Brown looks like I banged him over the head with his axe. "From a polar bear."

I clear my throat. "Several of them, actually."

His stunned gaze shifts to my mate. "And you knew."

Ben nods.

He knew about everything, even the back alleys where I went to fence some of the stuff I didn't dare sell online. Not once did he ever try to clip my wings, even when my going clipped his. I offer up the only defense I have, one more time. "The pups were hungry."

"You lived on the street?" Mikayla presses her lips together. "Katrina did, too. She's told me some stuff."

Hopefully not the worst parts. This pack doesn't need any more nightmares.

Brandy sits down really abruptly. "You stole from polar bears to feed our pups."

I wince. They're my pups, too.

Ben's arms wrap around me, strong and true. "That's not what she meant, love."

Brandy's forehead wrinkles as she looks at him, confused. Then her eyes widen as they fly back to me. "Wait, you don't think you're part of us?"

I swallow, a bug on a really uncomfortable microscope.

She rolls to her feet, her hands fisting and fire in her eyes. "Are you fucking kidding me? You stole food to feed our pups and you don't think that alone would make you family, even if you weren't family already?"

My raven stares, her beak open.

Righteous fury blazes out of her every pore. "Are you out of your ever-loving mind, Fallon? You're Ben's *mate*. You're my *sister*, and you insist on being one even on the days when I'm completely useless. You sounded more alarms than I can remember in the last six years and you attacked a fucking alpha wolf when he got too close to where Stinky was hiding and you got skinnier than any of us when there wasn't enough food."

I try to close my beak. It doesn't work.

She sits back down again and takes a slow, deep breath, never taking her eyes off me. "You are Fallon *Dunn*. You're my sister. I've already got one of those wandering in the woods who probably can't remember who I am, so if you don't want to be my sister, you're just going to have to suck it up and deal."

My bird manages to regain enough control of her head to look at her mate.

Ben just chuckles. "What she said."

I dare to look at the others. Brown and Mikayla and Wrinkles all cross their arms and glare at me, a unified wall of disapproval. Wrinkles harrumphs loudly. "Did you actually think for one second that we wouldn't have your back on this?"

I shake my head in a direction that isn't yes or no, completely overwhelmed. "I'm sorry. Kel said I was a stupidhead."

"You were a complete stupidhead."

I cringe. Bailey never pulls her punches.

She snorts. "I don't know how you think that disqualifies you from being a Dunn, though."

Brandy snickers. "Seriously."

"Hey." Ben scowls at both of them as he nuzzles into my neck. "Some of us are law-abiding, prudent, well-behaved members of this clan."

Bailey side-eyes Brandy. "Are you sure he's related?"

Brandy grins. "Nope. But can we keep Fallon?"

I duck my head into Ben's shoulder, befuddled and bewildered and entirely off-balance. Never, in any of the ways I ever imagined this might play out, did I expect anyone to be cracking jokes. "But I'm a thief."

They all look at me like I just said I wanted salad for breakfast.

Wrinkles smirks. "I'm going with criminal mastermind, myself."

Brandy holds out a fist-bump. "I like that."

"Wait." Mikayla sounds gleeful as all heads turn her direction. "We haven't even heard the good parts, yet. You stole from a bunch of polar bears and one of them found you in town and Kel was there?"

I don't seem to have any brains left, but I manage a nod.

She leans against Brandy and sighs. "This is going to be the best story."

"I think," says Ben quietly, stroking my shoulders, "that she maybe needs to tell it later. Or you could go bug Kel for the details."

Mikayla wrinkles her nose. "Nope. He'll leave out all the good parts. I'll wait."

I try breathing, but it still feels like a polar bear is squeezing my ribs.

Bailey leans against Brandy's other side. "That was a pretty good rant."

Brandy smirks. "I learned from the best."

"Rennie was the best." Bailey's eyes are full of something wistful and determined and complicated and sad. "Remember that time she decided Hoot and Grady were the ones who stole all her socks and drew happy faces on the toes?"

"Yeah." Brandy lays her head on Bailey's shoulder. "Do we know who actually did that?"

I stare as the laws of gravity upend for the second time in the same freaking day. Rennie and Grady are names we speak only in whispers.

Wrinkles sits down behind the three younger wolves and cuddles them all into her lap like small pups. Brown stays where he is, emanating the gruff, solid presence that we all long ago learned to understand as love. Ben runs his fingers up and down my spine, finding all my prickly parts and telling them to rest easy. He tips his head against mine, his words landing quiet next to my ear. "Bailey got here a few minutes before you did. Lissa wants to tell Hayden and Kel and Rio what happened to our family."

My ribs collapse inward.

"She wanted to know how we felt about that." Ben looks over at the small wolf pile where his cousin and his sister are telling halting stories of socks and love. "I think that maybe this and Brandy's rant are our answer."

I wrap around him, dazed and confused and wildly uncertain of everything except for where my arms need to be. "Are you sure?"

He huffs a laugh into my hair, which is mostly feathers as my bird scrabbles to stay human. "No. What do you think?"

I close my eyes. I think that I'm a dweller of the shadows and his family used to be citizens of the light. I think that this is all too fast, that if we yank the hiding places away too quickly, something important will shrivel or cringe or shrink away forever. I think that there will always be distance between the murk and the sunshine, and I'm already grieving that he will live on the other side.

But those answers aren't the right ones.

Because already, these wolves I love, they're reorienting. Already, the answer that they've given matters. Brandy yelled and Bailey got soft and even though neither of those things will last much longer today, they're both absolutely precious. Citizens of the light, finding their way back to the country of their birth. "I saw your dad."

Ben's breathing stops. "When?"

I squeeze in closer, holding the shape of who we are like he always does for me. "Last night. I flew over the rocks where the ghost wolves sometimes lie in the sun."

His swallow sounds so loud in my ears.

"I showed him some photos I had on my phone. From the knitting circle. Of you, and Brandy, and Hoot." Daughter, son, and niece. I take a deep breath and place my palm against Ben's heart. "He looked at all of them. He remembers you, love."

A quiet, anguished whimper.

I press my cheek against his. For six years, we haven't known if anything more remained of his father than a wolf. My own grieving doesn't matter. I touch the heart of the man I love and fan the terrible hope that needs to step out of the shadows along with the truth. "When I showed Cleve the picture of Kelsey, he reached out and touched his granddaughter's face. He was human, Ben."

12

HAYDEN

I stare at my calm, taciturn beta, who just told me a story that would give a bear reporter the scoop of several lifetimes. "You've got to be kidding."

Kel grins. "Nope."

My wolf feels like he accidentally ran into a revolving door getting out of bed. "A woman whose bird isn't much bigger than Robbie's wolf broke into a polar bear's den, took something that matters to him, and then stood on a sidewalk and pretended she didn't know him."

Kel nods cheerfully and eats more of the muffin he swiped from Kennedy when she was dumb enough to take her eyes off him. Which happened shortly after Ghost swiped his, so I'm pretty sure the teenage gang in our midst is considering that a win.

I tell my wolf that he can't go steal a muffin until I'm

done staring at my beta in disbelief. "Do I need to talk to Ivan?"

He shakes his head, talking around his food. "Don't think so."

Growing up in Whistler Pack, you hear a lot of crazy stories. Fallon might have just won that competition without even trying. My wolf is a pretty tough dude, and he's breaking out in hives at the mere thought of doing what she did.

That she did it to feed pups that the former leadership of this pack considered less important than their next beer isn't helping. I scrub my fingers on my forehead, trying to process that level of dereliction of duty and failing utterly. Fuck. "We can't let why she did it be the story. This has to be about her courage." Her courage and her insanely reckless, beautiful service to her pack.

He grunts. "Duh."

Which is why he told it the way he did, and I'm being slow on the uptake again. "Does Ivan know why she did it?"

He nods. "Before he found us, I think."

My wolf shudders. Polar bears are the most feared hunters on the planet for good reason, and the shifter version isn't a whole lot more civilized than their wild cousins. A very few, like Ronan, learn to balance those instincts with human niceties. The rest hang out in Inuvik and consider Ivan their leader. "You said she stole from more than just him."

"Yup."

Troublesome beta. "Since you're here and not setting

up illegal gizmos on our northern border, I assume you're not worried about the others."

He smiles faintly. "Ivan will deal with them. He won't let any of his bears trouble her."

I try to wrap my head around the insanity of what she did. Earning a polar bear's respect generally involves at least a minor act of war, but I can see why this impressed him. I'm also looking at a guy who would have been willing to start that war if respect hadn't been forthcoming. "How are you?"

He glares at me, which is exactly the response I expected. "Eamon tried to close down the perimeter."

Of course that's what's eating at him. The power-hungry act of a man seeking absolute control. The kind that's prelude to something even worse. "His lieutenants had shit for brains, but they would have been able to scent anyone leaving on the ground."

"Yes."

The slow-burning fury contained in that single word is nearly infinite. I study the most lethal man I know, polar bears included. If Kelvin Nogues ever comes face to face with Eamon Martins, Eamon is going to have a very bad day. "Starving pups would have shredded any resistance the pack had left." The submissive kind that was keeping hearts alive.

Kel just nods.

I don't know what he did as a soldier. I just know that he dreams, over and over again, of being too late. "How is Fallon?"

He sucks in a breath. "She thought we would think less of her."

He still thinks that some days. "We can fix that. A parade? Fireworks? A castle built out of shiny things?"

He chuckles. "She lived on the streets. She's still working on getting used to a tent."

I growl. "Thanks a lot. I had my wolf almost calmed down."

He snorts. "Take a number. My wolf had to sit there while I had a casual chat with a polar bear. He's currently planning a dozen ways to gut me in my sleep."

There are a whole lot of nightmares that have been trying to do that for twenty-two years. "Want a castle built out of shiny things?"

He eyes me wryly. "I don't think Jules sells those."

I grin. "She would if I asked nicely."

He sighs, the weight on his shoulders back to the usual levels. "Are you done yet? We need a plan."

I roll my eyes just to bug him. "Duh."

The growl that leaks out of him tells me just how twisted up his wolf got. Fallon might not understand that he would have gone to instant war for her, but I do. Saying so will just get one of my limbs chewed off, however. I'll let him put me through my alpha paces instead. He always finds that soothing. "Hinting at an interview with Reilly was smart."

His eyes turn solemn and sad. "It needs to happen."

I know those eyes. They're the ones I had to drag kicking and screaming back into the heart of pack. Kel of the dark places. Which is why he's so fucking good at helping others walk out of the murk and into the light. "Will she let us get away with it?"

He shrugs. "She'll sit with him. She'll just try not to say much."

There are a lot of ways to lean on that, and he knows all of them. He also believes, deeply, in consent. "What are you thinking?"

His eyes turn thoughtful. "That a bear reporter could maybe talk to Ivan first."

My wolf chokes. "Seriously?"

He shrugs. "It's going to happen anyhow."

Probably. Freaking bears and their idea of a suitable birthday gift. However, since the rest of our pack is currently re-watching video footage of Russian sand bear toddlers pushing each other down a dune, I probably can't keep treating Ivan like the threat he absolutely is. I sigh. "I want eyes on that call."

Kel smirks. "Duh."

I sigh again, but I'm also thinking. Other than the part about Ivan being one of the world's most terrifying predators, it's an excellent idea. It's been a really big week, and Reilly needs a headline that isn't about him. "Do I need to call Ivan first and make clear that Fallon is ours?" Bears have a bad habit of collecting objects and people that they fancy.

Kel's lips twitch. "You might need to tell your mother that, too."

I wince. Adrianna Scott is going to love every single moment of this story, except for why it was necessary— and that part is going to make her about as easy to influence as an intergalactic bulldozer. "Ebony is our liaison with Whistler Pack, right?"

Kel chuckles. "She is now."

I grin. "Great. She can deal with my mom. That makes Ivan your problem."

He snorts. "And you'll be doing what, exactly?"

I shoot him the most regal look my wolf can manage. "Stealing muffins."

I need fuel so I can figure out how to tell a raven that she's my hero.

FALLON

I wake up groggy and annoyed and more than a little surprised that I fell asleep.

I push up onto my elbows. Bailey's gone, but Mikayla and Wrinkles and Brandy are all in a pile snoring, and Brown is leaning against a log with his eyes half-closed. Which is a lot more alert than it looks, but this is still a really chill camp.

The wolf lying curled up against me stretches a little, sensing my movements, even if his human is still sound asleep. I run my fingers through the soft fur behind his ears. He doesn't have the true red of a lot of the Dunn wolves, but what looks brown at first glance catches hints of gold and silver and ruby red if you catch it in the right light.

I smile. My mate's jewels. I loved him before I ever

saw his wolf, but it didn't hurt that his fur is shiny. Fur that disappears as I stroke it, replaced by naked man.

"Hey, beautiful." He blinks slowly, his voice still gravelly with sleep. "Why are we waking up?"

I keep running my fingers through his hair. "Because some of us aren't nocturnal." The moon will be full soon. It tugs the whole pack toward the circadian rhythms of vampires.

His hand finds a path under my sweater.

I chuckle. "That's why we needed a nap, remember?" The aftereffects of blowing off some of the steam that was swirling inside my mate and his wolf, and an excellent way to get my brain to stop trying to puzzle out the new laws of gravity.

A blanket *thunks* on top of both of us. "Cover your ass and stop feeling up your woman. There's no time for that. We need to catch some fish for dinner, seeing as how our cook's still sleeping."

Brown feels up Wrinkles plenty while he fishes. "You don't need Ben for that."

Brown snorts. "You don't need him, either. In my day, messing around in the woods once in an afternoon was plenty."

Ben starts chuckling beside me. "And this, children, is why Brown doesn't get to teach you about the birds and the bees."

"Bees are smart and mind their own business unless you're a dumbass. Birds shit on your head." Brown shuffles by us on his way over to the cooking shack, which is as much privacy as he figures anyone needs.

I fumble around for a pinecone to toss at his retreating backside, but there are none to be found. Which is an oversight I clearly need to correct the next time I have a nap. Brown seems to have chased away my polar-bear hangover, though.

And some of Ben's ease. When I roll back toward my mate, his eyes are on his sister, and the rest of him has gone somewhere a lot further away. I cuddle up around him and wish, for about the billionth time, that I could share my wings. There are moments when his soul needs so very badly to fly. "I'm sorry."

He nuzzles into my hair, a man well able to be in two places at once. "For what?"

For so many things. "That your dad came to me."

A long, slow silence as he breathes onto the top of my head. "Don't be. He came to you because you know the shadows. Because you understand them in a way that I don't. That I can't."

Kel said something a little bit like that.

"I don't care who he came to, beautiful. I care that he came at all." Ben's fingers trail along my spine, which means he's breached the walls of my sweater again. "I don't know if he'll ever step out of the shadows, and I know that you don't really know if you will, either."

My breath catches.

"Of course I know that, love. I always have." A soft chuckle. "Apparently our entire pack is going to know it, now. My mate, the queen of thieves."

Guh. That's what chased us into the forest before our

nap. My baby packmates getting ridiculous. "I'm sorry for that, too."

He chuckles again. "Quit apologizing or Brandy will yell again, and I'm still trying to get used to the first time."

So is she. Her anxiety kicked up big time when Bailey left. Which is part of how I almost ended up with a royal title and why the napping wolves all smell like one of Wrinkles's sleepytime teas.

Ben strokes my cheek. "Your shadows make us stronger, Fallon Dunn. And I will always love you, no matter where you're standing."

RIO

My wolf rubs his snout on his paw and looks over at the trees again. He's not expecting danger. He's keeping his eyes on the glowing mate bond on the horizon. Kelsey keeps turning her head that way, too.

I don't know what Fallon's baby pack and her mate have done, but it clearly made an impression. My wolf is watching, trying to decide if it's big enough. A raven who lives in the shadows is about to find herself with precious few places to hide—and how she reacts will boomerang back through all the shadows that connect to her.

A situation that has my sentinel squirming. He still doesn't know enough.

That isn't going to stop these dice from landing, however. So I'm doing what I can. I had myself a very interesting conversation with a polar bear who is currently terrorizing the human population in town—or at least I assume that's the reaction to his discovery that gift bags come in forty-seven sizes and colors.

He would fill them all for Fallon if he could. Her bravery impressed him. Her absolute loyalty to the small and the weak flattened him. I had to do some fast talking to keep Eamon Martins alive.

My wolf ponders the glow on the horizon. Fallon has always stood for those in the shadows, but she's done it with her deeds. Today, she used her words. My sentinel isn't sure why that matters yet, but it does.

He also knows that she's not the only small, fierce packmate on the move today. Bailey passed through earlier and said something to Lissa, and now Lissa is pale and thoughtful and worried, and Myrna is nowhere to be found.

Something's up. Something that doesn't begin with the glow in the woods—but somehow ends there.

Which is why I'm lying here in my fur with my paws flat on the ground, and why Ravi is teaching Kelsey a song more appropriate for a guitar player with twice as many fingers as she's got, and why Shelley is mixing up a batch of cookie dough so big it barely fits in the kitchen.

Pack, trying to hold steady and be ready for what they can feel coming.

Which means I have one more thing to do before I sleep tonight, because there's a gravity beam I need to lean on that the sensitives of this pack won't understand.

It doesn't run through them.

ADRIANNA

I stare at the warning from Rio—the one that arrived just as I was tucking myself into bed, and made instantly sure I won't be sleeping tonight.

I stare at the words again. They're written with kindness and care, but that doesn't make them any less stark. I might feel my son shaking, and I need to stay where I am.

Which are fighting words, and there's no chance at all that Rio sent them lightly. He wants me to know that his pack needs to work some things through without a spare alpha arriving to muck things up, and I have the utmost respect for who he is as a man, a sentinel, and a wolf.

But none of that will matter at all if I feel Hayden cracking, and Rio knows that, too. He knows me, and he loves me, and perhaps better than anyone still living, he knows just what James's death did to my wolf.

I swallow. If he's asking me to put a hand on her scruff, I need to listen. I wouldn't harm the hearts of Ghost Mountain for anything, and I have plenty to keep me busy here. I'm still coordinating the rescue efforts for the shifters whose den fell through the permafrost.

I run my fingers across the words of Rio's text one more time. It's so very clear. I need to stay where I am.

So I do the next best thing to getting on a plane. I reach into my heart—and send the man who still lives there to watch over our son.

13

HAYDEN

I expected someone to come find me. When I told Lissa over breakfast this morning that I was putting Reilly on the trail of Fallon's story, she laid her hand on my heart and told me there was a story I needed to hear first. Then she told me to go find myself somewhere private to sit, and to not make a secret of where I'd gone.

All of which nearly panicked my wolf.

I'm not surprised to see the particular envoy who's walking toward me. I hold out a hand as Myrna approaches, gripping her warm fingers in welcome as she comes and sits beside me. She keeps some distance between us and wraps her arms around her knees, which has my wolf sharply scanning for predators, even though he's pretty sure the storm that just arrived is inside her.

I honor the space with all the silent attentiveness I can muster.

She doesn't look at me. She looks out over one of the prettiest valleys in our territory, her eyes haunted. "I'm going to tell you the story of what happened."

Fuuuuuck. I swallow hard. "Thank you."

Her faint smile is mostly a sad grimace. "Thank Lissa. She's the one who convinced Bailey that you need to know."

My green-eyed wolf, taking care of her pack even when it's obviously going to completely suck. I gaze sadly at the woman sitting beside me and wish I could somehow hear the words without her having to say them.

She swallows, still staring out over the valley. "I need you to let me tell it start to finish without interrupting. And then I think my wolf is probably going to need to go run for a while."

I get a tight grip on the yellow-gold scruff inside me. I'm going to hate the hell out of this, and that's not going to hold a candle to how she feels.

Myrna sucks in a shaky breath and blows it back out again. "My daddy started this pack. It was small at first, three families, and we were in no hurry to get bigger."

That was how most wolf shifters did things until Whistler Pack came along. How many of them still do things.

"There were five pups in the first generation. Anna Maria, who mated out of the pack, and Tara, and me, and the Dunn twins. Aaron and Cleve."

My wolf gathers the names. Cherishes them. Grieves.

"Tara and Aaron always knew they were meant for each other." Myrna's words are quiet and unquenchably sad. "They mated young, and Aaron ended up alpha after my daddy. He was the logical choice. He was the strongest dominant and a good man. He did well by us, even though his wolf wasn't truly alpha."

Family packs can get away with that if there's enough respect. Enough love.

I bow my head. Samuel broke so many things.

Myrna hugs her knees a little tighter. "The next generation had a lot of pups and a lot of strong-willed dominants. We didn't know quite how that would shake out, until the day Ruby walked into a diner in town where Aaron's son, Cody, was eating a burger, and announced that he was her mate."

My throat closes. Ruby is a name on Kennedy's white board. Cody isn't.

"She was a firecracker. A strong woman with alpha written all over her wolf, and her bond with Cody settled our pack. We were growing. New families were joining us, drawn by the strength of the two who would be our alpha pair when Aaron stepped down. We were earning ourselves a quiet name as a pack who welcomed immigrants and single parents and those like Dorie who collect strays. A pack that would have made my daddy proud."

Her agony is a living thing—and her fury. "Samuel picked us as his target. Shelley learned that later. Our true alphas weren't in charge yet, and we had a lot more juveniles and teens than most packs. In his eyes, that made us vulnerable. It made us weak."

I don't look at the slim, fierce elder who is somehow finding the strength to tell me this—I don't want to crack either of us. But I will spend every day of the rest of my life doing battle with the idea that open arms and kindness are weak.

Myrna's eyes aren't seeing the valley anymore. "Samuel didn't smell like pure evil when he showed up. He was charming. We prided ourselves on being welcoming to newcomers, and Cori was lovely. Too shy, but we didn't think hard enough about why. Ravi fell head over heels for her and we were distracted by young love."

She looks down at her lap, her voice hoarse. "We were distracted."

My wolf nearly rips straight through my chest.

When Myrna looks out over the valley again, my wolf can hear her silent, keening grief. "There was no warning. One day, Samuel walked into the middle of the den while we were eating lunch and issued an alpha challenge." Her hands curl into white-knuckled fists. "We didn't want to let it happen, but Eamon wrapped his arm around Cleve and told everyone not to move."

Aaron's twin brother. Fuck. I've heard the rest. The quick, utterly lopsided battle that left their alpha bleeding out while his pack tried desperately to save him.

Myrna closes her eyes, and what comes out next is little more than a whisper. "We didn't expect Samuel to kill him."

My wolf revolts. They were a generous, welcoming family pack, not an assault team.

Myrna inhales again, and when she opens her eyes, they're as late-summer dry as the valley below us. "We were in shock. Reeling. And we had our hands full trying to keep every dominant in the pack from challenging Samuel. None of them were strong enough to take him head on, but Cody and Bailey had just watched their father die."

I know what losing mine did to me. And I know what Adrianna Scott's claws did to the abandoned van on the side of the road that stole the life of her mate. It took two sentinels, a dozen betas, and a video of her weeping daughter to stand down the lethal rage of her wolf and bring her home.

Myrna picks up a small, yellowing fern frond and spreads it out on her knee, carefully smoothing each twisted leaf. "We were trying to make a plan. Our strongest dominants—Cody, Ruby, Milo, Bailey—they were going to work together. Wait for the right moment and take back our pack."

Shards of ice hit my heart. Myrna has three sons, and I only know the whereabouts and general health of one of them. The other two are only names. Xander and Milo.

She swallows. "A couple of weeks later, Samuel walked up to Cody and Ruby and held out his phone. It had a picture of Eamon on it, holding Daniel. Their little boy."

The ice in my heart turns to glaciers. That's Stinky's real name.

"He told Ruby that she needed to go find Eamon or her little boy would die. Told Milo the same thing when he arrived on the dead run." Myrna stares into space, a statue formed of rage and grief. "Ruby felt her mate die just before she got to her son."

Robbie. Lissa. My wolf scrabbles, frantic.

A small hand reaches blindly for mine. "It broke them, Hayden. All of them. Bailey was the only one left who was dominant enough and sane enough to give Samuel grief, but her family was in tatters and she had pups to save. Ebony made her see that. She was here visiting Ruby."

The hoarse whisper of sanity left inside my wolf knows that might have been all that saved his pack.

Myrna's sigh is the sound of hope running out of air. "We got some out. But not enough. Samuel and Eamon tortured any resistance they could find, and at the end of it, they had their claws in our boys. They turned them into their lieutenants."

She shrugs helplessly. "Kenny stayed with them, and the rest of us tried to plan. Then Jason died and Robbie and Kelsey were born and we didn't dare anymore."

Her fingers in mine are ice cold.

She slips them out of my numb grip and reaches into her back pocket to pull out a crumpled piece of paper. "I drew you a family tree. Of the Dunn clan. So you can understand."

RIO

I wrap my arms tighter around Lissa.

She thrashes in my arms. "He needs me, Rio. Let me go."

I hate my sentinel's answer on this as hard as I've ever hated anything. "He needs to listen. He needs to know."

She propels herself backward off my chest, her eyes pure wolf. "His heart is bleeding. And he's so angry."

And the mate bond between them is glowing like a fucking nuclear explosion, but none of that changes the work that Hayden Scott needs to do to lead his pack. "That's his job. He won't let you take it away from him."

Lissa's snarl isn't anywhere close to human.

The big black wolf of death holds up his hands and drops his gaze. *Respect, green-eyed wolf.* Submission, even, if she needs it.

She barely notices. Her eyes are too steeped in remembered trauma and boiling love and fiery pain.

So I do the only thing I can. I stand witness. My wolf gave up trying to process all of the story coming through his paws—but he got some. Bailey Dunn, daughter of the alpha who died. Sister of the alpha-elect who was murdered. Aunt of the pup who was threatened, a monumental act of evil that created half of the ghost wolves in this pack. And best friend of the woman who stayed to try to keep her alive.

Myrna didn't just tell Hayden the story of one family. She told the story of every wolf in this pack.

I reach for hands that are still ready to claw through me to get to the man she loves. "He needs to do this, Lissa. He needs to feel all of it."

To be worthy. To be ready.

Because it's not his strength that will make him the leader his pack needs next, or his unquenchable need to live in the light. It's the eight-year-old boy who lives inside him. The one full of remembered trauma and fiery pain—and the raw tenderness of the man who grew from those roots.

14

FALLON

My bird shakes her head as she spies yet another lone wolf, this time slinking along a ridgeline. She's spent the whole freaking day dropping care packages on their heads. Snacks, clothing that smells of pack, lightweight emergency blankets for the ones dumb enough to get caught naked in the rain.

She wants one of the blankets for her very own. They're shiny.

My baby pack is getting through the explosion the way they always do—in a pile of fur, doctored by intermittent cups of tea. Even Reuben is there. He showed up without a word while the aftershocks were still happening, pushed Wrinkles over to the pile of fur, and made her drink a whole big mug of what she poured down the rest of us.

I'll drop them some more cookies when I'm done chasing down this wolf.

Or not. I veer away as I figure out who it is. Bailey is out here for the same reason I am. Doing the job of our alpha and our beta and our sentinel while they reassemble themselves after the bomb blast. Myrna's story hit them really hard.

Which, somehow, after the initial scramble and wolves running naked into the woods, is soothing the rest of us. The three men who changed our destiny—they tremble, too. They hurt and they bleed and they know the taste of helpless rage, just like us. We knew that, but feeling it transmit through every gravity beam in this pack was something entirely different.

Now our wolves know.

I bank away from the mountain, catching the nice tailwind that usually blows off the ridge above Dorie's camp. Tara tried to run this morning, but a bunch of the sentries sat on her and Stinky ordered up some of his grandma's best hot chocolate, and that held her long enough for Rio to arrive and give her a fierce hug that nearly crushed her and mostly set her right again.

Rio isn't there when I spy their camp, though. Just a guy sitting in a tree, so still that Dorie hasn't seen him, or she'd be giving him hell for sneaking up on her like that. I'm glad to see him. He feels things really deeply, and he hasn't got Lissa practically glued to him or Robbie curled up in his arms or a wreath of Kelsey's flowers around his neck.

I circle over the camp and wave so that I don't incur

the wrath of Dorie. Then I land on a tree branch far enough away to escape if Kel's feeling moody. I wrap the last silver blanket around my shoulders and eye him. "You look like somebody made you eat swamp goo."

He doesn't say anything.

I track his gaze—the way it moves as Stinky dashes through the camp with a fork in each hand and Adelina chasing him.

Crap. "He's fine." He's been fine for six years.

"I know." Kel grimaces. "But my wolf is currently refusing to leave the damn tree, so I'm humoring him."

His shadows aren't the same as mine, but they're fierce. "Want a snack? Or some hot chocolate?"

He shoots me a dirty look.

I pitch a pinecone at his head. "We're taking care of you. Suck it up. You can't have my blanket, though." I pull the silver corners tighter around me. It's light and warm and shiny. My raven is enamored.

Kel's lips twitch. "You're impressively annoying for a bird."

That's a big improvement over his dead-eyed stare. "Be nice to me, or I'll get Hoot." She's the one who arrived at our camp after the bomb blast, handed me a stack of blankets and a bag of snacks, and told me to get my butt and my wings in gear and be useful.

"Damn." Kel shakes his head and shoulders, a guy walking out of a rainstorm into weather that's more hospitable. "Please tell me that Hayden and Rio are coping better than I am."

They're all human and talking and reaching for what

will steady them. They're doing just fine. "Nope. You're all a hot mess."

His eyes shoot to me, alarmed.

I snort. "You all tried to pretend you were okay, which is dumb. Now that we've got you being honest, it's all good."

Kel raises an eyebrow. "Says the woman who had months to mention that she's a polar-bear-robbing thief and didn't bother?"

I roll my eyes. "I didn't tell Wrinkles for years, so trust me, you aren't nearly the scariest person trying to have that conversation with me."

He smiles a little. "I'm glad you told them."

I move close enough to elbow his wolf. Which is a little hard to do while wrapped in a crinkly blanket, but my raven is not letting go of the crinkly shiny anytime soon. "There was this persistent guy in a truck who seemed to think that maybe I should."

He manages most of a wry grin. "I'm not even close to the most persistent person in this pack. Possibly not even in that truck."

I smile cheerfully. "It's good that you know that. So, do you want me to get you a snack, or are you going to head back to the den so that Shelley can feed you?"

He growls, but I can see the hit land.

I wait. I learned that from Ben.

Finally, Kel sighs. "You're good at this. Thanks."

I wrinkle my nose. "I haven't even brought you cookies, yet."

He chuckles. "People like you and me, we serve by

harassing others and moving them an inch or two in the right direction. You've got a talent for helping those of us who sometimes get stuck in the dark."

I stare at him. That sounds oddly like what Ben said.

His lips quirk. "I'll still growl at you the next time you try to herd my ass. Just so we're clear."

Ha. There will be no next time. I'm not trying to herd anyone. No inches and no directions.

My raven pecks my skull companionably and reminds me about honey-cake lessons and trembling tree-huggers and making up dumb photo captions in the dark.

I scowl at her. Maybe there were a few accidents. That's all. Helping out my fellow shadow dwellers in a topsy-turvy week.

She caws cheerfully about what I agreed to do tomorrow. And about the very quiet part I maybe didn't mention to anyone else. The part that suddenly needs to have three big, bad wolves in it. Which is going to be kind of tricky, to say the least.

Crap. I growl, mostly at her, but some at me and a lot at my newly crazy life. Being a thief was so much simpler. "If I organize something, can you get Hayden to come?"

Kel shrugs. "Sure."

My raven is shaking her head. Coming isn't enough.

Bossy bird. "He needs to be goofy and playful. Like he usually is. Not all silent and watchful like he is today."

Kel's eyebrows slide up. "Going to tell me why?"

Shortly after I sneak into Ivan's den in ballet shoes. "No."

His lips twitch. "Do I get to be silent and watchful?"

I'm guessing he turns that off about as easily as I chop off my wings. "Yes. But you have to stay where I put you."

That gets me a long, slow scrutiny that makes my bird want to tuck her head under her new blanket. "Rio?"

That one is strangely easy. "He'll know where he needs to be."

BEN

I stare at my mate as she flies off again, her bird trying to wrangle a half-eaten snack in her beak. She landed long enough to kiss me, arm-wrestle Brown for the last berry bar, and leave. "What got into her?"

Wrinkles chuckles. "Same thing as got into the rest of us. She's just processing it differently."

I look at the wolf who sat me down shortly after Fallon landed in my arms, and told me just what it was going to be like to love someone who isn't a wolf. I was young and dumb and I laughed. "It's not just that. She's changing. She feels different, somehow. More open. More fierce."

A brisk pat on my arm. "You would know. You've got a smart wolf inside you. You've done very well by Fallon."

Those are huge words of praise from a woman who always means them and rarely says them. My wolf sits down and stares, a little off-kilter.

She huffs out a laugh and ruffles my hair like I'm

Stinky's age. "I forget that you're a little too likely to believe your own advertising. You're a wonderful man and you need to remember that. She's lucky to have you."

I look up and then down. The sky and the ground are still where they usually are.

She snorts and hands me a dish towel. "Here, you finish up with these. I need to go make another kettle of tea."

She's brewed up at least four different kinds already, and we've had a steady supply of visitors filling cups and flasks and canteens. "Do you need me to make a den run?" She's been sending them most of her tea fixings.

She shakes her head. "This will pass quickly enough. We'll steady, soon, and we'll be stronger for having told our newcomers."

I lean against her solid warmth and close my eyes, trying not to think of all the ghosts who share my last name, and failing miserably. "Do you think any of them will ever come home?"

It's the plaintive question of a small boy, but I can't seem to take it back.

The hands that caught that small boy when he was born pat my head. "They're already coming closer, Benjamin Dunn. Don't you dare give up on them now."

FALLON

"I need your help."

Bailey shoots me a suspicious look. "What for?"

My bird keeps a careful distance. When I first met her, she was all snark and no bite. Today, that's maybe not a sure thing. "I want you to help me teach a class on shiny rocks."

She rolls her eyes. "Right. Because ravens don't know anything about shiny things."

Annoying wolf. "I know about rocks. I don't know about school, okay? I hardly ever went."

Something softer sneaks into her eyes.

I manage a decent growl. "Don't feel sorry for me, or I swear I'll spend the rest of my life dropping pinecones on you while you sleep."

Softer flees, replaced with amused wolf. "What is it with this pack and pinecones?"

I snort. "Those are Kel's fault."

She laughs and tosses me one of the ropes she's untangling. "If you're going to interrupt my work, you get to help."

My raven stares at the rope mournfully. It's not shiny, and it's really tangled. "What happened to it?"

Bailey snorts. "Stinky started a game of tie up the bear."

At least it wasn't a skunk. That kid has no sense of self-preservation. Which is both a miracle and a curse, and none of us have ever been able to find it in ourselves to teach him any different. Including his tough-love, survival-obsessed favorite aunt.

Bailey considers her own impressively snarled rope. "Maybe we should just fix this with a knife."

It's going to take more than a few weeks to ditch the habits of six years. I find one end of my rope and start backtracking it through the tangles. "Why isn't Stinky doing this?" Bailey is big on consequences falling on the shifter who set them into motion—the little ones, anyhow. She's spent most of the last six years beating herself up for not being able to stop all the big ones.

"He mutinied," she says dryly. "Aided and abetted by his alpha, who swung by with Robbie."

Those two are pretty irresistible, even for tough aunties. "Want me to track them down and pelt them with pinecones?"

She chuckles. "Maybe. After you tell me about this rock lesson that's been on the school schedule with your name beside it for weeks."

She always knows everything. Which is probably a useful skill for a teacher and less fun when you're trying to carefully herd one. "It started out as an excuse to get the pups and juveniles out of the den. Then Reilly decided that all the fun things are school, and I got put on the schedule."

Bailey snickers quietly.

I shake my head. "Mikayla said that Kelsey got sad last night when she discovered school doesn't keep going after supper."

A laugh squirts out of Bailey. "Poor pup. Reilly's really been pushing the idea that school is great. He talked most of Dorie's crew into signing up, and they're hardly even complaining."

With all the bright and colorful supplies they have,

he even has my raven half convinced. My human knows better. Supplies are just accessories. The rest is hard chairs and droning voices and dust-coated windows that are never open.

And eyes. So many disappointed eyes.

Bailey glances over at me. "Most of Dorie's strays came to us when they were babies, but there are a couple who were older and have some big holes in their education."

Pushy wolf. "I'm not here to talk about that."

"Too bad." She shakes out a section of rope and scowls at the part that's still tangled. "I'm not going to pat you on the head, and I'm not going to ask you what happened. I don't figure you'd tell me, anyhow, and I know you've told Ben. I assume he told you that we're not snobs and we don't judge people by how well they can spell."

They've never made me feel excluded. "Still not talking about it."

Her lips quirk. "The crew that's going to school will maybe start throwing around a lot of topics that you didn't spend a whole lot of time learning." A pause. "If you let that make you feel like more of an outsider, I will find you and chew on your tail feathers."

My raven scoots back in alarm.

I snort. "Quit making my bird nervous."

Bailey rolls her eyes. "She steals from polar bears."

The Dunns are way scarier than polar bears. "Not talking about that, either."

"Right." Bailey's lips quirk. "Anyhow. My threat

stands. Now tell me about this rock lesson so that I can turn you down and you can go away and stop mangling my rope."

I look down at the mess in my hands. Oops.

My bird caws a protest. It's ugly and it smells like bear.

I shake my head. If it was delicate jewelry chains, she'd sit here for hours untangling them. "I'm taking them to Rambling Creek. It got a nice dump of pretty rocks in the spring runoff."

"That's a nice run from the den." She smirks. "I hear that students learn better after they've gotten some of the energy out of their paws."

She can smirk all she wants if she keeps thinking like a teacher. "It's not their energy I'm worried about. Mikayla's been looking up some of the rocks on the internet, and then Hoot and Reilly got curious and suddenly they're all throwing around big words about volcanoes and minerals and sedimentary layers."

I only know what the valuable ones are worth and which ones should be sold in a dark alley instead of online.

"Sounds like a science lesson." Bailey's voice is casual, which I don't trust for a minute. "I can give you a couple of good resources to read, if you like."

I glare at her. "No. I want the smart teacher who's read the good resources to come and explain fossils and sedimentary layers and why we have a lot of really weird minerals in our water around here."

Bailey's eyes brighten. "Rambling Creek has fossils?"

It will after I drop a few from the sky. "Some."

She shoots me a suspicious look.

I sigh. I should probably tell her the rest before she figures it out for herself and threatens my tail feathers again, but I can't. I need the shadows to stay where I put them. "Please?"

She growls. "Fine. How many are coming?"

I roll my eyes. "At last count, half the pack." Somebody needs to figure out how to remove our bear cub's admin privileges for the online classroom. Although the word puzzles he puts up are pretty cool. My raven likes those. They flash pretty colors when she finds a word.

Bailey works out another knot. "How many of them know what a mineral is? Or a sedimentary layer?"

I grin brightly. "If you come, one more."

She yanks on the rope hard enough to scare it into obedience, but I can already see her brain working out how to teach two dozen students about pretty rocks. She glances at me casually. "You'll make sure that we don't take too many rocks from the stream?"

"Hello, I live with Wrinkles." Who has strict rules on what we take from the land and even stricter ones about the respect we need to have while we do it.

Bailey smiles down at her rope. "Then I'd say you've been to plenty of school."

I scowl. Sneaky, tricky wolf.

Which means I need to be an even trickier raven.

15

FALLON

Darn brain that woke me up at the crack of dawn. I should still be asleep, curled up next to my warm, cozy mate and not thinking about potential disasters at Rambling Creek. However, since my brain apparently hates me, I get to lurk in the forest trying to be useful instead.

I squint at the sat phone screen, moving it into deeper shade to try to get a better look at my current auction listings. I grin when I finally make out the details. One of the signed books Ben found in town has already been bid up to double what I expected it to sell for, and the others are tracking nicely.

I tap into the book auction to check on the history of the top bidder. It's hard to claim moral superiority when I've spent most my life selling stolen goods, but online markets are getting seriously swampy. It's a buyer with good history, though. There are still some of those left, especially if you're selling cult-classic science fiction paperbacks.

My bird shudders. She has no idea why anyone wants to collect dusty paper.

I chuckle and switch to a different browser tab. She perks up as I log in to ShifterNet. There are pretties there. I take a quick look at our baby pack's trade items, which is easy—they're all gone. That will make some shifters I know very happy. Except for Brown. He doesn't know what Mikayla did with the toy blocks he carved and then tossed onto the kindling pile.

I transfer our credit balance to the pack's main account. Lissa set us all up so that each baby pack can trade independently if we want to, but Myrna's got her eye on some step stools for the new kitchen. Probably because half the kitchen help is under three feet tall.

I tap into Brandy's timid question in the trade forum about whether anyone might be interested in some pencil sketches. I snort as I read the replies. Mikayla made her add a cute drawing of a baby owl to her post, and there are at least five people arguing over who saw it first. I add a comment suggesting that a smart buyer might name a price they're willing to pay.

I grin as little dots show at least two people typing furiously, and switch over to my private messages. A request for more boring rocks with pretty insides, so clearly Wrinkles is ignoring her messages again. A reminder link to the sign-up sheet for cookies, which I ignore. That's the kind of ordinary pack-in-the-light stuff that Mikayla handles, or tries to, anyhow. I don't think she really knew what to do when she asked me for my favorite kind of cookies and I had no idea how to answer her.

I sigh. I shouldn't be digging myself into a mood. Those are infectious. I have dishes to wash and a sexy wolf who wants help rigging a new drying line, and those are both jobs I can handle without tying my brain in a knot while I wait for Hoot to show up.

I go to stick the sat phone in my pocket and pause halfway there. The hair on the back of my neck is doing funny things. My raven doesn't have a good nose like wolves do, but she's got a way of sensing things, and she thinks we have company.

A branch cracks in the woods, and my head snaps around just in time to see a shadow step out of the trees.

It's my freaking alpha.

HAYDEN

I hate sneaking up on people. I tried to be loud, but Fallon was pretty absorbed in whatever she was doing on her phone, and now she looks like she expects me to chomp on her any second.

Way to make a piss-poor entrance. So not what I need to be doing after blasting every wolf in my pack with emotions I couldn't contain. "Hey, Fallon."

She tilts her head, her bird watching me cautiously.

I hold out the small bag of goodies Shelley sent out with me. "Cookies, chocolate, and jam. Myrna and Braden just made a batch."

Fallon opens the bag and pulls out the jar of jam, grinning at the slightly sticky paw print on the label. "He's such a cutie."

He's a berry-fueled menace, but only his moms and his alpha seem to think so. "We'll see if you still think that after he comes out to help Brown smoke fish."

She looks a little surprised.

I chuckle. Orbital communications have done wonders for spreading information in our pack, but sheer volume still leaves some holes, especially when communications try to go through a very taciturn bear. "The next time he fires up the smoker, Bailey is bringing a bunch of the pups to help." Which everyone is carefully not calling school.

Fallon's eyes spark with amusement. "Brown agreed to that?"

I grin. "He did. I hear Bailey agreed to help with your lesson, too."

She rolls her eyes. "I didn't realize we were all ganging up on her."

I suspect that's what it's going to take. For Bailey, and maybe for Fallon, too. "I heard a pretty interesting story from Kel."

She sighs. "Why are wolves so freaking chatty?"

I hide a grin. "Bears are even chattier."

She looks at me in absolute horror. "Ivan is telling people?"

Probably. "This isn't going to stay a secret. You know that, right?"

Her arms start flapping. Wings, readying for escape.

I sigh. I owe Kel cookies. He figured this would scare her worse than staring down a polar bear. "Yesterday, Myrna told me a really hard story."

She eyes me suspiciously, perplexed by my sharp turn.

Rio said she was up in the skies all day yesterday, taking care of wolves who got tossed around by their alpha losing his shit. Which means I might not want to hear her answer to my next question. It might not be the same as his. "How did it affect the pack?"

Fallon cocks her head. "We're fine. You know that, right? You're allowed to have moments when you can't deal, just like the rest of us."

I say some version of that to Kel every damn day. Which probably means he sent me out here to talk to her just to get even. "It hit a lot of wolves pretty hard."

She shrugs, the layers of street so obvious now that Rio told me to open my damn eyes. "It wasn't so bad. We had warm blankets and chocolate and that video you recorded to hand out."

Hoot made me do it. A way to apologize to dozens of shifters all at once, and to explain why my wolf went off the rails. I didn't see the edited, annotated version until later—the one with a lead-in by Reilly, a really fantastic shot of Myrna's pale, steady face, and Kelsey singing a song for anyone who needed to hear it.

Which I only growled about a little, because it's so

damn obvious why those parts mattered. I look at my raven packmate, who navigates the shadows with easy skill and casual bravery and thinks herself entirely unremarkable, and wonder how to gently help her consider letting her pack embarrass her, too. "Myrna's story mattered. So did that damn video."

She crosses her arms over her ribs. "Some stories matter more than others."

My wolf walks very gingerly through the opening she's given him. "Why?"

She scowls ferociously. "Some stories help everyone pull in the same direction, or know where the fragile places are, or they settle our wolves. Others are just a raven doing dumb things that nobody should ever contemplate doing again. There's no reason to tell that one."

My wolf grins. He likes her. She's tricky, just like all his favorite birds. "Really. There's no reason to talk about an act of mesmerizing defiance that happened during some of your pack's grimmest days?"

Her dark eyes glare holes through my skull.

I smile as gently as I can. "Let your pack celebrate who you are, Fallon Dunn. Let those who lived through those years know about the resistance they helped fuel, and let those of us who arrived too late be really fucking glad that you were here."

She swallows three times before she speaks. "You play really dirty."

I chuckle. I won't tell her about all the practice I've had. I'm not sure she's ready to be compared to Kel and his stack of medals, quite yet. "That's why I get the fancy paycheck."

She scowls. "You don't get paid to be alpha."

I grin. "I do. I get to deliver berry jam to reluctant ravens and convince them to talk to our intrepid bear reporter."

The aggravated look I get would give Kel a run for his money. "A small story. That I get to read before it goes out."

My wolf growls.

I pat his head. Not my first rodeo. "Nope."

She glares at me again.

My wolf grins. Feisty raven. I pull a rock out of my pocket. One I dug out of the bottom of my backpack this morning. It's been traveling with me for a very long time. I hold it out on my palm.

She looks at me suspiciously, but her raven is already swaying toward the orange-red, translucent fire in my hand. "What is it?"

"Carnelian." I wrap my fingers around it one last time. "It's a crystal. My dad told me it was full of bravery. He said that when I held it, it would help the bravery inside me to be strong, and I would be able to speak the truth that others need to hear. I think that it's meant to be yours, now."

The faint whisper of touch that followed me all the way out here brushes against the back of my neck. It got to me before Lissa did yesterday, and it hasn't left me alone since.

Fallon stares, dumbfounded.

I hold out the rock. It's a hard thing to give up, which means it's exactly right. My dad taught me that, too.

She shakes her head wildly. "I can't take that."

I smile. "Sure, you can." I drop it gently into a palm that opens reflexively to catch it. And then I run like hell before she gets enough control over her raven to try to give it back.

FALLON

Annoying. Tricky. Sneaky. Obnoxious. Pushy. Aggravating.

My human has been generating a pithy list of words to describe her alpha, and I don't think she's repeated a single one, yet. My raven is just rubbing her cheek on the pretty rock and sighing happily. I grumble. I tried flying after him. She acted like she had two broken wings and six missing tail feathers. It was just embarrassing.

It still is.

"That's really pretty."

I growl. "It belongs to Hayden and I need to give it back."

Hoot giggles. "I don't think your raven agrees with you."

My raven has given up plenty of shinies. She's traded them for food, and bandages, and wool to make warm hats. I hold up the gorgeous rock that glows like orange fire and let the sunlight play with it. I've never had a dad give me anything, and even though Hayden isn't much older than I am, that's totally what this feels like.

Tricky, sneaky, aggravating wolf.

Now I *am* repeating myself. "Thanks for coming."

Hoot bumps my shoulder. "You ask, I come. Especially when you spent all day yesterday helping me get everyone settled back down."

She did the hard ones. "How are the ghosts?"

She shrugs. "Haven't found them all yet. Teesha has a couple who are still missing, and I only saw Grandpa Cleve from a distance."

My heart aches. All the pups used to call him that. Now the littlest ones don't even know him. "How's the den? You guys were ground zero for the Hayden blast."

She rolls her eyes. "Nope. That was Terrence, who was apparently sunning himself in the valley right below where Hayden and Myrna had their little chat. He woke up from a nap and thought he'd been hit by lightning. He nearly streaked through the den. Which freaked out his wolf, because his human can be there, but his wolf totally can't."

I wince. Poor Terrence. He's a sweet, proud man who hates that his wolf is so damaged. His word, not mine.

I sigh. There are so many shifters in this pack who feel damaged and broken and worse, and some of them can't get anywhere near the den in either of their forms. Which means my freaking bird is insisting that I try herding people and helping them move inches again.

I lean against Hoot's shoulder. I don't do big thoughts —I do small, shiny ones. I reach into my bag for some small squares of paper, leftovers from the origami project. They're beige, and nobody wanted to fold them. I used some of the fancy new pencil crayons to write on them so they wouldn't look so boring, but my raven is still mad that we didn't use shinier paper. "Could you help me deliver these?"

Hoot takes one, her wolf curious.

I wait while she reads. It doesn't take long—there aren't that many words.

Her eyes meet mine, and her face looks like I felt when Hayden handed me the fire-orange rock.

I swallow. "I won't do it if you think it's a bad idea." She might. One of those papers is for her twin brother. They were out in the woods with Bailey when Eamon took Stinky hostage. Grady, sensitive and psychic and submissive like Kelsey, felt every moment of what happened to both of his parents.

He won't come. His inch will maybe be sniffing the paper.

"It's a really great idea," she says, very softly, looking back down at my messy handwriting. "I wish I'd thought of it."

I swallow again. "It needs to stay quiet. It won't work if people know." It's going to be hard enough for Hoot to keep secret, and she'll understand better than anyone why I'm doing it this way.

She nods silently. Then she leans in and rests her head on my shoulder, cuddling the papers into her chest with infinite care. "I'll deliver them. I can help with the rest, too."

She'd probably do a better job than I would, but for some reason, my raven needs that part to be her very own. I shake my head. "I'll do it. I need you to be a goofy student who splashes Reilly and sings with Kelsey and heckles Bailey when she tries to explain about rotting fossils."

Hoot lifts her head and wrinkles her nose. "I don't think fossils rot. Isn't that why they're fossils?"

I snort. "They're not shiny, so I have no idea."

She giggles.

I hold tight to that. I know where this pack wants those of us who live in the shadows to go. If I'm truly honest like the shiny, orange fire rock in my hand wants me to be, I don't really believe we can get there.

But I think that maybe the inches matter anyhow.

16

FALLON

"This is a really pretty one, Fallon. Can I put it in your pile?"

My raven shakes her head. Silly pup. Wolves clearly don't understand the principle of hoarding their own shiny things at all. The diligent students are finding rocks in the river and heading over to Bailey for a science lesson, or to Mikayla and Adelina, who are trying to match wet pebbles to the classification list Reilly made. The future traders are making deals with Wrinkles, who is doing a brisk business swapping cookies for the more valuable stones and crystals that will go up on ShifterNet.

The rest of them are making a pile of pretty rocks in front of my raven. It's almost as tall as she is. I look down at Stinky and sigh. "Did you ask Bailey what kind of rock it is?"

He nods solemnly.

I'm getting wiser. "Do you remember?"

He grins and shakes his head.

I ruffle his hair, which is wet, because all the stones he's retrieved so far have come from the deep part of the river. I look over at where Hayden is snagging pups, as the swifter current in the middle catches them, and tossing them back to safe waters. He's caught a few teenagers who got surprised by the brisk flow, too.

I cuddle into my sweater. Silly wolves. I didn't expect them to go swimming in September. However, Hayden is standing in a place that will make him wildly visible up on the ledge, and there's nothing that says adorable, safe alpha quite like him booping Kelsey or Stinky or Hoot on the nose before he ferries them to shallow waters.

I squat down so that I can boop Stinky's nose, too. "You know the rule about my pile, right?"

His head bobs. "We're going to make it as tall as the sky and Reilly will take a picture, and then we're going to put them all back in the stream so we're not like the robber barons."

Someone has taken serious creative liberties with the original rules. Putting the rocks back was Brown's idea, but his version was a lot more pragmatic. Catch and release, just like with fish we don't need.

My raven pouts quietly in the back of my head. She is *not* happy about the release part. "What's a robber baron?"

Stinky grins. "They were bad guys in the olden days who took lots of stuff from the land and from poor folks and from the indigenous people who were here first, and they got richer than sin and we don't want to be like them because being rich doesn't sound like very much fun. You have to wear this thing called a tie around your neck and shoes every day and nobody wants to be your friend because you're kind of mean on the inside, even if you smile when they take your picture."

Wow. "That doesn't sound like anything I learned in school."

He leans in, his eyes bright, and whispers conspiratorially. "That part isn't school. Hayden said he learned it from a movie. He said that maybe we can watch it when we get our new den."

I let myself glide for a moment on the warm thermals of his bright, easy dreams. Stinky is one of the wolves who will make it all the way back to the den. Dorie's camp has already moved inside the inner perimeter, and his big sister Hoot is a master at marshmallow bribery and impromptu sleepovers. "Add your pretty rock to my pile, and then go see if you can find one that Bailey and Mikayla and Adelina can't identify." That turned into a competition about two minutes after we got here. So far, the winner is a set of three deep-purple stones that Ghost found.

Stinky flashes me a grin as he dashes off, neatly avoiding a collision with Lissa and hurtling headlong into Kel and Ebony instead.

I laugh as our betas catch him in fluid unison and toss him over to Hayden.

Ebony breaks off to go help, because there are at least

three rock collectors who are going to land in the fast flow in the middle of the river any second. Kel angles my way, which puts my raven on alert.

He's stayed where I put him, but he hasn't been happy about it.

He isn't going to be happy about this, either. I flash him a grin that I hope looks all cute and innocent like Stinky's. "Guard my rocks?"

He shoots me a disgruntled look. "Where are you going?"

Nowhere I plan to tell him about. There are already enough quiet glances up in the direction of the ledge. Hoot when she can't help it, and Ghost and Kelsey because they always know. I don't, which is driving my bird crazy enough that she's actually willing to leave a pile of pretty shinies bigger than she is to go investigate. "To check on some things. Don't let anyone put a rock on my pile that hasn't had a science lesson yet. No ugly ones, either."

His lips quirk. "I'm a soldier. All rocks are ugly."

Those are fighting words. Ones that are interrupted by a big splash that has us both looking. I shake my head as Shelley stands back up, grinning bashfully and holding a rock the size of her fist that has Wrinkles whooping. "How is everyone not freezing?"

He chuckles. "Wolf fur is pretty warm."

None of them are wearing it. Paws can't pick up rocks. "It's part of your job description to make sure nobody dies of hypothermia, right?"

He pats my shoulder. "Go. I won't let them steal your rocks."

That's not why I'm suddenly hesitating. I've been desperate to know for hours, and now that the answer is a thirty-second flight away, I'm not sure I want it.

"Whatever you find up there," says Kel quietly, "don't forget what's already happened down here."

I take a deep breath. He's right. Half a dozen wolves have quietly come and watched from the river bank, or found a pretty stone, or in Moon Girl's case, chased away a couple of wild ravens who thought they'd found the mother lode. I also spied a really quiet, tree-dwelling human who was holding an origami-paper invitation in her fist.

I sigh. My raven isn't easily satisfied. She wants more shinies, always. I nod at Kel, which is as close as I can manage to gratitude, and head off downstream. A few people notice me leaving, including my alpha, but nobody comments. Another one of today's rules. Which probably aren't really fooling anyone anymore, but they've done what they were meant to do.

They created shadows.

I stop beside a handy bush and pull my sweater over my head. My fragile human skin squawks about the sudden cold as I squiggle out of my jeans, too. I shift into my raven to finish the job, which makes her caw in protest. She thinks socks are ridiculous. I hush her as she flaps skyward. We don't need any curious wolves following us. We're not going far.

I land on the pale skeleton of a long-dead tree,

tucking myself against one of the long scorch marks on its trunk. It's not easy to hide a large black bird in a forest, but I've gotten better at it, and nobody down at the river or on the ledge should be able to see me from here.

I take another look at the short flight path I practiced a dozen times last night. It didn't get a whole lot easier with practice, but at least my bird got herself familiar with the twists and turns. Nothing ruins stealth reconnaissance quite like accidentally running into a tree.

I take one last look at the run I'm about to make, paying particular attention to the rock outcroppings. Along with the scraggly bushes and scrubby trees that somehow grow out of cracks in a mountain, they provide enough cover that maybe a bunch of wolves focused on the river below won't notice.

If they do, hopefully they'll deal. I drew a raven on the origami-paper invitations.

My bird snorts. That was not a raven.

I scowl. It was the best I could do on short notice.

She ignores me and launches herself off her perch, somersaulting in the only open space on this flight path just because she can. Then she steadies. We did plenty of stealth flying in the city. She knows when to be serious.

I stay as close to the rocks as I can, which isn't easy. They're a bumpy mess. My raven tucks in a wing sharply as she turns a really tight corner between a sheer slice of rock and a row of hanging tree branches that are a really fantastic bird trap. The hole I tested last night still works, though. Barely. My raven is definitely wider than she used to be.

I land on a tree that has almost as many carnivorous branches as the one I just flew through, and hop forward until I'm well tucked under pine boughs. Then I shift, because there's just no way to do the next part with wings. I slither down, pushing pine fronds out of the way and cursing as a stray pinecone bops me on the head. A squirrel chitters madly and chases after it, unimpressed at what I just did to his dinner plans.

I set my feet on the branch I'm trying to reach and wince as it bends alarmingly under my human weight. I shift as I let go of the much sturdier one I was holding on to and trust my wings and claws to do their job.

They do. My raven shakes, happy to be back in her feathers.

The rest of me is too busy peering through a screen of pine needles to care. I gulp as my bird eyes focus on the ledge. There are wolves there. More than one. And every last one of them has their nose hanging over the edge, looking down at the river below.

I hop closer, squinting through pine needles across the expanse of sun and into the deep shadows of the ledge. Trying to count. Trying to name. Closest to me is a gray wolf with red glints in his coat, and from the way he's lying, his right hip painfully cocked, that can only be Grandpa Cleve. Beside him is another wolf of indistinguishable color that I can't identify. And lying companionably beyond them, a wolf as black as night and twice as big as his companions.

I huff out a quiet breath. I guess Rio figured out where to put himself.

My raven grumbles. She hopes he didn't eat all the cookies. She made eleven flights to the ledge first thing this morning, delivering snacks, trinkets, a few wild wishes, and an entirely foolish pitcher of sun tea.

I tell her to quit grumping. I couldn't find a canteen with a handle she could manage, and the pitcher wasn't that bad.

She caws, which scares the crap out of the poor squirrel again.

The black wolf raises his head and looks right at me. Then he settles back down. Neither of the other two wolves so much as cock an ear. They're too focused on the river below.

I let out a breath full of relief and a few other things I don't really want to think about. I knew the view was good from up here, but I didn't realize how well the sound was going to carry. The high, rocky river banks are doing a fine job of funneling the sounds of mischief and chatter and glee up to the avid ears on the ledge.

Something that's been flying dizzy in my chest since I came up with this idea finally settles. These are good inches. Really good ones. The ghost wolves I invited didn't all come, but my sights weren't set nearly that high. Two came, and they're watching pack and hearing pack and feeling pack, and that matters. A way to belong, even just for a little while, without needing to get close to the den or even leave the shadows.

I back up slowly, taking one last look at the ledge as I retreat. It's time to return to my pile of shiny rocks, but my raven hasn't properly touched these shinies yet, and she wants to. I could maybe do a flyover. Rio will know who the second wolf is, but I can't ask him, and Hoot is quietly turning inside out down below as she collects rocks and makes jokes and tries to be nothing more than a playful student on a sunny fall day.

It's too big a risk, though. I'm a big, black object in the sky, and there's no way to get any closer without pulling two dozen sets of eyes in my direction. Which might not reveal the wolves on the ledge, because they're pretty well screened by the shadows from the scrubby trees above them, but I won't take the chance.

Shadows matter.

I shift to human again to squirm my way up to a branch where my raven can actually fly out of this tree— and freeze.

There's another wolf. A fourth one, tucked so far back on the ledge that I can't really see her, but an errant ray of light just broke through the scrubby overhang and landed on something unmistakable. A wolf snout lying on an object I left down there as an act of silent, foolish hope.

One of the wild wishes.

I gulp, swiping at the sudden tears in my eyes that will for sure botch a stealthy retreat. I don't know the identity of the wolf in the shadows for certain. It's possible she doesn't know, either. Some of our most wounded have lost all of themselves but the faintest embers, or at least that's how Wrinkles explains it. I don't know who it is that got my invitation, and came, and still can't bring herself to look over the edge.

But I do know that she's cuddling a hot-pink knitted square in her paws.

One that smells of Kelsey Dunn.

RIO

Some day I'll stop underestimating the wolves of this pack, including the ones who love us enough to stick around and be pack even when they don't have fur.

My wolf breathes, very gingerly. Fallon has left her tree. She's back down at the river, guarding her pretties and joking with Brandy and eating one of the sandwiches Ben brought her when she returned.

Ben and Brandy don't know. Ghost does, and Kelsey wonders, and Hoot's hope is so strong I can taste it, but the rest of them are playing fluid, easy, goofy pack to perfection because they don't know that they're putting on a performance.

My sentinel hates the dishonesty—and bows his head to the thief and shadow dweller who understood it was necessary. It isn't neat and it isn't tidy and it isn't instincts that come from the light, but it's pure brilliance, and as soon as I'm done giving a raven hell for lobbing a fastball that nearly whacked me in the head, my wolf is going to lick her until she splutters.

I sigh. I have work to finish before I can consider giving anyone hell. Critical, delicate work that a raven who doesn't trust easily is trusting me to do, and I need to not fuck it up.

The wolf beside me is fading. She arrived glued to the older wolf's side and hasn't left it, but her ability to be here is just about done. I lean against her as gently as a black behemoth can manage and try to pass a silent signal to the grandfather wolf on her other shoulder. He isn't done yet, and I wish that he could stay and drink more of this precious water into his parched soul.

The earth murmurs what I already know. His wolf can come and watch again. He's done this before—he's too easy with it for this to be his first time. And if he needs reminding, I have his scent now.

A grumble. A protest as much from his hip as his wolf.

Another good reason to get moving. This ledge is sheer genius as a viewing location, but it's not all that kind to old bodies, or young ones, either. Especially when we haven't so much as twitched for more than an hour.

The young wolf between us slides back a careful, quivering inch. The elder wolf turns his head and scans his much younger charge. A solemn brown eye meets mine, and an old, ragged snout nods. He will take her. They will go.

I don't move as they do. She's not ready for the big, black wolf to show her his full size. But as soon as they disappear into the shadows, I rise to follow them, because there is one who isn't done here yet.

I carefully don't look her way as my wolf pads over to the narrow goat trail that brought him here and will take him away again. He doesn't pause for the cookies, or for the small objects that smell of wolves he knows and wolves he has never seen, or for the half-drunk glass of tea sitting on a flat rock.

But he listens to the earth, and he offers silent words to the ravaged heart in the deepest shadows.

You are seen.

17

FALLON

I wasn't ready for tears.

I shoot Ben a frantic look over Hoot's head as she cuddles into my chest, holding a small carved wolf in her hand and wailing. He just reaches over and tugs my head against his, his grip fierce. His lips brush against my cheek. "Thank you."

My bird flaps desperately, trapped by fur and complicated feelings.

A hand settles on my shoulder. "I've made tea. Hoot, you'll pour it into mugs. Ben, let go of your mate before you pull out all her feathers."

They both let go of me, looking sheepish, even though there are still tears streaming down Hoot's face.

Wrinkles wipes at them gently with the sleeve of her flannel shirt. "Careful now, or you'll break more legs off that carving and Brown will growl."

Hoot manages a sniffly laugh. "Grady broke off the leg. The tail was my fault, though. I threw it at him for stealing my chocolate cake. I missed and hit Moss Rock instead."

Moss Rock is a small mountain. A carving the size of her palm didn't have a chance.

She looks at me. "I can't believe you stole it."

I wince. So much for being a retired thief. "I'm sorry. You weren't at your camp to ask. I should have taken something else."

She shakes her head fiercely. "You can steal my things any time you like if you bring them back smelling like my brother."

I didn't know about that part until I got back and Ben intercepted me, his eyes glued to the small bag where I'd gathered up the wild wishes that weren't taken.

Hoot throws herself into my arms again, a little less frantically this time, squishing the small, carved wolf between us. "I delivered the invitation out to his rocks, but I never thought he'd come. I read it out loud when I dropped it off, but I didn't think he even heard me."

I can't believe they all managed to find a random ledge on the side of a mountain. The map was almost as bad as the ones Reilly drew for the treasure hunt. Which makes me think that a big, black wolf did a lot more than he admitted to when he swung by our camp a little while ago. "Did you talk to Rio?"

She nods, sniffling. "He didn't see Grady. But he said Grandpa Cleve is wise and kind and he remembers us just fine, and his wolf thought it was really funny when

Kelsey chased the wild ravens away from your pile of pretty rocks."

Those were two really persistent birds. "I think he might have eaten some of the cookies, too." Someone did, and washed them down with some of the tea that was so stupidly hard to get up there.

Mikayla dips her head, but not before I see her quiet pleasure. She made the cookies. I stole those, too.

Ben moves closer and rubs Hoot's back, but he's smiling at me. "Thank you."

He's been saying that every two minutes, ever since Rio showed up and confirmed what I was too scared to tell anyone. I didn't want to be wrong.

"He watched us." Brandy hugs her knees a little tighter. "Dad watched us, Ben."

Happiness blazes out of my mate. "I know."

Hoot pats my arm with the hand that isn't clutching the wolf carving and wipes her face on my shirt. "You're the best aunt."

I laugh. "I'm your first-cousin-once-removed-in-law. Or whatever you call it when Ben didn't actually marry me."

He snorts. "I tried."

Hoot looks up and smiles. "We call you family."

I hug her shoulders, not entirely sure what to say or what to do or anything else. When I first got here eight years ago, Aaron was the alpha and his twin brother Cleve was everyone's grandpa, and the rest of the Dunn family was a big, jumbled mess that took me ages to figure out because they threw around words like sister and cousin and dad and uncle with terrible lack of precision.

Which was overwhelming and uncomfortable and awkwardly, hesitantly wondrous for a raven who had just fallen out of the sky. And absolute hell when their family got gutted. Mess with one Dunn and you really and truly mess with them all.

I take a deep breath and reach for Ben's hand, because he's feeling this just as deeply as the teenager in my arms—he's just trying really hard to help me stay in my skin. He knows how wildly uncomfortable the emotion and the inclusion of this are for me.

I take a deep breath and try to get a little easier with both. A whole lot of inches happened today. This is mine.

HAYDEN

I shift and yank on the hoodie and pants I carried with me. I'm warm from the run, but that won't last long. I also rein in my wolf, because his instincts are still running hard and the woman who just spun to face me needs words, pronto.

Or at least those are what I'm going to try first. I'm not convinced they're going to work. Bailey's eyes are pure wolf and her movements are fluid like a panther. She's half a breath from furry, and I'm out here because her wolf is spewing violence Lissa could feel all the way back at the den.

It's not less intense up close.

She's scratched and bloody and obviously fresh from a brawl that didn't dim her need to fight at all. Which means she was keeping herself under tight control to protect whoever was desperate enough or angry enough or far enough gone to attack a wolf as dominant as Bailey Dunn.

Someone skilled enough to make her bleed. Fuck.

Her hands close into fists. "Get out of here. Lissa likes your face pretty and my control sucks right now."

I keep my movements easy and respectful. "I know. I came to help."

The growl that comes out of her throat is nowhere near human.

I listen with ears that have a lot more information than the last time they faced her. Bailey's generation of the Dunn family had three strongly dominant wolves. Cody, the alpha-elect, is dead. His mate, Ruby, is a ghost out in the far reaches of our territory who doesn't recognize her own children—or perhaps can't bear to look at them.

I'm looking at the third. The one who pulled it together when her family needed her, who rose to be the fierce leader and protector they needed. Until Myrna talked to me, I didn't have any idea how much personal trauma Bailey had pushed aside to do it. "It was either me, or let Lissa come out here."

Shame and guilt mix with Bailey's fury.

Fuck. It took fierce trust for Lissa to send me out here to do the job she's done magnificently for the last six years. I need to not screw this up. I look into fury and offer the one thing that Lissa can't. Willing claws and teeth. "If you wanted to be alpha, you could give my wolf a damn good run for his money. Since you don't, we both know how this ends, and you can trust me to stay until it's done."

Shock lands in Bailey's eyes.

It's an honest offer. I'll fight if that's what she needs. But I know another wolf who strangled his own trauma because he was needed, and I have a weapon in my arsenal that sometimes works even better than teeth and claws. I flash her a grin. "Maybe punch me in the nose before we get furry, though. If I go back with a black eye, everyone at the den will feel sorry for me for a while."

The category-five hurricane inside her teeters.

I wait. She has the absolute right to decide what kind of storm she needs to be right now.

The next growl out of her is a lot more human and very reluctantly amused. "You're a jerk. And an idiot. My wolf could have jumped you while you were pulling on your pants, and then where would you be?"

Kel trained me better than that. I hope. "A guy with a wolf bite on his ass?"

Her snicker is still leaning hard toward the dangerous side of annoyed, but her eyes aren't wolf any longer. "You would have deserved it."

"Probably." I toss a pinecone at her head. "Are you going to do this every time you have a really good day being a teacher?"

She snatches the pinecone out of the air and glares at

me. "How did you manage to stay alive long enough to grow up?"

A pack with a really high tolerance for shenanigans. "Kel says I lack a self-preservation gene." Which was an insult that made ten-year-old me go look up several words the first time he hurled it.

She shakes her head. "It figures. We get the alpha with gummy bears for brains."

I need to remember that one. "Sucks to be you. Want the update?"

She scowls. "Dunns are losing their shit all over Ghost Mountain territory?"

Some more violently than others, apparently. Bailey's scratches are starting to heal, but someone got in a few good swipes. "How's Cleve?"

She shoots me a dirty look. She probably thought her alpha didn't notice her sneaking off down the old wolf's trail as we were all leaving rock school. "He's fine. Annoyed that I tracked him. I probably wouldn't have if I hadn't found a crumpled piece of paper on the ground last night that smelled like Fallon."

Oops. Operational-security loophole. One that means Bailey knew there might be stealth visitors today. She put on a damn good act. "Did you keep the paper?"

A disgusted look that slowly turns into a wry grimace. "Yeah."

I wait. Fallon shook mountains today, and my wolf is pretty sure there are a couple of avalanches that haven't happened yet.

Bailey scuffs her sneaker in the dirt. "Damn raven, trying to fix things that can't be fixed."

I'm looking at a wolf who doesn't believe that for a second. And one who thrives on the small details of her family and her pack. Which I carefully collected before I came out here. "Brandy got a little overwhelmed by the news that her dad showed up, but her baby pack is on it. Kelsey is happily toasting tiny marshmallows with Myrna, which is even harder than folding origami bears, and asking what grandpas are like."

Bailey's grin is lopsided, reluctant, and real. Then she sobers. "Stinky?"

It's so good to understand why she needs to know. Her brother's youngest son and the first pup she took to safety. "He drew a picture for Raven to take to Grandpa Cleve. Then he fell asleep with his head in his snack, which is going to be messy, since it involved melted cheese."

Her snicker is wet and wavery. "That kid and cheese."

She made that possible for him. Allowed him, against all odds, to become a happy-go-lucky kid who remembers little of the time before Samuel and was kept far away from what came after. "Reilly found a recipe for cheese cookies. Stinky's already trying to convince Shelley that those would be a nutritious breakfast."

Bailey raises an eyebrow. "You can stop herding me any time now."

Smart wolf. "Not herding. Inviting."

She rolls her eyes. "Yes, I love pack gossip. No, I'm

not going to be your teacher. I'm not moving any closer to the den, either. If Stinky wants to see me, he can use his legs."

The blood she's wearing makes it a lot clearer why her camp is as far from the den as Kel would let her put it. So I push on what feels safer to lean on. "You might want to use your legs and pay Fallon a visit."

Bailey's eyes narrow. "Why? What else did she do?"

I prepare to exit my pants in a hurry, just in case. "She left some special items up on the viewing ledge. Hoot's came back smelling like Grady. The crocheted pink square that Kelsey made didn't come back at all."

Tears spill down Bailey's cheeks, hot and fierce and instant.

I don't step any closer. Nothing in her wolf or her body language is giving me that permission.

"That fucking raven." Bailey spins away, far happier to expose her back to me than her shuddering sobs.

It kills me to stand and watch, but I know that's exactly what Lissa sent me out here to do—and in her own way, so did Fallon.

Stand witness and learn.

I thought I had learned. I sat down with Dorie and Ravi as soon as we got back to the den. There will be more school field trips. Lots of them, with a published schedule and nearby shadowy places with a good view. But that isn't enough. I watch Bailey's back as she fights to lock the feelings of devastating loss back into submission. And I let myself remember.

The aching emptiness of a father, gone. The overwhelming, hopeless sadness.

And the rage.

Ever since I took Myrna's scribbled family tree and laid it over the shape of the baby packs Kennedy made, I've been worried about Hoot. She's the Dunn who travels the woods tending to wounds and daring to hope and standing for her family with gentleness and fierce love, and she's got way too many gravity beams in her small hands.

I didn't realize that she didn't have all of them.

The brokenness runs into Hoot's hands. The fury runs into Bailey's. And Fallon, adopted Dunn and outsider and denizen of the shadows—is asking us to make better space for all of it to belong.

CLEVE

My hip complains bitterly as I zigzag slowly down the hill. It prefers the flats these days, but I make this journey each time the full moon wanes.

I dig for the human word. *Months*. Each month, I come to check on the two who worry me most.

I left Molly sleeping. Reuben will watch over her. He's a good wolf, even if he doesn't believe it of himself. He's the one who brought Molly to me, a lost and starving youngster who came to these woods because she heard that we were a good pack for strays.

She was three months too late.

My wolf shakes his head. Enough.

I listen. My human thoughts can dig me into the dark places so very quickly, and there are those who need me yet, even if my hip would rather find a sunny rock to enjoy the last of the day's warmth. The warm days will be fewer soon. The cold comes, and with it, the constant hunger and fear.

My wolf nips at my nose. This winter will be different. Even Reuben thinks so.

I want to believe him, I do, so very fiercely. There are two pups of my line that I don't want to be hungry and afraid. One who swims like a fish and laughs easily at himself, and one who sings of flowers as she hunts for pretty rocks. She enchanted my wolf today, and broke my human's heart. She looks so exactly like her mother as a small girl.

Rennie.

Fingers of darkness reach for my human.

I snap wolf teeth that are long used to the task of chasing those fingers away. I shifted today, long enough to eat the cookie and drink some of the tea that smelled of berries and strange grasses. That time in my human skin gave the darkness a foothold, just as it did when I shifted to touch the strange object of metal and glass that held the small girl's face.

I hadn't shed my fur in years. Too afraid of the darkness.

But it was worth it.

For the touch. For the word.

Kelsey.

I will give Rennie this word. Not today. On a new one, when I have the strength to be human again, and her eyes are clear in that way they sometimes get.

I take a left at the goat trail that leads by her caves. There's no sign of goat hooves here on the rocks, but there's a scent that's clear enough. Rennie lets them be. She chases only rabbits and the odd squirrel foolish enough to get lost above the tree line.

Next time I'll bring her a rabbit, before the cold comes and my hip pains me more and I have trouble catching them.

Reuben promises there will be food.

I shake off the words. Promises are human things. My wolf can't let human things matter.

I head for the gap in the rocks that will lead me to the small cave den of my youngest daughter. I know before I get there that Rennie isn't inside. A faint scent trail runs up into the naked rocks where only goats and tormented wolves with young hips can go.

I sigh. I had wanted to see her, but she will scent my wolf and know that I came by. I hope she took the small knitted square of pink with her into the high mountains. My wolf wanted very badly to claim it, but it wasn't meant for him. He sniffed it, though. Memorized the scent of the small girl who sings of flowers. He will know her as she travels his forests now.

I turn to go, and my wolf catches the faint scent of blood.

My head drops. It's been two full moons since I last

smelled Rennie's blood. Two moons since she last hurt herself. Which can only mean one thing.

Ruby was fighting again.

The fingers of darkness reach for me, and I don't snap at them this time. I let them come. Let them drown me in the discouragement and the guilt and the empty, echoing sadness that my twin and my pups once filled. The dark feelings flood in, as thick and fierce and suffocating as ever.

But somewhere in the darkness, something different also lingers.

The faintest whisper of a song about flowers.

18

FALLON

Crap. I'm so not ready for this. I stare at the bear cub who just walked into my camp, holding the notebook he uses for interviews. I have no idea where nice, normal days went, but I want them back.

Wrinkles greets him cheerfully. "Hey, Reilly. We're finished breakfast, but Mikayla made berry bars with extra honey if you want one."

When I lived on the street, there were some people who hoarded food, and others who couldn't stop eating when they finally got a decent meal, even if it made them sick. We're still a little bit crazy like that about food here in this camp. We got low on rice the other day and panic hit Mikayla's eyes, even though the den has a huge bin we can take from anytime we want. "They're pretty good if you like stuff so sweet that it makes your teeth ache."

Reilly grins. "I'm a bear. My teeth love sweet stuff."

My raven shakes her head. Spicy is so much yummier.

Brown grumbles as he walks in, carrying his buckets from a trip to the river. "Sure. Show up when the fishing's done, kid."

Reilly's eyes light up. "Do you need more? I can help."

Brown actually looks disappointed, which makes Wrinkles hide a smile behind her sleeve. "Nah. Smoker will be full with this load. If you come by tomorrow, you can help me turn them."

"Can I bring Stinky?" Reilly carefully sets down his gear. "And Robbie, maybe?"

Brown rumbles out a sigh. "They can come, but only if they work hard and don't eat all my berry bars."

Reilly looks almost insulted. "We always work hard."

He does. I have no idea when Kennedy's baby pack finds time to sleep. They're always running out to the base camps with videos and gossip and cookies. We send cookies back with them, too, which makes literally no sense, but it makes Mikayla hum happily, and Brown runs to the den for all the flour and butter and sugar that she wants, and Brandy loves the stories about silly things that happen at the den.

I look up and realize I've missed how the fish-turning duties were sorted. Which means a bear cub's attention has turned back to me.

He smiles, a little uncertainly. "Hayden said that he talked to you about my story."

I sigh. "He did. It's not you, I promise. Pretend that I'm just cranky like Brown."

Wrinkles sets down two glasses of sun tea and a honey berry bar. "What story are you chasing? Do you need quotes from the people who know Fallon best?"

That makes me feel strangely warm in my discomfort.

Reilly beams at her. "You can give me all your best quotes. I'm telling about how Fallon snuck into a polar bear's den and took three really cool bear coins so that we would have enough food to eat, and then when Ivan asked her why, she said she wasn't sorry, and he thinks that's exactly the right answer."

Dread pools in my stomach. "You talked to Ivan?"

Reilly's eyes shine. "I did. He's going to send me a picture of the coins. He was really proud to be my second polar bear interview. Ronan was my first, but Ivan said that's as it should be."

The extremely scary polar bear clearly didn't scare Reilly at all, which I should be grateful for, except I'm too freaked out about what else he might have said. "You know that bears like to add things to their stories that aren't necessarily true, right?" Brown tells whoppers on a regular basis.

Reilly nods solemnly. "Ronan says that the real truth of a story is in its deeper meaning, and sometimes you need to embellish details so that people who aren't bears can see the true meaning, nice and clear."

Brown snorts. "That is some serious bear bullshit, right there."

Wrinkles laughs and tosses a dishrag at him.

He scowls and throws it back at her. "If you wanted a mate with good manners, woman, you picked the wrong bear."

She shakes her head, amused. "You were the only bear in sight, my dear, and I picked you for your ingenious skills in the woods, not for your manners."

Reilly tilts his head. "Are you talking about sex?"

Wrinkles doesn't even blink. "That I am, but you aren't supposed to figure that out for a few years yet, even if you are an adorable bear cub. So you can pretend that I'm talking about how well he fishes."

Reilly grins. "I know all about sex. Rio explained it after Stinky wanted to know why Hayden and Lissa keep coming back from the woods with leaves in their hair."

I probably shouldn't find that hilarious, but I do. "Maybe you should make that your next headline."

"Myrna says that everyone already knows about sex and they'll be way more interested in how you snuck into Ivan's den." He picks his notebook back up. "Ivan really wants to know that, too."

Brown grunts. "I bet he does."

Reilly carefully writes something at the top of his page. "I looked up some things online about how to be a good thief, and it said you should scope out a location before you rob it. Did you do that?"

Sweet holy hell. "You shouldn't be Googling things like that."

Curious bear eyes. "Why not?"

Wrinkles snickers. "She's worried that it will lead you into a life of crime."

Reilly frowns. "I look up all kinds of stuff. About outer space and how to help a friend who's scared and what little brown speckles on lettuce means and why some ravens migrate and others don't."

That is some kind of list. "Lettuce with brown speckles is usually fine." I don't have a clue about outer space or why ravens do anything, and scared friends are the only kind I've ever had.

He nods cheerfully. "That's what I told Shelley, but she still wasn't sure, so they decided to feed those ones to the bunnies that Ghost adopted."

We all stare at him.

He grins. "That's what Hayden's eyes did, too. And Kenny's. And Ebony's. Ghost thinks that the bunnies are juveniles who don't have a mom, so they didn't know better than to wander into a garden that smells like wolf. Besides, they're kind of cute. One has this nose that wrinkles just like Mellie when she gets mad, and another one has an ear that falls over when it hops, and one is white, just like Robbie."

The giggles that Wrinkles has been trying to hold in finally escape. She falls over, holding her belly and laughing all the way from her toes. "Bunnies. BUNNIES."

Reilly whips out his sat phone and takes a picture. "I'm going to put the story about the bunnies in next week's edition. I don't have a really good picture of them, yet. I have one of Shelley where she's all mad that they got into her cucumber patch, though. They took a tiny bunny bite out of each one."

Brown rolls his eyes. "I can't imagine how a wolf could take care of that problem."

Reilly shakes his head solemnly. "Any wolf who does that will face the wrath of Ghost. That's what Hayden said, and since Shelley really loves Ghost and Shelley makes all the cookies, those are three really safe bunnies."

I wince. There are so many predators in the woods, and not all of them can be dissuaded with cookie threats. "You know that wild owls and hawks will eat bunnies, right?"

He nods. "That's why Kendra is going to come and put hawk sign around our garden."

I only met the messenger hawk alpha once. It took my bird a whole day to start breathing again. "That will work."

Reilly smiles happily. "That's what Rio said. But he also explained that maybe the bunnies will get eaten, because that's the way of the woods. We're supposed to do our best and be kind and let them be the wild things that they are."

I look down into my lap, feeling tender and not at all sure why. "That's a really great story." One that lets innocent kids be kids and still prepares them for the way the world rolls, and somehow gives three really lost bunnies a fighting chance, too.

"Yours is really great, too," says Reilly quietly. "But if you don't want me to tell it, I won't."

Guh. I spent ten years on the streets and I know how

to fight darn near everything—except gentle. "I'm just not used to being the center of attention. I'll deal."

"Why?'

I look up into sweet, curious eyes. "Why what?"

His head tilts. "Why does it bother you to be in the center?"

I stare at him. That isn't what I said, at all—but it's what I meant.

He waits quietly, a gentle bear with kind eyes who truly wants to know.

I have no idea how to answer that in a way that lets him keep believing in the bright innocence of cucumber-eating bunnies. "I'm used to living in the shadows. It's uncomfortable to have everyone looking my way."

He drops his gaze to a point over my shoulder, just like a polite dominant would do with an uncomfortable submissive wolf. It's entirely wrong for my raven, and sweet all the same. "Did you learn how to steal when you lived in the shadows?"

"Yeah. I did." Which is absolutely all that I'm saying about living on the street to a sensitive eleven-year-old, no matter what he's lived through. "You wanted to know how I scoped the job at Ivan's den, right?"

He nods eagerly.

I walk him through it, in enough detail to be inter-esting and hopefully not enough to lay out a blueprint for a life of crime. I point out the advantages of having an animal far smaller than any of the other shifters in my pack, and how freaking cold it is up north, and how handy it is to have wings.

None of which makes his eyes shine any less. "Wow. So you scouted everything before you took the coins, but you didn't have time to do that before you put them back. And that's a lot riskier, right? Which means you were really brave."

Someone has been feeding this reporter way too much information. "It's going to snow up there soon. I wanted to return the coins before winter set in."

Wrinkles snorts. Apparently I'm failing at trying to make this sound like a casual trip.

Reilly cocks his head. "Why?"

I sigh. Persistent bear. "Because Ivan is our friend. I don't steal from friends." Unless her name is Hoot, and those were special circumstances. "It would have bugged me all winter."

Reilly grins. "He thinks it's really awesome that you consider him a friend."

That sounds ominous.

Reilly flips the pages of his notebook until he gets to one covered in scribbles. "He also said that he will excuse you for not understanding the terms of bear friendship, just this once. If you try to return any of the other items you took, he will not be so understanding. Specifically, you took one very ugly belt buckle from a bear who lives north and east of him, in a large den that smells of wood shavings."

Crap. I remember that one. My bird was so enamored with that belt buckle. My human was a lot more excited by what it was worth. That was one of the really bad times. Both parts of me shoot a suspicious look at a reporter and his notebook. "Why does the belt buckle matter, specifically?"

Reilly's eyes gleam. "Because it belonged to Phil. He's a polar bear who makes furniture. He's making our couches, so that makes him a friend to our pack, and you don't steal from friends, right?"

My raven freezes.

Reilly smiles cheerfully.

Awesome. I've just been neatly boxed into a corner by an eleven-year-old bear eating a honey bar. I scowl at the sat phone that's just recorded my self-disgust for posterity.

Reilly takes a second photo for good measure. "Ivan said that Phil hated that belt buckle, and he'll get an entire winter's pleasure out of knowing his alpha was bested by a raven. I have quotes from all the other bears you stole from, too. They're really funny."

I drop my head into my hands. "Just tell me all of them and get it over with."

"Nope." Reilly grins at me cheerfully when I look back up. "They're my scoop. You'll have to read my story to find out."

Wrinkles makes funny choking sounds.

I glare at her, which is useless. She's a healer and mated to a bear. Glares stopped working on her before I was born.

Reilly writes something in his notebook. "It's a really big list. Ivan says that some of them are perhaps not factually correct, but I told him about Ronan's embellishing details that help to make the story more true, and he said that's exactly right."

I stare at him. "Ivan told you lies and you're going to publish them?"

Wrinkles snorts. "That story isn't going to resemble the truth for five minutes after Reilly tells it. And besides, those quotes aren't about what you stole. It's a list of polar bears who are honoring what you did." She pats Brown's arm. "Bears are wonderful that way. I bet they arm-wrestled for spots on that list."

"They did." Reilly beams at her, delighted. "And a throwing contest. And something with ice floes that Ivan said maybe wasn't wise to put in a newspaper."

My raven is speechless. This is worse than flying in bright sunlight over snow.

Wrinkles chuckles. "It's good to know that he's showing some self-restraint."

Reilly grins at me. "Ivan says the bears will drink vodka in your honor every night this winter. They tried to claim you as a bear sister, but Hayden called him and growled and said they couldn't have you, so I guess that means you don't get any vodka."

My human has no words, either.

Which doesn't seem to matter. Reilly leans toward Brown and asks something that generates a whole lot more scribbling. Wrinkles shoots me an amused glance and adds her two cents.

I groan quietly. This is going to be an utter disaster.

A gentle hand lands on my back. Ben, back from

taking Brandy over to visit with Dorie's crew. "I heard enough. Are you okay with this?"

I lean into his touch and sigh. "I'll deal. I'll just hide in the woods for a couple of weeks when this edition goes out."

He grins. "Good luck with that."

I growl. "Whose side are you on?"

He chuckles and plants a kiss behind my ear. "Yours. Always. Want to run away to the woods right this minute?"

I snort. "Not unless you want our sex lives in the next gossip column. Rio told the juveniles what it means to have leaves in our hair."

I can feel his grin. And another kiss behind my ear. "I think Reilly's got more questions for you."

I groan. "I'm not sure I can handle any more embellishing details."

Ben chuckles. "Maybe steal from turtle shifters next time. Or sharks. I hear they don't talk much."

There isn't going to be a next time, because pups in my pack don't go hungry anymore. Which is a big enough deal that I can suck it up and answer whatever the world's sweetest bear cub wants to ask.

I look back over at Reilly. I know how much food he needed these last six years, and how hard he had to work to keep his bear under control. I don't even want to think about a hungry teenage grizzly. "Two more questions, hot stuff, and then I need a break."

He smiles at me. "I only have one more. Thanks for being really patient."

Guh. "I'm ready. Lay it on me."

He looks down at his notebook. "Myrna says that it's always good to tease your next story, so can you tell me how you feel about the ravens coming to visit?"

My feathers ruffle in an instant. I sit bolt upright. "What?"

Reilly looks at me uncertainly. "Hayden got a call from the raven flock that lives over in Desolation Inlet, right before my birthday week started. They want to come for a visit, just like the cats did."

I feel like I just drank a glass of alley slime. "I didn't know that."

Ben strokes my back. "They didn't used to want contact with us. I guess that's changed."

Reilly nods. "They have a new alpha and she likes working with other packs. They do lots of trades with the cats, and Myrna knows their beta from back when she was a rampaging teenager."

I try to smile. It doesn't work. Too many inches.

"That sounds useful." Wrinkles shoots me a concerned look. "And it sounds like den business. Nothing that needs to affect us way out here."

My bird grabs on to that with all her claws. I can stay in the shadows. Trade with them online, maybe. "Okay, yeah. That makes sense."

Reilly looks perplexed. "Don't you want to meet other raven shifters?"

No. I have no freaking clue how to be a raven, and they'll figure that out in about ten seconds and there will be more disappointed eyes, and worse, I'll be letting down my pack. But I can't say that to a kid who desperately wants to meet more bears. "Maybe one day."

Reilly's eyes are still full of questions—but he shuts his notebook anyhow.

Which somehow makes me sad.

19

FALLON

There are days I feel like a reasonably competent grown-up. And then there are the days I'm quaking in my boots about something that should be simple and normal, and totally isn't. I look over at the guy who quietly stayed by my side all of last night and through this morning. Letting me quake. "I'm doing okay. I just have a lot to think about."

He rolls his eyes, which looks funny and lopsided because he's bent over digging out a couple of mushrooms from under a nurse log. We're on our way to the den to pick up supplies, but we're taking the long route so we can harvest enough to feed the whole pack while still following Wrinkles's ironclad rules about leaving plenty in the ground to make mushroom babies for next year. She only trusts us to do that without supervision for a couple of species, but early fall is prime season for one of them, and someone has put in a request for their birthday dinner.

My mate is gathering more than his fair share of mushrooms, but he's leaving plenty of space for me to do the talking. Which isn't a general thing—Benjamin Dunn is a plenty chatty wolf when he wants to be.

I sigh and start with the part I least want to think about. "One of my babysitters, back when I was little and still living with my aunt, was a raven shifter. She liked to sing silly songs, and she told me stories about her flock. On my birthday, she braided about a billion beads into my feathers. I could hardly fly when she was done, but I was really shiny."

I've never forgotten how that felt. Or how it trampled something vital when my aunt got home and saw the beads and yanked every last one of them out, muttering nasty things about uncivilized animals as she did it.

Ben comes over behind me and nuzzles his chin against my shoulder.

Not once in eight years has he failed to offer me comfort when I need it. "Pretty much everything I know about being a raven shifter, I learned from her. Which isn't very much."

He strokes my arms. "What was her name?"

I close my eyes against the pain. "I don't remember. I was really little and she was only around for a few months." But I remember her stories, and how it felt to have her touch my feathers and tell me they were beautiful. The next person to do that was the man who is currently holding me. In between were a lot of people who hoped that if they ignored my raven long enough, she might disappear.

I guess they didn't expect the rest of me to head out the door along with her.

I tip my head into my chest, seeking the comfort of feathers that aren't there. I did fine. I learned how to survive on the street, and I held on to those few stories I had of raven shifters like talismans. "I don't know what will happen when the ravens come to visit. I feel ignorant, and also like my bird wants things I can't give her. I'm scared that will make me do something stupid."

Arms wrap around me, the same sturdy ones that caught me on that first day when I fell from the sky. "There are no right answers, beautiful. It's okay to want whatever you want."

He means it. He always has, even on the days when his life was hanging in tatters. I take a deep, shaky breath into lungs that are feeling tight and prickly. Today is for new discomforts, not old hurts. I turn and kiss his cheek. "We have mushrooms to collect. You promised you wouldn't let me wallow."

He snorts. "I promised I wouldn't let you pick anything poisonous."

I flash him a grin. "Same difference."

Ben angles toward a patch of mushrooms that's big enough we can both take a few for our bags. He takes a good look to make sure they're not one of the more dangerous lookalikes and starts competently harvesting.

I tug on a couple that are crowding their neighbors.

Bullies deserve to turn into food first. Especially ones who are bullies in the shadows.

I snort quietly. That makes the mushrooms sound like some strange sort of kin.

I feel around another small grouping, trying to find the ones that can be taken with the least harm. That's not something I ever worried about in the city. There was always another abandoned lot that could provide earthworms and dandelion greens, and all I ever wanted in those days was a cheeseburger that was warm and whole and still in its wrapper.

If I ever get brave enough to ask for a birthday meal, that's what it will be.

Ben reaches over and tugs on the feathers I wove into my hair this morning. My bird is molting, and Kelsey loves it when I bring her my discards. "It will be fine. We can stay at our camp, or we can go spy on them and pretend you're a wolf, or you can introduce yourself and let Hayden chew on any ravens who don't think you're good enough."

I link my fingers through his and keep ambling toward the den. At this rate, it's going to take us a week to get there. Which would be fine by me, but the mushrooms would miss their birthday dinner. "I can't pretend to be a wolf. I don't smell right."

"Ravens have crap for noses, remember?" Ben lets go of my hand to swing up into a tree and slice off one of the humongous mushrooms growing out of its trunk. It looks like it has a very lumpy and likely fatal disease, and it definitely isn't what we've been collecting.

I peer at it, temporarily distracted from worrying about uncomfortable visitors. "Are you sure that's safe to eat?"

"It's not poisonous." He tucks it carefully into a reusable container. "Wrinkles says it tastes like dirt, but it's excellent for dyeing. She's got a weaver down in New Mexico who wants them. Some artist friend of Muriel's."

Muriel is the world-famous painter in Whistler Pack who insists on being Shelley's chief enabler of art supplies, so if she has a friend who wants mushrooms, I'm happy to help collect them. "Do they know that shipping vegetables across borders can be tricky?" I learned that the hard way. Never ship illegally acquired goods and claim they're food.

He grins. "Do I look like the brains of this operation?"

I snicker and kiss his cheek, because it's there and because he's always been irresistible. "Nope. I picked you for your strong, sexy arms, remember?"

I just got really lucky with what came along with those arms.

HAYDEN

I watch the two mushroom pickers headed my way. They both carry signs of trauma, hers older than his—but the love between them is a thing of beauty and wonder and fierce strength.

Their eyes flicker to me as I step out of the trees. I

don't miss Ben's instinctive step in front of his mate, or Fallon's arms rising behind her—or how quickly those reactions fade as they register who I am.

A trust my wolf cherishes.

Fallon shoots me a mildly dirty look. "If you give me another rock, I'm throwing it in the first stream I can find."

That's not the intel I got from Hoot, who thinks I'm a cute alpha. "No rocks." Although I did contemplate bringing some, given that I'm out here to apologize like hell. In the midst of Reilly's birthday extravaganza, I somehow forgot to mention to our resident raven that we're about to have the local flock drop by.

Poor Reilly is seeing this as a failure of orbital communications, but it's not. It's alpha failure, the kind that runs far deeper than an oversight in communication, because Kel and Rio both had the same amorphous gut sense I did—that Fallon doesn't know much about being a raven. Which we didn't fucking chat about until Reilly showed up at the den, out of breath and worried about his packmate.

Smart bear. Dumbass adults. "I'm sorry. I should have let you know about the visit from the Desolation Inlet ravens. It slipped my mind, which isn't even kind of an excuse."

A bland shrug. "No big deal."

She's way too good at that. And my wolf is way too in the dark. "Do you have any thoughts on them coming for a visit?"

This time I don't even get a shrug, just studied indifference. "You're alpha."

"Yup." One who knows when it's time to shoot straight and honest. "I'm an alpha who likes to make decisions that support his packmates, not steamroll them."

The indifference cracks as her lips quirk. "I'm a bird. We don't just stand there when steamrollers are headed our way."

I grin. "Are you saying that wolves are dumbasses?"

She flutters her eyelashes at me innocently, which makes my wolf bust up laughing. I wrap an arm around her shoulders, still chuckling. Feathery packmates don't always appreciate touch like furry shifters do, but this one does, even when she's still tense.

She nestles in for a moment, and then she backs away.

My wolf doesn't like the wary light in her eyes at all. Fallon decided he was cute and trustworthy weeks ago, and this is a clear setback. I meet her gaze. Ravens play power games differently than wolves do, and I've never met one who didn't want me to look them straight in the eyes. "You have all the power here."

The corners of her mouth turn down. "I don't want it."

Fuck. "Let me try saying that a different way. Something about this visit clearly has you uneasy. It's my job to deal with the ravens. I can do a better job of that if I understand what you want and need."

Ben heads toward a tree covered in lumpy mushrooms. Offering me a little space to work. Or harvesting something that might kill me. I don't underestimate even the most easygoing submissive wolf, especially when his mate isn't all that happy to see me.

Fallon watches him leave and makes a face. "You're smooth like Ben."

My lips quirk. "I hope that's a compliment."

She huffs out a laugh. "Most days."

I lean against a tree. She's moving mountains for our pack right now. The last thing I want to do is have some visitors dump her on her ass, or make her feel more like an outsider, or push her any deeper into the shadows. Which is a conversation Kel or Rio should be out here having, because they both have more of a relationship with her than I do, but I got outvoted. "I'm thinking about postponing the visit. It's been a big week. It might be good to have some downtime before we deal with anything else."

Her wariness grows tentacles. "I'm fine."

Damn. "Talk to me, Fallon. I'd like to help."

FALLON

Hayden is watching me so carefully, like he can see the turmoil inside me and hopes, so very gently, that I might be willing to share it.

I turn away, because my bird is terrible at resisting kind eyes. It doesn't help, though. The man who uses them on me most often is walking back toward us. He wraps his arms firmly around me before he spares any attention for his alpha. "What's going on?"

The thunder that rolls through Ben's eyes clearly surprises Hayden. It doesn't surprise me. My guy is gentle and funny and easygoing, right up until he's not. He stares down his alpha with a look that has to be giving his wolf conniptions.

I make a face and pet his wolf. "He wants to know what I need."

Ben keeps his arm around my waist, but I can feel his thunder ebbing away. "Thank you for asking her."

Hayden rolls his eyes. "Duh."

Ben kisses my forehead. No pressure to find my words. Just the silent reassurance that any of them will be fine with him.

I lean into his warmth. "Myrna and the raven beta were friends, and the ravens trade some great stuff online. I don't want to get in the way of that. I'll deal."

Hayden reaches out and touches my shoulder, in exactly the right way to speak to my bird. "Your pack is here for you. I hope you can give us a chance to prove just how steady we are behind you, even those of us who are new and just learning."

Shamed anger rises in my ribs. "You haven't done anything wrong."

He looks almost surprised. Probably because half of me just sprouted feathers.

Ben's hands skim my back, offering all the touch my bird will allow when she's this riled.

I face the guy who's somehow trying to make what I

lack into his fault. "You've done nothing but stand for all of us since you got here. You don't have anything to prove." My hands are in fists, my fingernails digging into my palms. "Neither does this pack. They took me in and they loved me and I won't embarrass them."

I crash to a halt. I didn't mean to say that last thing. Oh, I didn't mean to say it, but I did and it's out there and I can't take it back. I try not to cringe. There's no backing down on the street, not ever, and not from dominant wolves, either.

Hayden just calmly meets my eyes. "I know quite a few ravens. My sense is that you would fit in with them just fine, but I can't say for sure. What I can say with absolute confidence is that you're one of the finest wolves I know, and there is nothing you could do that would embarrass this pack."

I stare at him.

His lips quirk. "I thought we had that covered with the whole stealing-from-a-polar-bear deal."

My raven squawks weakly.

He stuffs his hands in his pockets. "I don't know what it's like to be on the periphery, or to be excluded. I was born James and Adrianna Scott's son, and that puts a guy right in the middle of his pack. I'm trying to imagine what it would be like to grow up without knowing very many wolves, and my brain can't really get there. It's too different from what I know."

He doesn't know—but he wants to. I can hear it in every word. Utter, aching sincerity.

I just don't know how to tell him.

Ben's hands stroke my shoulders, literally and figuratively holding me together.

Hayden studies me for a while. "Here's my bossy alpha opinion, which you're free to reject. Come to the den when the ravens visit. Listen from the trees or throw pinecones at them or stand at my side or help Myrna negotiate the trade deals."

My raven perks up.

Crap. He's found her eternal weakness. "Myrna's solid. She doesn't need help."

Hayden grins. "She thinks you're better. She was cackling all morning about some exchange of smoked fish, healing teas, and waffle recipes you pulled off with the hawks. She also told me that if you don't agree to head the trade delegation, she's going to get Shelley to hide zucchini in your cookies. I might be able to talk her down from that, but no guarantees."

I roll my eyes. "Wolves are so annoying."

Hayden grins at my mate. "We are."

Ben snorts. "Speak for yourself. I'm helpful and thoughtful and I eat my zucchini like a grown-up wolf."

Hayden shudders. "It doesn't even grow in the ground like a respectable vegetable. It lurks under innocent watermelon plants, waiting for unsuspecting wolves to pass by."

Ben shoots his alpha a wry look. "So, just to be clear, we have an incoming local pack to impress, and you believe Shelley is growing carnivorous zucchini in her kitchen garden?"

Hayden nods cheerfully. "Yup. The ones in the second row are the meanest."

I can feel the silent laughter shaking my mate's ribs. Goofballs, both of them, putting on a comedy show, casually proving that this pack is really hard to embarrass, and carefully giving me time to find the answer that Hayden needs from me. I sigh. I already have it—I just needed to pout a little first. "They're coming tomorrow, right? I'll be there."

"Your baby pack could come spend the night at the den." Hayden's offer is nonchalant, but his eyes aren't. "I think Shelley's planning a waffle breakfast. We got a big delivery of fresh strawberries from the cats."

I look at him carefully. "Those are Brandy's favorites."

He smiles a little. "I know."

Tricky, maneuvering wolf. "You do know who's in our baby pack, right? Brown would need at least a dozen people to growl at, and he's way nicer than Reuben." I try to imagine either of them lasting a night at the den, or Brandy or Ben, for that matter. Wrinkles and Mikayla make almost as many trips in as I do, but the rest of our baby pack has issues.

Hayden nods, like none of those are a big deal.

I can't deal with explaining more shadows today. "I'll come in the morning. A little early so that I can sit down with Myrna and make some plans."

Ben clears his throat.

I roll my eyes. "Fine. *We'll* come in the morning." Ben's wolf won't like being there any more than I will, but there's no chance he'll stay home, and I know better than to rile my mate's thunder. Especially when I'd lose.

Hayden smiles and tugs on his backpack straps. "I have supplies to deliver out to your camp. If you stop by the kitchen when you get to the den, Shelley is experimenting with some new muffin recipes. She's looking for testers."

My raven cocks her head suspiciously.

He walks off, humming innocently.

Ben watches him go with thoughtful eyes.

Crap.

20

FALLON

Never let an alpha talk to your baby pack unsupervised.

Hayden walked the entire lot of them into the den, carrying their sleeping rolls and smiling cheerfully, an hour after we got here. I don't think they even heard my squawks of protest. They were too busy being assimilated.

I can't complain about that, because they've been assimilated in ways that are so very obviously thoughtful and intentionally calibrated to who each of them are, and the individual challenges they're facing being here. They've done the same for Ben, too, and I didn't realize anyone at the den had any inkling about why he rarely comes here.

I'm also trying not to think too hard about the assimilation they're casually wrapping around me. Myrna and Lissa are having an animated conversation about the avalanche of fall vegetables coming from the cats and whether we should be sending them more smoked fish or knitted blankets in response.

It's not an accident that they're having it right beside me.

I do my best to ignore them, even though they're totally underestimating how good the newest batch of smoked fish is, and keep watching the shenanigans in the river. I shake my head as Braden falls off Brown's back into the chilly stream, yipping at the cold. It doesn't stop him from clambering back up, though, the naked toddler eagerly scaling black-bear mountain like he's been doing since my baby pack arrived.

Assimilators 1, Brown 0. I can't think of any better way to keep him here than a toddler who smells of berries and thinks bear growls are funny.

Brown stands perfectly still until a small brown wolf materializes on his shoulders. Braden shakes off the water in his fur and yips a challenge at Mellie. The far more dominant pup is riding on the furry shoulders of a gangly grizzly, wearing a pretty sundress and some of my feathers in her hair. She flaps her arms and aims a darn realistic hawk cry at her challenger.

My bird shudders. She's met several hawk shifters in the past few weeks, and all of them made the atavistic part of her brain quiver. Which she needs to get over, because they're happily making all kinds of trade deliveries for us, and that means she doesn't have to lug clunky packages to the post office.

Brown feints a charge, which gets Braden all excited

and makes most of the watching adults chuckle. Mellie growls as they close and Braden promptly tries to roll over and show her his belly. Which topples him off into the stream again. Hayden scoops him up this time, wearing bright orange swim trunks that Kelsey apparently found for him at the thrift store. "You need better tactics, little dude."

The pup in his arms shifts to human. "Cookie?"

Hayden grins. "Those could work."

"Hayden Arthurius Scott." Shelley marches over to the edge of the stream with her hands on her hips. "What did I tell you about cookies right before dinner?"

I glance over at Brandy and Mikayla, because Shelley is just joking around, but it doesn't take much to set off the trigger-happy alarms in Brandy's brain. She's fine, though. She's sitting over by Ravi with Kelsey in her lap, eating apple slices and braiding raven feathers into small-girl hair.

Hayden snorts at his accuser. "My sister is in so much trouble for telling you my middle name."

Shelley's glare doesn't budge.

Our alpha shoots a long-suffering look at the pup in his arms. "I guess that means we have to eat our cookies after supper."

Braden tips up his chin and howls mournfully.

Shelley's lips quirk. "Boys who want cookies after dinner can help carry all the food and dishes over from the kitchen."

Reilly shifts and whoops, neatly catching Mellie before she lands in the stream. She pats his cheek as he carries her over to the edge of the water and sets her down on dry land. He ruffles her hair and shrugs his way into a big flannel shirt and a pair of cozy pants the same color as Brown's fur.

Myrna chuckles beside me. "It always surprises me when such a shy, skinny kid emerges from that big, fierce bear."

Lissa grins. "He's not quite so shy anymore."

He isn't—and he isn't alone. These weeks are changing all of us. Which is good, and also sad. Some of us won't ever change fast enough to catch up.

Lissa's fingers reach out and clasp mine. "I'm so glad you're spending the night."

They all are. The entire den has been wrapping us in appreciative warmth since we got here. It's been a potent reminder of just how much they think those of us in the far orbits matter. And just how much they want us to come home.

I swallow. We're trying.

"No pressure," says Lissa quietly. "Truly. One night is a gift, or dinner, or an hour sitting by the river. We'll wait as long as it takes for you to feel ready for more. Or not. Hayden knows that some will likely stay out at the base camps forever."

I would have included most of my baby pack in that count, but tonight is putting some dents in that certainty. I look over at a low, makeshift table assembled from a long board and a couple of stumps, where five heads are focused on copying the intricate movements of Ebony's hands. "I can't believe Reuben is folding paper flowers."

Lissa grins. "I can't believe Ebony is sharing her new origami paper."

My raven can't, either. It's the most beautiful paper she's ever seen, small squares of iridescent, metallic shimmer that fold into flower jewels. She's trying to figure out what she might offer up in trade for one of the shiny purple ones.

Lissa looks at me carefully. "Is there anything that would make tonight easier for you?"

One night is easy enough. It's the thought that my baby pack might not give me an excuse to live in the shadows forever that's hard. I shrug. "This works. A chance to hang out and eat good food and not think too much."

She chuckles. "Is it working?"

Some. My raven drags my reluctant eyeballs over to where Ben is showing Lissa's son how to thread leather laces for some new carry pouches. All the tension that was in my mate when we crossed the inner perimeter is gone.

Lissa exhales softly. "He's really good with Robbie."

My heart aches. Ben would love living at the den. He mentors younger wolves as easily as he breathes. But he won't come until he and Brandy are both ready—and that day might never arrive for either of them. Not with the memories that are literally soaked into the ground of this place.

"Oh, listen to that." The pleasure in Lissa's voice is soft and bright.

I follow her gaze over to Kelsey, who is still sitting in

Brandy's lap. She's got a hot pink guitar in her hands, and she's playing along with Ravi—or he's playing along with her. She looks entirely in charge.

It's not the adorable four-year-old oracle we're all suddenly watching, though. It's the slightly embarrassed trio singing along. Shelley, still in her apron, finding a beautiful, haunting melody line. Brandy, her cheeks as pink as Kelsey's guitar, picking out a careful harmony. And Brown, adding growly low notes.

I stare. I didn't even know he could sing.

HAYDEN

I don't look at my two betas. I know they're watching the same magic as the rest of us—and the big fucking mirror it's holding up to our challenges. "Tell me that tomorrow isn't going to fuck this up." Fallon is holding steady, despite her screaming discomfort, but if our morning guests don't embrace whatever clumsy raven ways she might have, it could go south fast. And if it does, her whole baby pack will go under with her.

Ebony makes a noncommittal sound. "It might."

Not the answer I wanted, but if there are any two betas in the world less likely to tell their alpha what he wants to hear, I haven't met them. I wait on Kel's reply. We have seven packmates finding a foothold in the den tonight, and he'll fight anything that tries to mess with that at least as hard as I will.

He exhales slowly. "Depends what hits the fan tomorrow. If our visitors are idiots, that's easy. We chew on them and escort them to the road."

I can't speak for ravens I don't know, but I can very definitely speak for Fallon's pack. "If they're idiots, they're going to find themselves facing some very cranky wolves."

Ebony snorts. "And a black bear who makes us all look like amateurs."

Brown could definitely throw in a few wrinkles. He's pack because his mate is pack. His bear is a loner who respects no authority and loves Fallon absolutely. Which is fine. I'm good with love that's a little rough around the edges. I just hope it waits on my signal before it chomps on any tail feathers.

"I don't think the ravens are idiots." Ebony frowns, her eyes scanning the den like a soldier on alert. "I've been talking with them. They're eager to know us."

That doesn't always mean accepting what they find, but my wolf liked what he saw in my brief conversation with their beta. "If they're not idiots, it gets more complicated. There are lots of ways for polite and kind and well-meaning to get under Fallon's skin." The fiercest shadows are the ones that live inside us.

Kel nods. "Her baby pack is more solid than I expected. That will help."

Ebony's eyes soften as Kelsey's song dissolves into giggles and hugs. "I rolled Brown and Reuben into the security team and reviewed our basic hand signals with both of them."

I nod. "Good. Family at her back."

Kel smiles as Kelsey blows him a kiss. "I don't think this is going to come down to teeth and claws, even the dumbass posturing kind."

I don't either, but they're going to have Fallon's back anyhow.

"What's your gut smelling?" Ebony is still watching the gentle musical antics, but like all good betas, she can do six things at once, and she has as much respect for her co-beta's innards as I do.

Kel snorts. "Noses smell. Guts eat and keep you from ending up dead."

Ebony pitches a pinecone at his head.

He catches it before it bonks his ear, and shoots it and her a disgusted look. "This den has way too damn many of these things."

She snickers. "You started it."

He absolutely did. An impromptu fighting lesson in coping with distractions that has somehow wormed its way into pack daily life. Which I think secretly delights Kel, because most of the submissives have way better aim than the rest of us. I think he's given them lessons in the woods. "We can always throw them at the ravens."

"There's a thought." Kel's dry tone is coupled with a grin at Kelsey, who's sending him not-at-all-subtle hand signals about how the hot chocolate needs to have extra marshmallows tonight.

I shake my head. She landed a pinecone in Kennedy's soup yesterday. And giggled. "That pup is turning into a menace."

"She is, and if she doesn't think we're doing right by Fallon, she'll probably take over." Ebony shoots me a look. "So maybe we should get our shit together and come up with a plan there, Alpha."

"We have a plan." Kel fires back a hand signal I don't know, probably because he just made it up. "We watch, we have Fallon's back, and we're ready for anything she needs."

I hide a grin as Kelsey mimics his new hand signal and turns to teach it to Robbie and Brandy. "So basically our plan is to stand around like wolf lawn ornaments and roll with whatever shit hits the fan?"

Ebony's lips quirk. "Isn't that always the plan?"

My wolf refuses to answer that.

RIO

Fallon offers me one of the ridiculously large coconut–peanut-butter balls that Shelley and the pups made for dessert. We're supposed to be delivering them to Dorie's camp, which is clearly why I got sent out with supervisors. "Nope. This is a test, I know it."

She snickers, which does as much to release the tension in her mate as getting farther away from the place in the woods that my sentinel now understands is so very fucking haunted. Which he is kicking himself over. Hard. I knew about the spot at the den—the one Brandy can't stop herself from looking at, and every time she does, her hands shake. I just hadn't pieced together what it meant until we passed by a second one.

Fallon elbows me. "Spill. Your wolf is really loud when he's chewing on something."

My wolf is oddly reticent to take the opening she's given him. Partly because he's trying to process what the haunted places mean, and partly because there are depths swirling inside his raven packmate tonight that he doesn't fully understand, yet—and he's not sure he should disturb them.

I scratch behind his itchy ear. He's not going to get the time he wants. More swirling is coming for a visit in the morning, and she's going to be at the epicenter. "Hayden taught you the new hand signals?"

She rolls her eyes. "Yes, including the one to show how many of their tail feathers I want chomped. You know that's ridiculous, right?"

I grin. "That one was my idea."

She shakes her head, amused by my silly wolf, as intended, but I can feel the determined cheerfulness she's been wearing all night starting to give way to something gentler.

I let my energy mellow along with hers.

She walks quietly for a while, her eyes on the forest floor. My wolf is happy to walk alongside. Fallon thinks best when she's in motion, and the guy walking beside her thinks best when his mate is breathing normally.

It takes most of the rest of the way to the perimeter, but she gets to wherever she was heading internally, emptying her lungs and filling them again in the way that only a body built to fly can do. "It will be fine. My baby pack is here. That matters."

So fucking much. I put thanks into the earth every damn day for the fourteen-year-old genius who formed them.

Fallon shakes her head ruefully. "I can't believe Hayden convinced them all to come."

Ben snorts.

I hide a grin. Somebody's been chatting with his baby pack.

Fallon side-eyes him. "What did he bribe them with?"

"Nothing." Ben links his fingers through hers. "He strolled in and casually mentioned that the ravens were coming for a visit in the morning, and since the two of us were already at the den, they were welcome to come for dinner and spend the night. Mikayla said everyone was holding their sleeping rolls by the time he finished his sentence."

Hayden said it happened faster than that, and even though Brandy was gulping hard, she was the first one with her gear ready.

Fallon blinks quietly in the dark.

It can take newcomers a really long time to believe in the true depths of loyalty in a wolf pack. Hayden knew exactly what he was doing when he casually invited her crew, and her baby pack knows enough about why they were needed that they didn't ask a single question. They just came, even the three of them who haven't been across the inner perimeter in years.

My wolf followed them in. All of them shook as they stepped across that line—and none of them hesitated.

Fallon exhales slowly. "I'm trying to not be an idiot. Now, or later tonight, or in the morning. I could use some help with that."

Brave raven. I don't think she uses those last words very often.

Ben wraps his arm around her waist and nuzzles into her neck. "We can invent a hand signal for being an idiot. Just think how often you could use it around camp."

A wolf who would die for his mate—and who clearly knows a lot more about what swirls in his raven's depths than I do. "We already have one."

They both blink at me. Fallon's lips quirk. "Seriously?"

I grin. "Yup. Kennedy and Hayden are the most frequent recipients."

That earns me an amused eye roll.

My wolf preens. "Hayden promises to be on his best behavior tomorrow. So long as he gets to be immature after the ravens leave, he should be good."

Her lips quirk again.

Bless Hayden and his penchant for convincing his packmates that he's an adorable, overgrown pup. Tomorrow won't be one of those days, though. Hayden Scott traverses interspecies shifter dynamics better than anyone I know, especially the kind that involve making very clear who his teeth and claws support—and the kind that help potentially clueless visitors navigate boggy ground.

There was a reason teenage Hayden got assigned as the schoolyard buddy of half the new kids in Whistler Pack, and it wasn't because he paid attention in class.

Fallon walks a little further in silence, her fingers laced with those of her mate.

My sentinel listens to the sound of her steps on the earth. The answer they give is succinct and solid. Her raven was smart enough to fall out of the sky into Benjamin Dunn's arms, tough enough to feed a starving wolf pack by whatever means necessary, and brave enough to answer a bear cub honestly when he looked straight at her soul. A meeting with a few birds might rock her, but it isn't going to break her.

My wolf breathes easier. He'll be ready afterward. In case she needs him to cast a comforting shadow or two.

She squeezes Ben's hand as we get close to Dorie's camp and bumps her shoulder against mine. "You two need to find the sentries. My nose isn't any good for that."

Hayden is right. She's a damn fine wolf. I grin at Ben. "All I can smell is coconut."

He smirks, but I can see the other messages in his eyes. He sees the swirls inside the woman he loves, and honors them, and will do battle with them or fight beside them, whichever will love her best.

I nod in acknowledgement. It's been an edifying night—and a humbling one. "If you two deliver the cookies, I'll take a run out to the perimeter." I need some thinking time.

Fallon eyes me, her head cocked. Then she nods,

whatever she's picking up from my wolf enough to leave him be.

She is so very easy, and so very kind, with the shadows of others.

I watch them walk off, their heads tipped together in quiet communion. Then I shed my clothes. This kind of thinking requires my paws on the earth, and so does the detour I need to make on my way out to the perimeter.

My wolf needs to stand in the tainted place. The haunted one.

It doesn't take long to reach the spot. It's an innocuous collection of trees, unremarkable in every way, except that it doesn't smell like wolf, and this close to the den, it should. My sentinel shivers as he figures out why. Even for the wolves who live at the den, it's a place to be avoided.

Not by their wolves. By their humans.

I shift into my human skin and crouch down. I take a deep breath, put my hands on the earth, and let my human emotions rush in. I've been told the story of this place, the one pulsing with betrayal and excruciating choices and blood running into the earth. This is where the alpha-elect pair of Ghost Mountain Pack was standing when evil came for them.

I say their names.

Cody Dunn, executed by a madman.

Ruby Dunn, forced to choose between the life of her mate and her pup.

My tears spill. I let the earth have them. A sentinel's grief for each of them, and for all the others. The shrapnel of that moment hit their family and their pack with devastating force.

When I finally look up, it's toward the den, where I thought I was going to be spending the night easing the way for the visit of some ravens in the morning. I don't know why this is reaching for me instead, but I trust my wolf and the extra layer of woo he was born with. I press my palms more firmly into the dirt, acknowledging what my human heart can finally see so clearly. I don't know what to do with it yet, but I won't look away.

For the wolves who were here when we arrived, the den is a place of bad memories, but it's also the hill they chose to fight on. For so many of the wolves in the woods, this is the place they ran from. The place that broke them. I've seen the quaking, but I didn't fully understand it. I thought Hayden was the problem, or dominant wolves in general, or the struggle of integrating back into pack—and I was right. All of those things are huge and ongoing and true.

I missed this much simpler truth.

For the wolves in the woods, the den itself is haunted. A place of bloodshed and trauma and failure. A place that is anything but home.

I exhale, long and slow and worried, into the deepening night. I don't know what this means, yet. I only know that it matters.

21

HAYDEN

I scramble out of my sleeping bag, peering sleepily at my beta. "What?"

Ebony smirks. "They're here. Apparently, you didn't specify a time for this meeting, and they're quite eager."

I look around at my strewn, sleeping pack. "Fuck. I forgot that ravens are lunatics who sleep at night and wake up at the crack of dawn."

Shelley snorts from the small fire she's starting. The rest of the day, she makes coffee on the stove in the kitchen, but the first caffeine of the morning is always fire-brewed.

Which I normally sleep through. I glare up at the pretty colors streaking the sky. "I don't suppose they can be persuaded to go have breakfast in town?"

Ebony rolls her eyes. "Stop being a grumpy alpha and get your shit together."

Right. "The next time I decide to stay up half the night trying to decipher your terrible drawings, remind me why I need to go to bed."

She grins. "I wasn't on your team. That was Myrna."

I scowl, because it's all coming back to me now. "You had Brandy. And Shelley. Two artists who can actually draw clues that their team can decipher." My team degenerated into reckless and bawdy guesses that turned the teenagers purple with laughter.

Purple teenagers make for really unhelpful teammates.

Ebony snickers, which is really mean at the crack of dawn. "Poor alpha."

Alpha who needs to display at least minimal adequacy at being a pack leader. "What did you do with the ravens?"

"Left them standing by their truck looking eager. Adelina and Reuben are keeping an eye on them. Which came with coffee demands, since I was supposed to be relieving them."

I shake my head. When I first got here, most of this pack hadn't seen coffee in six years. You'd never know it to look at them now.

Ebony glances over at the pup pile, which has two bears in it this morning. "We can leave them sleeping, maybe."

I snort. Pups never sleep through anything exciting, and neither do crotchety black bears. "No, let's get everyone moving. Slowly. I'll go out there and make raven small talk until things are ready in here."

"I'll come."

I turn to face the speaker. She's standing behind me, her eyes clear and her hands shoved in her pockets.

"No way." Shelley's hands keep briskly tending to her fire, but her words brook no argument. "Your pack stands with you. No sneaking off to meet the birds by yourself."

I exchange a look with Ebony and hide a grin. I love it when my submissives decide the pack hierarchy can go stuff itself.

Shelley stands up, a pot lid in one hand and a ladle in the other, and starts banging them together. "Rise and shine, people."

Bleary heads poke out of sleeping bags.

She points with her ladle. "Mikayla, go get some pancake batter started up. We'll cook out here this morning. Shark squad mamas, see if you can keep Brown and Braden away from the strawberries long enough that the rest of us get some. Robbie, show Kennedy and Ben how to make a gigantic bowl of whipped cream, and don't the three of you dare make a mess of my kitchen."

I shake my head in awe. She's weaving the baby pack into her orders without even missing a beat.

She's also not done. "Hoot, you and Brandy and Reilly can transport dishes."

Reilly tries to follow instructions and runs smack into Kennedy, which sends them both to the ground in a pile of giggles.

Shelley shakes her head wryly. "Lissa and Kel, see if you can make this den look a little less like we had a pillow fight last night. Ghost and Fallon, since you started that fight, you can join them on pickup duty. Wrinkles, I need you to take over this coffee so that I can get the pancake griddles warming. Anyone whose name I haven't mentioned, find something useful to do."

I take two steps before I realize that doesn't actually include me.

Shelley bangs her lid with the ladle again. "Move it, people. We have ravens here, and we are not going to embarrass our pack."

Two dozen sets of eyes snap her way.

She nods. "Good. You're finally awake. They're at the road. We have ten minutes." She turns to face me. "It will take you that long to walk them in. We'll be ready."

I reach out and gingerly extract the pot lid and the ladle from her hands. Then I do what any self-respecting alpha would do in this situation.

I back up very respectfully and make a run for it.

FALLON

I thought I would have time to get ready.

I yank my fingers through my hair, trying to smooth it into some semblance of raven who didn't end up on the wrong end of a pillow fight.

Ben leans in to kiss my cheek. "You look fine."

Says the guy who never manages to get all of the leaves out when we come back to camp after shenanigans in the forest. I look down to make sure that my shirt isn't on backward and my shoes are on the right feet. Two months ago, I woke easily into instant alertness. This morning I feel like a trampled blackberry after a bear passes through.

"Here." A steaming mug lands in my hands. "Coffee with lots of sugar."

I stare at it suspiciously. "You let Wrinkles make the coffee." That means there could be any number of things in the mug that didn't start off as coffee beans.

Shelley chuckles. "I can get you apple juice instead."

Right. I'm being ridiculous. "Thank you."

Her hand pats my shoulder. "I've been chatting with Martha about that mural I need to go do for the ravens. She's good people. I don't know about the rest of them, but I like her well enough."

I never had a mom—and yet, somewhere deep, I know that I just got stood on my feet by one. I nod word-lessly over my mug.

She gives me one last shoulder pat and turns to my mate. "The second round of coffee is coming right up. The den looks very nice. You've got a touch with the pups. They listen to you."

Ben quietly turns pink.

I set my head on his shoulder, watching Shelley as she walks away. I wish this for him—this kind of life where there are a dozen others to help him hold the center—even though I know better than to wish for impossible things. I hold out my mug so he can take the first sip. "I'll share."

"Lucky you," says Kel dryly, joining us.

I shrug and hold out my mug to him, too.

His eyes soften. "I'm good, thanks. My brain is more used to waking up hard than most of this crew. I'll wait for a batch that Wrinkles hasn't doctored."

I knew it. I sniff my mug suspiciously, wishing I had a wolf nose.

Ben chuckles. "It smells like coffee and tastes like coffee. I think you're safe."

It's always better to make someone else go first. I take a tentative sip. It's got some oddly bitter notes, even through the sugar, but thinking too hard about stuff like that is never a good idea when you share your camp with a healer.

"You have some choices this morning." Kel's words are casual, but his eyes aren't, and his eyes are pointed at me. "Hayden will be arriving with the ravens shortly. There are three of them. Tressie is alpha, Martha is their beta, and Emma Jean is the last of their group."

I have no idea how he found all that out while I got my shoes on. "Emma Jean is one of their traders. She posts a lot of their items in the ShifterNet store." She's a fierce negotiator with a fondness for purple and a deep soft spot for people who don't know what their goods are worth. Especially if they're young and promise to send a drawing as part of the deal.

"That would make sense." Kel nods easily. "Ebony says that's one of their interests this visit. Exploring more local trading opportunities."

He's repeating things that I already know, and I'm

finding them soothing, darn it. "We could package some deals together instead of single trades. It would be more efficient, and we could include items and services that don't usually go up on ShifterNet."

Kel's eyes smile, even when the rest of him doesn't. "You can save those thoughts and share them with Myrna later, or you can go stand up front with her when the ravens arrive. Whatever you decide, take Ben with you, since he's sharing your coffee."

My mate huffs out a laugh as he meets my eyes. "Let's go join the chaos. We can always climb a tree if the view isn't any good. Or flash hand signals at Myrna if she's making awful trades."

"That doesn't work." Kel falls in beside us as Ben neatly herds my raven over to the assembling crowd. "The other day she traded cookies for some herbs Wrinkles wanted, and even Reilly and Kennedy pretending that they just got stabbed didn't stop her."

I sigh. Wrinkles is really excited about those herbs. She gets to make salves this winter. Proper ones in jars that we can store without worrying that we might be giving ourselves away to some randomly wandering lieutenant. "Did she at least trade the cookies with the raisins in them?" My raven has no idea why any sane person would put withered fruit in cookies.

"Nope." Myrna closes in on my other side. "I traded the triple-chocolate-chunk ones, and my pack will be very grateful when flu season hits and all they have to do to feel better is put gunk on their chests."

Kel groans. "I hate the gunk."

I grin at Myrna. "Good trade."

She rolls her eyes. "Thank you. Come stand right here beside me. I need backup who recognizes a good trade when she sees one."

Kennedy grins at me as I get stationed at the front of the chattering pack. "I thought Fallon was in charge of trades, and you were her trusty sidekick."

Myrna eyes me. "That could be arranged."

I'm being completely maneuvered. I know that, and yet I somehow can't find the words to protest. I dig for instincts honed by years on the street and in a forest gone bad—and gulp at the answer sitting there as clear as day.

I don't want the ravens to be here. I don't want to learn just how much I'm not like them. But if I have to face them, I'll do it like I did on the street.

From the front.

KEL

Some soldiers lead from the back. Fallon isn't one of them. I watch as she finds her steel, a subtle straightening of her backbone that says this isn't her first battlefield and she doesn't plan to die here.

I wish she didn't see what's coming as a battle, but I can't do anything about the fact that it could be. Acceptance and belonging are as important to hearts as breathing, and the lack of them can be wielded like a blade. And there's always the possibility, pulled away from her comfortable shadows, that she might see glinting weapons where there are none.

I surely did.

I hear the quiet owl hoot that says the arrival of our guests is imminent. I take a quick scan of Fallon's baby pack. They all have buddies this morning, people stationed to back them up or hold their capes or add their weight to whatever might be required. I grin as Mellie pats Reuben's cheek. The poor guy is still trying to work out what hit him, but it's no accident that he's holding a wolf who will assume that strange birds are our friends.

I see Hayden's head cresting the rise first, but there's one not far behind it. A tall, rangy woman with a sharp gaze that pinpoints our defenses, our welcome commit-tee, and our cute pups, all in a single, quick scan. The other two women are shorter, and softer in every way, one a grandmother right down to her t-shirt that says so, the other offering a tentative smile and already waving at anyone who smiles back.

They're all carefully not singling Fallon out, so Hayden must have made himself useful on the short walk to get here.

They come to a halt in front of us and Myrna steps forward, wrapping the woman in the grandmother t-shirt in a huge hug. "You look exactly the same, Martha. Exactly the same."

Martha's chuckle is as watery as Myrna's greeting. "Not a day over twelve, huh?" She leans back enough to pat wizened cheeks. "How long has it been, fifty years?"

Given the love flowing between them, there's obviously been more than one boneheaded alpha in these parts over the years. Raven shifters have reasons for the isolation they often choose, but the costs can be so very high.

Myrna smiles and steps back, reluctantly releasing Martha's hand. "I see you've met our alpha. He's a good man, despite teaching the pups more swear words than I do. I'm glad you've come."

Brilliantly done. She's broken the ice, greeted a long-lost friend, and swung us back toward a protocol that will keep our wolves happy, all in the space of a few sentences. And neatly kept attention off the utterly still raven tucked in behind her.

Hayden exchanges a look with the tall woman beside him.

She nods fractionally and faces our pack. "I'm Tressie, alpha of the Desolation Inlet ravens. Martha is our beta, and Emma Jean is our best trader, although she grumps at me when I call her that."

The woman on the end turns pink with embarrassed pleasure, which instantly endears her to our entire pack.

I keep my eyes on the alpha who was smart enough to bring Emma Jean along.

There's a glimmer of a smile as she momentarily meets my gaze. "We come in welcome, and in gratitude that your lives have taken a turn for the better, and in hope that we can forge new connections between our flock and your pack."

Nice acknowledgement of the past six years without dwelling on them. My wolf is impressed.

She pauses a moment. "I know that there were once deep bonds of friendship running between us." She smiles at Martha and Myrna. "I also know that old attitudes in our flock were responsible for those connections eroding and disappearing. I want you to know that we come here humbly, acknowledging our past mistakes and having done the work to hopefully not repeat them. We are not ravens who desire to live shut off from those around us."

Someone has clearly read Adrianna Scott's definition of what constitutes a worthy apology. She's also young enough that she likely wasn't a driving force in those years. Owning them anyhow is going to earn her a great deal of respect from the alpha wolf beside her.

Myrna takes Martha's hand again and clasps it tight to her heart. Their joint sniffles say all the words that are necessary. Kelsey walks over to Emma Jean and takes her hand, smiling brightly. Then she gives her alpha a very pointed look.

Hayden grins and takes Tressie's hand.

She looks at him, amused. "Does this mean I get pancakes?"

FALLON

My bird has no idea what to do with herself.

We're seated in a loose semicircle around the three visiting ravens. Ben is beside me, his presence a gentle, steady anchor in what suddenly feels like a storm. It's not our visitors' fault. They're waiting politely with plates in their laps as we all get settled, nodding as names are said and we ease toward some kind of conversation that won't require us all to stand and stare at each other.

I can't seem to do a whole lot about the last part, however. I can't take my eyes off any of them. Off their easy closeness. Off the shiny, riotous beads in their hair. Off three women who couldn't possibly look any more different from each other—and yet are somehow the same.

Raven shifters.

Like me.

I had dreams last night, ones where the words they said and the words I said found nowhere to meet and kept ending in anger and confusion and disappointed eyes. I never expected just looking at them to undo me.

Kelsey and Robbie walk over with the first of the pancakes, hot off the griddle, and deposit them, more or less accurately, onto Tressie's and Martha's plates. Reilly follows behind them with a bowl of strawberries and a large scoop spoon.

Tressie adds berries and calmly passes her plate down to Emma Jean.

Kelsey beams at the alpha who got it exactly right.

The next pancakes don't actually hit their intended plate at all, but Brown just picks them up and dusts them off and pats Robbie on the shoulder. The raven alpha notices and approves, and so does the shy trader who took Kelsey's hand. My bird likes that. Robbie is her friend.

He always has a pebble in his pocket for her, and if they aren't shiny enough, he spits on them and polishes them with his tongue.

He learned that from his alpha.

Myrna sits down on my other side and eyes our visitors. "You've come to talk trading, and it will be a while until we all have our pancakes. Do you want to start with knitted items first, or shiny things?"

Tressie chuckles. "Trading is high on our list, but there's one thing we'd like to do first, if you don't mind."

Myrna waves her fork regally, which makes everyone laugh.

Except for the ravens.

They all look at me, and as one, the three of them reach for beaded strands in their hair. I stare as they undo some kind of clasps that allow suddenly freed beads to tumble into their hands. Beads they catch carefully, almost reverently, and stir with carefully questing fingers.

Tressie stands and walks the short distance between us, dropping to her knees in front of me. Delight shines in her eyes as she holds out a beautiful, translucent orange bead. "Congratulations. We didn't know, or we would have come better prepared, but please, let us add to the birth beads. We would be so honored."

My bird stares at the orange bead, her beak wide open, trying to parse the words and utterly failing.

It's Ben who somehow finds his voice. "The what?"

Her eyes flick to him, and then to me, clouding with worry. "Perhaps the traditions of your flock are different. In ours, we set them around the nest of the mother as she gives birth, and then they begin the first strands of life beads for her hatchling."

I cling to Ben's hand, the only solid thing in my world.

Tressie's dark eyes flood with horror. "You didn't know. Oh, Fallon. I'm so sorry."

I shake my head wildly, not at all sure what I mean or which direction my head is going or what I would be trying to say if I could think at all.

"We're—" My mate clears his throat, his fingers a death grip on mine. "We're having a baby?"

Tressie nods, very slowly. "Yes."

The single, disembodied word wraps me in a thousand layers of numb, thick fog. Fog with arms, fog with hands, fog with a hundred voices, all of them talking at once, a gray and impenetrable curtain between me and the rest of the world.

Until the blazing joy in Ben's eyes punches through.

22

FALLON

"Congratulations," says Hayden cheerfully to the raven alpha, taking a seat beside Lissa and holding a mug of tea that's probably for me. "As grand entrances go, I didn't figure anyone was ever going to beat Reese."

Tressie makes a wry face. "As a rule, I try not to compete with the cats."

Martha snorts. "You might add a rule about delivering unexpected news to pregnant mamas before they've had their pancakes."

She's currently spoon-feeding me mine. I can't find my spine yet. Or most of my other body parts. I'm curled up in Ben's lap, trying to process the impossible. Somehow, in six years of war, I stopped thinking about having babies with this man.

So did everyone else, apparently. They keep sneaking in for awed touches and quiet sniffing. Which Kelsey and

Hoot are supervising. The baby in my belly might be only two minutes old, but she has cousins and they are fierce.

Which is good. Her parents are still having trouble breathing.

Tressie looks as thoroughly rueful as I've ever seen anyone look. "I'm so sorry. One of the consequences of growing up mostly in isolation is that I forget far too often that not everyone knows the same things."

I'm the one who doesn't know things. I make a valiant attempt to pick my head up off Ben's chest and say so.

He settles it right back over his heart again. "How did you know?"

Tressie smiles. "We can feel it. It's hard to explain, but it's something really obvious to my bird. There's a second presence inside Fallon."

Martha makes a quiet sound of pure happiness.

Myrna adds another pancake to the plate that Martha is feeding me from. Her eyes narrow as she looks at her friend. "You know. You know whether she's having a wolf baby or a raven baby."

The part of me that was sort of managing to breathe gets stuck again.

Martha makes a face. "Yes. But I'm doing my very best to keep quiet about it. We've already overstepped our bounds once, and maybe Ben and Fallon don't want to know."

I feel Ben's answer in the same breath as mine. My hands settle over his on my belly. "Please."

Tressie's eyes move to him, first. "There's something I

need to say before I tell you, because it wouldn't have been clear at times in our past. We yearn, always, for ravens to mate with each other, because it's the surest way for there to be ravens in the next generation. But we value love above all. We're delighted that the two of you found each other."

Hoot clears her throat. "What does that mean, the part about ravens in the next generation?"

Something shows up in Tressie's eyes and disappears again as fast as it came. "The science is complicated, but raven-shifter genes tend to be recessive. So if we mate with non-ravens, generally the offspring takes the shifter form of the other parent." She smiles at me, and there's pure joy in her eyes. "But not this time."

My heart stutters. I don't know how to be a raven.

"Quit scaring her," says Martha dryly, patting my knee. "Open up."

I open my mouth obediently as the fork swoops in again, loaded up with whipped cream and berries.

"You'll have questions," she says briskly. "Go ahead. I've got all the answers in the world."

HAYDEN

I'm going to kiss Martha, just as soon as I get a chance. She took Fallon's panic out at the knees and bought the rest of us a chance to get our shit together.

I look into the eyes of the wolf taking the mug of tea

out of my hands, thinking that she's an excellent candidate to go first, and then grin as Reilly scoots by us both. Perfect. I don't know who gave him a nudge to come forward, but Fallon can't possibly know less about this than an eleven-year-old bear, and he'll happily ask smart, curious questions until sundown.

Which needs to happen. Whistler Pack has quite a few ravens, so Kel and Rio and I know some of what's coming, but judging from how calmly our pack took the news that Fallon has a raven baby inside her, I don't think anyone else does.

"I have questions. Lots and lots." Reilly flips to a new page in his notebook and holds his pen ready. "Are raven babies born in eggs, or like a wolf baby?"

Martha smiles at him. "We call them chicks or hatchlings, but they're born just like a human baby. Is that true for wolves, too?"

Definitely kissing her.

Reilly nods solemnly. "And bears. We sometimes take longer to shift into our bears after we're born than wolves do, though. Sometimes they even shift before they can walk. But sometimes they wait a really long time, and that's okay, too."

Robbie grins happily from his log.

Best bear cub ever.

Martha blinks slowly. "Well, you're in for a very interesting treat with Fallon's baby, then. Ravens usually shift for the first time when they're a few days old."

Lissa sucks in a shocked breath beside me.

I hide a grin. She has no idea.

"What do they look like?" Reilly's eyes are as big as his head. "Are they kind of small like Fallon?"

Martha's eyes twinkle as she looks at our intrepid reporter. "They're little round balls of black fluff, just the right size to sit on your hand. They can't fly for a couple of years, but they learn to hop very quickly, so they tend to get underfoot."

Reilly looks down at his sneaker-clad feet in absolute horror.

Rio gets his words out before I do. "You don't need to worry, Riles. They're really loud, so you just have to pay attention to where they are. Which will probably be on top of you. Raven chicks love bear fur."

Martha's eyes widen. "Do they really?"

Rio nods. "The nests at Whistler Pack mostly end up lined with polar-bear fur. Ronan would get his brush out every time they needed more."

Reilly looks enchanted. As he should. He'll get the nice, sweet, sleepy baby raven. The rest of us will get the version that needs to be fed every ten minutes and makes more noise than an air-raid siren when they're hungry.

Rio pats him on the head. "You can help with manners lessons for the pups, too. We have to teach everyone to be just as careful with the new baby as you are with them."

Reilly looks a little daunted by the size of that task.

Kelsey and Hoot look like avenging warriors.

I snort. Nobody is going to accidentally make it through those two.

Layla looks down at the two rambunctious pups in her lap, worry in her eyes.

Rio sits down beside her and bumps her shoulder. "No worries. We trained Hayden Scott. If he can learn not to squish a raven chick, anyone can."

My whole pack looks at me and giggles.

I roll my eyes. We'll need to borrow some birds to practice on. Ones big enough to fly away if the smaller pups get too rough. I'll ask Tressie about that later, though. There's no need to panic Ben and Fallon with descriptions of raven toddlers just yet. Kel has two whole years to get ready for fuzzy lightning with wings.

I miss Reilly's next question, but Kel launches into an explanation of how to train baby wolves to see a fuzzy ball of down as a packmate instead of as food. The ravens seem as interested as everyone else. I slide backward and let the voices fade out a little. Kel and Rio have both spent way more time with the babies of Whistler Pack than I have. I always got kicked out of the nursery. Something about the babies requiring calm and sleep.

I angle my scoot backward until I'm sitting beside the raven alpha.

She glances at me, amusement mingling with a touch of sympathetic horror. "You're going to have a juvenile grizzly. And a baby raven. In the same pack."

That last sentence is going to be the tricky part. Right now, Fallon's baby pack lives three hours away from the den. But that's not the part of the equation Tressie's looking at. I've seen Kendra with the hawk babies of Whistler. They're always a little bit hers. "Yes. And a cat auntie who adores babies." Just so that all of our tricky cards are on the table.

Her lips quirk. "I spoke with a couple of ravens from your old pack. They swear you're a good guy and you know your birds, so I'm not going to kidnap Fallon and lock her in my aerie."

I growl a little. "You can try."

She snorts. "Tell your wolf to chill. First babies when you're a new alpha are hard, but he needs to suck it up."

He already knows that.

She looks over at where Martha is still feeding Fallon and answering Reilly's questions and not looking at all claustrophobic as a dozen wolves try to touch and sniff the belly that will one day be their new packmate. "She can be here in three hours. Any time of the day or night. A dozen others, too, but she'll disown me if I don't put her at the front of the line."

My wolf is feeling a little possessive at the moment, but he hasn't sat on all my brains. "Thank you. Fallon might really appreciate that."

She smiles faintly. "She's not sure about us."

Good. She didn't miss that. "Not my story to tell."

"Thank you for letting me know that there's one there," she says quietly. "I'll think carefully about who I send over. Ravens who are easy to trust and know how to tread lightly. I've got some who are good at protection detail, too, if you need that."

I shake my head. It's a thoughtful and generous offer, but keeping a small black ball of fluff safe is the least of our worries. I can already see Myrna recruiting people for her frying-pan brigade, and nothing will get through Kelvin Nogues when he's got a baby to protect.

What's grabbing my wolf by the ears and shaking him is the timeline.

There's healing to be done in this pack that's going to take years. A tiny, unborn raven is about to ask some of it to happen in months—and it's going to make that ask most strongly of the family who got hit harder than anyone.

This baby will be pack, which is more than enough to stir our deepest pack waters. But this baby will also be a Dunn. I can see Kelsey's eyes from where I'm sitting, and Hoot's, already dreaming of their fluffy, adorable baby cousin. And I can see Brandy's, right beside her brother, already trying to figure out how she can shake and fight her way through every day so that this baby can live at the den.

Which Fallon is going to veto the second her head comes out of the clouds, and she's probably right to do it, but it's going to break the hearts of a couple of my favorite young wolves, and two dozen more besides, and it's going to shine such a hard light on the work we still have to do —and the brightest light of all is going to land on our wolves who need the deepest shadows.

A pressure cooker of fluffy black hope.

FALLON

Ben's hand strokes my belly, awed and reverent.

Wrinkles chuckles as she sits down beside me with a fresh mug of tea. "Since these two still can't manage to speak just yet, what do I need to know?"

Martha eyes the steaming mug. "You must be the pack healer."

"I am." Wrinkles wraps my fingers around the cup's warmth. "I don't know nearly enough about how to support a raven pregnancy, however."

"Lots of food." Martha winks at me. "She'll be starving around the clock for the first few months, even in the middle of the night."

"Nausea?"

I make a face. There are teas for that. Dreadful, stinky teas.

Martha laughs. "No. That seems to be one of the pleasant side effects of the shorter pregnancy."

Wrinkles's eyebrows fly up.

Martha smiles and feeds me another spoonful of berries. "Raven shifters gestate faster. Seven months, usually, so this little one will likely arrive in about six."

My brain turns to garble.

Six. Months.

Martha pats my knee. "It's a good thing. We can't fly for the last few months, which tends to lead to really cranky ravens."

Reilly turns to a new page in his notebook. "Why won't she be able to fly?"

Bless him for asking everything. And for taking notes

so that he can tell me again on some day in the future when I have a working brain.

Martha sets down my empty berry bowl and smiles at him fondly. "I bet your bear is bigger than your human, right?"

Reilly nods vigorously. "Lots bigger."

"Well, Fallon's bird is smaller than she is, but the babies in our bellies don't change size when we shift. So for a bear, that's not a problem. For a wolf, I've heard it can be a tight fit toward the end."

Myrna snorts. "I'll say."

Martha shoots her a wry grin. "At least you didn't have to try flying with your belly so big that you couldn't see over it or around it. I would land and roll like a bowling ball."

"That wasn't bad for your baby?" Reilly's eyes are huge.

My brain sticks its head back in the sand.

"Nope." Martha pets his shoulder like he's a bird. "Babies are tough. Raven-shifter babies tend to be on the small side, especially if you insist on flying as much as I did, but they're healthy and strong."

"I didn't." Emma Jean's words are hesitant, but her smile is sweet and genuine. "I put my feet up for the last two months and let my mate fetch me snacks, and I think I wore every sweater the flock owned."

I shiver. Six months is somewhere in the dead of winter.

"We'll knit more sweaters." Wrinkles sounds amused. "Ben will be delighted to fetch and carry, and I'm thinking that Mikayla might make a trip over your way to learn more about what snacks are best for pregnant ravens."

My head finally makes it off of Ben's chest. "I can eat whatever."

Three ravens, twenty-six wolves, and two bears all glare at me.

Martha chuckles. "That will never work, dear. Just so you know. It's okay to let yourself be pampered a little. You're growing a whole new being inside you."

Wrinkles pats my knee. "We'll let you practice in small bits. It's just like Brown learning to use his nice manners. Over time, it will get easier."

Brown's rumbling growl makes the ravens jerk to attention.

"It's okay." Reilly smiles at them. "He's a nice bear. He's a little cranky sometimes, but he does anything Wrinkles tells him to do and he loves Fallon really a lot and he'll make sure her hatchling is safe and has carved wooden toys to chew on and everything."

Emma Jean's eyes light up. She pushes up on her knees so that she can get a better look at Brown. "You're the one who carves all those wonderful blocks? I tried to buy the last set on ShifterNet, but I got outbid by a cat."

Brown's next growl is more like a roar. "Woman, what have you done?"

Wrinkles rolls her eyes. "Calm down or you'll scare the baby, dear."

His mouth snaps shut.

She grins at me. "That's going to be quite useful for

the next six months. If I can also convince you to develop a craving for ham-and-split-pea soup, it will be a very good winter."

Ben chuckles by my ear.

"I have an excellent soup recipe." Martha looks around. "Which one of you is Mikayla?"

The squeaking noise doesn't sound a whole lot like my baby packmate, but it makes everyone laugh.

Martha beams at her. "We'll chat, sweetheart. I'll give you all my best recipes for hungry mama birds."

Four people start talking all at once. Shelley, who wants the recipes, too. Braden, who doesn't want anything to have to do with peas and says Robbie doesn't, either. Ravi, who has a question about raven babies and music. Ebony, asking something complicated about flying and center of gravity that makes me sound like some kind of strange, experimental arrow.

Pack being pack.

Somehow, that's what finally chases the last of the fog away.

Martha smiles at me gently. "Good. That didn't take you too long. Some newly pregnant mamas stay in that haze for days." She winks at Ben. "Daddies, too."

The way that word beams into his heart is pure magic.

Martha holds out her hand, a single purple bead on her palm. "I think you're maybe ready for these, now."

I stare. It's swirly, like purple fire somehow got caught in the glass. My bird is enthralled. "What do they mean?"

It's a different raven who answers. Tressie, holding

out her original orange bead beside Martha's. "They're a symbol of belonging. To flock, but we would very much like that definition to be a fluid one that welcomes those outside our boundaries as well as within. They're a promise, if you will. To you and your hatchling."

I can't hold the words in any longer. "I don't know how to be a raven."

She chuckles. "It's all optional except for the flying. This isn't something you have to earn."

Emma Jean holds out a ruby-red bead that makes my bird drool.

I'm wolf enough to look at my alpha before I take them.

He snorts.

Kelsey looks up at me, her eyes shining.

Tressie smiles and removes a strand of beads from her hair. "I see you already have feathers, sweetheart. Would you like to decorate them?"

Kelsey reaches for the beautiful rainbow of beads. She touches each one of them in turn, making small, wordless sounds of joy.

The raven alpha helps her clip them into her hair—and then she looks at me, her eyes solemn and bright as she holds out a single orange bead. "It truly is this simple, Fallon. Belonging is your right."

23

FALLON

I think we might have traded all the things. There are strands of beads in every pup's hair, and Reilly's, and Brandy's, and even possibly in Brown's. Emma Jean is clutching a single carved wooden block and fiercely refusing to give it back to him, despite his periodic rumbling. Martha is contemplating six small knitted blankets like making the wrong choice might start a war, and Tressie is deep in a conversation with Eliza that involves blowtorches and chainsaws.

The blowtorches are for making beads. I have no idea about the chainsaws.

My bird is settling. Or she's so full of pancakes and strawberries and baby that she can't move, which is more or less the same thing. Ben has left me for a whole two minutes to check in on Brandy, who's trying so very hard to keep her hands busy and her mind calm—and slowly sliding off that cliff.

I touch the beads in my hair. Some kinds of belonging are going to need to take a back seat soon, but I'm pretty sure my bird is going to insist that I sleep with my new hair adornments right where they are.

Tressie watches my fingers and smiles. Then she casts an eye up at the noonday sun. "I think we need to be going shortly, but we have a gift for your pack before we go."

She glances at Hayden.

He looks up from tickling Braden's belly. "Are there vegetables involved?"

Her lips quirk. "No. Well, perhaps down the road, but that choice will be up to you."

He waves a hand. "In that case, speak freely until you get to the part that might involve zucchini."

A whole bunch of wolves giggle. Cute ravens. Silly alpha.

Tressie looks around until she spies a big, black wolf. "You're working on a small design project. A tiny house nestled on a cliff ledge that will be heated by hot water."

His eyebrows go up. "I am, but I thought that was just Jules messing with me."

Tressie chuckles. "No. It's for us. We have a small underground hot spring not far from our main nests. We've carefully encouraged it to come to the surface in a location that will make for a very nice bathing pool, and we're hoping that there's enough leftover to heat the floor of what will essentially be a glass-enclosed nest."

Rio grins. "There's enough. I sent the final specs on the design to Jules last night. I came up with a way to use the cliff as an insulator. That will make the heat exchange more efficient with the pipes under the nest floor."

I'm not following most of what he's saying. I'm way too focused on what I think it means. "The floor will be warm?"

He smiles at me. "As toasty as they want it to be."

My raven melts. That's the pot of gold at the end of every street person's rainbow—and also the bird who just found out that she's going to be pregnant in the dead middle of winter. Murmurs spread through my pack, too. They know what it is to sleep cold and shivering.

Hayden turns to Tressie, his smile a little lopsided. "Please tell me we can work out some kind of exchange where a bunch of rowdy wolves can come use your bathing pool if they promise to clean up afterwards. And maybe build you a really nice poolside hut, designed by HomeWild's best?"

Rio nods like a big puppy.

My raven is madly dancing inside me. Water. Hot water. Enough to make her whole body warm, even in the middle of winter.

Tressie smiles, and there's something enigmatic and deeply satisfied in her eyes. "I'm going to hold you to the poolside-hut design, but I may have another option for the rest."

She suddenly feels bigger. Regal, almost.

My raven freezes.

HAYDEN

I have no idea what's about to happen—but I'm watching a woman who absolutely knows how to make a moment count. Every single wolf and raven and bear in my pack is staring at her, silent and awestruck.

I really need to learn that trick.

She holds her rapt audience for a breath. Two. "We have a young raven who has an unusual talent. He can sense the places where water flows hot inside the earth. He sees them as a heat map of sorts. He found us two small sources near our nests, and a larger one over on the edge of our territory that we'll be sharing with our indigenous neighbors."

Eyes light up all over my pack.

My wolf holds his breath.

Tressie reaches into the messenger bag she arrived with and pulls out a scroll. She sits on her heels and holds it out on her palms. "This is our gift to you, the shifters of Ghost Mountain Pack. A map specifying the flow of the underground hot spring in your territory."

Rio's eyes widen, and he practically trips over himself rolling to his feet.

Our entire pack leans toward a rolled piece of paper.

Rio sits down right next to Tressie and takes the scroll with hasty reverence. He unrolls it over his lap, his eyes scanning swiftly. Reilly scoots in beside him, which is a stunning lack of protocol from our rule-abiding bear, aided and abetted by a pack elder and a grinning baby alpha.

Two sets of dark eyes scrutinize the map avidly.

When Reilly sucks in a breath, I know it's big.

When Rio looks up, his eyes full of fierce glee, I know that it's polar-bear big. "It's under Ghost Mountain. It's closest to the surface just in behind Banner Rock."

My wolf runs frantically to catch up. "We can have a bathing pool? Fifteen minutes from the den?"

Tressie laughs. "You can have a dozen of them if you want. My ravens are insanely jealous. We have trickles of hot water. You have an underground river."

The sound that comes out of my pack is pure, unfettered delight.

My wolf sways where he sits. Warmth—an unlimited supply of it—for the pack who has known so much cold. An antidote to the awful, horrific shed they slept in for years. To the tiny, inadequate fires they built in the woods to evade detection. To the tattered clothing and even more tattered blankets they once guarded as treasure and, even now, struggle to leave behind. To the pathetic excuse for a lukewarm shower that's still all we have, and a den that's nothing more than ashes and dreams with winter coming.

Fuck. This is a gift for the ages.

One that my pack hasn't even begun to comprehend the size of, yet, although given the happiness in the eyes of three ravens, they don't need any more thanks than the sounds of pleasure that are rapidly building to a roar. I hold up my hand to stem the thousand questions that are nocking their arrows. "Could someone please give me the really simple explanation of what we can do with this, for an alpha who doesn't speak engineering?"

Tressie grins. "Don't ask me. I threaten our engineers with a fork on a regular basis. But I have a young raven who just started an internship with HomeWild who swears that this is the biggest deal ever."

The big, black wolf tears his eyes away from the map long enough to grin. "That's Indrani, right? She's going to catch up with the rest of us in about two more weeks, and then she's going to be an absolute menace."

The three visiting ravens nearly glow.

Smart sentinel. I clear my throat so that he keeps being smart.

He lifts his head back up, his eyes sheepish. "Indrani is right. This is a huge deal. We can use the hot water directly, so long as we can bring it to the surface and return it back to the water table in ways that are sustainable and respectful. But there are other uses. We can do like the ravens are doing and maybe put up some small cabins near Banner Rock with heated floors. We can also build a heat exchange system that will generate electricity from the geothermal energy."

I paid just enough attention in class to know what that means. "We can use this to power the den?"

He nods. "Yup. It will be a job to get it set up, but if we're careful and willing to bury a lot of cable, I think we can do it, and cable is way cheaper than solar panels."

The green-eyed wolf beside me sits up straight.

I know how big that line item is in her spreadsheets.

Tressie smiles. "That's what Indrani said."

Rio looks at Danielle and grins. "Excellent. She can come up here and help you plan the route for the cables."

Danielle looks terrified—and ready to die of excitement. "You need a real engineer for that. For all of this."

He shoots her a casually puzzled look. "Well, sure. They have to sign the paperwork. But somebody has to get their hands dirty with where all the pipes and cables are going to need to go, and I'm going to be too busy rejiggering the den design and trying to keep Jules from killing us all."

Danielle's mouth opens and closes, but nothing comes out.

My wolf snickers quietly. I'll deal with Jules. Rio will make sure that Danielle gets to quietly shine, and anyone else in this pack who wants to learn a new trade or apply one. There are three sets of very interested eyes in Fallon's baby pack alone.

I grab his scruff and meet the gaze of a pair of dark, intense eyes that belong to a raven who, as far as I know, has never held the business end of a tool.

He shrugs. She works hard. She'll help.

I shake my head. Those aren't eyes that are thinking about how to swing a hammer.

Or maybe they are.

FALLON

I saw a video clip of a man who went over a waterfall in a barrel, once.

I think I know how he felt.

My bird scratches at the inside of my skull.

I shake my head, trying to focus, trying to follow half a dozen conversations about water and pipes and hot soaks in the middle of winter and laying cables without disturbing the forest and how long it takes to run from Banner Rock to Shelley's cookie jar and back again.

My bird raps her beak this time.

I scowl. I'm a raven, not a woodpecker.

She caws. Loudly.

Tressie's head comes up.

Crap. I pull my head down into my shoulders, wishing for one of Ben's really big sweaters.

My mate leans in. "You okay?"

I don't know. "It's been kind of a wild day."

He leans his forehead against mine and sighs. "Yeah."

This is so big. So overwhelming. Babies and hot baths and I don't have any idea how to feel. The den wolves are moving so fast to make this gift from the ravens real, and that's just going to leave the rest of us further behind, except my insides want warm floors and hot baths like crazy, so maybe, just maybe, this could help us catch up, too. I glance around, trying to find my baby pack. "Where's Brandy?"

His fingers smooth my shoulders. "Up in a tree with Hoot."

That's one small step away from needing to bug out of here.

My eyes close. That's part of the scratching. Part of the abuse my bird is landing on the inside of my skull. "This hot springs stuff is going to be weird."

Ben's eyes are careful. Concerned. "Yeah. A little. Brown's pretty excited."

Brown will have things to build. And Wrinkles will have a way to keep her sick patients warm. "Maybe we can have hot soaks instead of nasty teas."

Ben snorts.

My bird hops around impatiently.

I sigh and try to listen.

My mate's fingers trace along my collarbone. "Rennie comes to Banner Rock sometimes. I've scented her trail."

My raven yanks my ears to his words. *Shiny.*

My eyes narrow. "You think she might come watch the bathing pool? Just like at the river?" I don't wait for him to answer. I can already see it. "We need to pick a place with a ledge. Somewhere the ghosts could watch from."

One with warm floors.

I pull my hoodie off, suddenly stupidly hot. "I'll go look." It's two minutes away on raven wings. I don't know anything about pipes and cables, but I can find ledges. Somewhere to watch from.

Good shadows. Safe shadows. Shadows closer to pack.

I hop around, one foot to the other. My bird caws, pushing feathers through my scalp and out my shoulder blades, frantic to take the raging energy inside her to the sky, but I don't need to go. I already know all the ledges. All the shadows. Ghost Mountain is full of them.

Shiny.

Wolves who can't come to the den. Who shake and tremble and fight the darkness inside them, but won't win, because the call to their wolf can't ever be louder than the voices that are already yelling. Who will be left behind with every forward step they take, because the others will always walk faster.

Shiny.

Warm floors. Warmth for aching hips and ravaged hearts and shivering mamas and pups who kick their blankets off in the night. A bear who can sleep as a man and hold his mate because his fur isn't needed to keep his pack warm.

Shiny.

Three bear coins, taken to feed the pups. I gave them back, but I didn't apologize. I looked a polar bear in the eyes and told the truth.

Shiny.

It's all optional except for the flying. Belonging can be simple.

Shiny.

Eight years ago, my raven made the choice to fall out of the sky into the arms of a wolf, and that made her family, and made her pack.

Shiny.

There's a raven baby in my belly. A Dunn. Kin to the ghost Dunns. The broken ones. Cleve. Rennie. Ruby. Grady. They deserve for me to speak the unthinkable truth, the impossible inch, the unbearable step that might make it so the ghost wolves can get closer to home. So that the wolves my baby is related to don't have to do awful battle with their own scars just to pay her a visit.

Shiny.

Six months. We don't have time to do this the den way.

I reach into my pocket and wrap my fingers around the rock that's been in there for days. The fiery orange one that holds the power to speak. "We could move the den."

24

RIO

Fallon's words hang in the air, quiet and poignant and utterly expecting to be rejected.

I stare at the woman with feathers sprouting out of her head and rise to my feet, the building designer who lives inside my head crashing headlong into a sentinel's dawning realization. I shake my head, the chaotic details trying to smooth themselves out inside my brain. She just spoke five words of utter heresy that have my wolf howling, and he shares space with a sentinel who speaks heresy on a regular basis. "Explain a little more."

Fallon thrusts her hands deeper into her pockets. "It won't work."

I smile a little. "It might not." My sentinel puts as much calm into the earth as he possibly can through lime-green socks and sneakers. It's not easy. My wolf isn't feeling very calm. But my sentinel is absolutely certain that the truth she just spoke needs to stay out here in the sunshine where we can grapple with it.

Fallon takes a deep breath and lets it out again. "We could move the den to Banner Rock. Close to the hot water. So the whole den could have warm floors."

I wait a beat. Two. Three.

Myrna's mouth drops open. "You're serious."

Fallon turns green—and doesn't look away from the woman whose daddy founded the pack on this particular patch of grass and rock. An act that forever set compass center for our wolves. We don't move dens. That would be like cutting out our hearts. An unbearable surgery— and maybe a brilliant, lifesaving one that just might start to heal the most pernicious wounds in this pack.

Tressie's brow furrows. "That seems like it would make sense. You could take full advantage of the geothermal that way." She looks around, a little confused. "It's not like you have a lot of infrastructure built here."

Ravens are happy to move to better nesting grounds.

We're not ravens.

Myrna hisses in a breath—and then lets it back out again, slowly and very visibly grappling with every instinct of her wolf. "You're right. We don't."

Shelley whimpers.

Myrna swallows and nods, every movement costing her in blood. "This has always been our den, and that matters to our wolves. But some in our pack can't even cross the inner perimeter. I keep hoping that will change, and it has for some." She looks around, finding Ravi. Kenny. Brandy. "But not for all."

My sentinel bows his head, honoring the elder who's holding the scalpel and considering the first cut.

"We would move the whole den?" Lissa's arms wrap around her ribs. "All of it?" She looks at Hayden, her eyes huge and wild. "Can we even do that?"

Hayden wraps his arms around her. "Let's ask that question after we ask the important one."

A long, thick silence. One full of wildly swinging gravity beams and doubt and ratcheting panic.

My sentinel shoves my wolf out of his way and grabs my brain. Words won't get us to where we need to go, and neither will howling. Words are too human, too precise, too linear. Howling is too embedded in the present and can't see all the scars. It isn't our wolves or our words that will decide this. It's where they meet. In our hearts. And most importantly, in the shadows inside those hearts, which we need to set on the scales of pack and weigh and measure with absolute clarity.

To a sentinel, that can only mean one thing. Paws on the earth. "Let's walk there."

Every head turns my way. I pause for a moment, gathering the rest of my words. "We need to listen. As wolves and humans both, to our own hearts and to those of our pack."

Kelsey, her entire being solemn, kicks off her sneakers and stands quietly, her bare feet on the earth.

Yes. Exactly like that. I bend down and unlace my shoes and free my feet from lime-green socks. All over my pack, confused and tangled and thoughtful and anxious shifters do the same.

When we're all ready, I look at the raven who will lead us.

She pulls her hands out of her pockets and reaches for Ben's hand. They pivot as a unit, the bond between them already growing tendrils around the tiny presence in her belly. The pack forms up behind them.

My sentinel bows his head again as they begin moving forward. Leading us into the trees. Into the shadows.

Of course.

We walk slowly, solemnly, a procession that isn't yet sure what it will become, but every pair of bare feet on the earth is making a promise, all the same. *We are here. We look. We listen.*

I put that same message into the cool dirt with a sentinel's power. And I open. To my own heart, first, and my wolf's howling confusion. I stroke him gently. He's new here, but he loves every inch of this den, and he's spent every day of the last three months pouring sentinel cement into the cracks in its foundations. Which might have looked an awful lot like eating cookies and making shy mamas giggle, but he's invested. Deeply.

I know that's a bare whisper of what some of the wolves around me are feeling, but this isn't a contest. *We are here. We look. We listen.* I dig my toes into the earth with each new slow, stately step and let myself listen deeper.

To Myrna, walking close beside me. To the vibrant, primal connection she holds to the earth we're walking away from. Land her daddy chose and her own submissive heart shaped into a home. Dirt she's bled for and loved and let soak up her tears, and the place she waits for her lost sons to make their way home.

To Shelley, who mated with evil so the den wouldn't turn into her pack's burial ground.

To Lissa, who's trying to pull herself out of her deep love for the woman she counts as her mother, and truly listen. My wolf sends her what little help he can. The heart of the pack might not decide this, but she'll be an enormous part of holding us steady.

She smiles, and my feet hear what she's picking up from the man holding her hand. Hayden Scott, alpha wolf, is flatly refusing to weigh in on this decision at all. He'll love his pack no matter what, and he will be so very proud of them. Hayden Scott, man, is remembering where we found Lissa and Robbie, facing down Samuel in a clearing in the shadow of Banner Rock.

My wolf smiles. Hayden doesn't think of that day as the one where he became alpha. He remembers it as the place where his new family was born.

Eliza moves closer to me, a gray, furry presence who makes no noise at all. Her heart speaks of her son—a wolf the den couldn't hold and couldn't protect and had to send away.

Ghost reaches down to pat Eliza's head—and allows my sentinel a view of the crystal-clear image she's holding. The one of Kelsey Dunn at the base of Banner Rock, standing between her alpha's knees with a single flower in her hand. The flower she gave to a polar bear in trust for a man who will never earn it.

My sentinel reacts on absolute instinct and pushes that diamond-bright image out to the others. Every submissive in the pack sucks in a breath as they catch a piece of Ghost's memory.

The bad man has no power here anymore.

Cori trembles. And smiles. Her heart remembers the view from the ledge, looking down as a polar bear roared and a good alpha stood and she took the first safe breaths of her life. She also listens to her mate, who is walking quietly with his pup in his arms, ashamed that he feels easier with every step we take away from the den.

A red wolf emerges from the shadows on the edge of the slowly traveling pack. Bailey shifts to human and pulls a t-shirt over her head, her eyes huge and staring straight at Fallon's belly.

My wolf grins. Someone smarter than me obviously went to get her. I put words into the earth. *We look. We listen. We choose.*

She shoots me a dirty look, but her feet are already listening—and she brought gravity beams with her. I can feel them. Fragments of thought and emotion and faint awareness that stretch all the way out to the very edges of our territory. Our deepest shadows.

Cori takes her mate's hand, amplifying the easing in Ravi's soul as we cross the inner perimeter. The line that was used as a weapon against his heart and his wolf and his family.

He's not the only one easing. Brandy is back in human form, with Kelsey on one side and Hoot on the other, the three of them following in a tiny baby raven's wake. None of them are thinking about the den at all. They're daring to let us hear their quiet, aching hope—for a family that just might rise from the ashes.

With all the gentleness my sentinel has in him, I use my feet on the earth to help us hear each other. To listen to deep, abiding roots and the cutting of them. To the scared needs of brave hearts and the barely whispered wishes of cautious ones. To scars and disbelief and silent, fragile yearning.

So many feet on the earth.

We step out of the trees, Ghost Mountain and Banner Rock majestic in front of us. A ripple moves through the pack, complicated and beautiful and holy.

We are here.

25

FALLON

"Well." Shelley looks around, hands on her hips, as two dozen heads swivel. "I'll need some help moving the pantry. Rio, I assume you can figure out how to make my kitchen work out here?"

The big, black wolf smiles and nods his assent.

Myrna grins. "Excellent. I need a steady supply of cookies while I'm lounging in the hot pool. I hear long soaks are good for old bones."

My bird clutches Ben's fingers. We're supposed to be here so we can think and feel. They're acting like we've already made a decision.

Ghost exchanges a look with Kel. "We could move some of the base camps here."

He shrugs. "Sure. Tents and sleeping platforms are portable. They'll probably get here faster than the den."

Shelley snorts. "Is that a dare?"

Myrna grins at her. "Sounds like one to me."

Jade puffs out her chest. "My help. My carry 'mallows."

Reilly giggles and ruffles her hair. "We need to bring all the stuff, silly. Beans and rice and dishes and the refrigerator, which might be kind of heavy."

Rio nods. "Yup. I might need a bear's help with that."

Reilly sticks up his hand. So does Robbie.

Brown sighs. "I suppose you'll be wanting a cooking shack, too."

My raven's beak can't seem to figure out how to close anymore.

Wrinkles grins. "If we're moving, dibs on the spot over there that gets the early morning sun in winter." She points to one of my raven's favorite spots on the mountain.

Brown growls. "Speak for yourself, woman."

Brandy pats Brown's shoulder. "You can stay out in the woods by yourself, if you want. I'll be in the hot pool." She looks over at Reilly. "Orbital communications will still bring us cookies, right?"

His head nods wildly as he beams at her.

Wrinkles elbows her mate. "Quit pouting. You can still head out to the woods to smoke fish all you want, but I'm liking the sound of warm floors."

Rio chuckles. "Those might take a few weeks."

My stomach does some kind of weird flip that mostly ends up a belly flop.

"Huh." Ebony tilts her head at my baby pack like a beta who just woke up from a nap and found herself in a mildly interesting conversation. "Would you really move your camp?"

Six sets of eyes swing to me.

I glare at all of them, including my mate. "How is that my decision?"

Brandy grins. "You're our fearless leader, remember?"

Freaking wolves. "We live out there for reasons, remember?"

"My wolf feels pretty good about this idea." Wrinkles takes a casual sip from her canteen. "What about yours, Ben?"

He does an excellent imitation of a moth about to land in a candle flame.

Brandy snickers. "He'll go where Fallon goes. Reuben will slink around and pretend he's not part of our baby pack, but he'll come anyhow, and Mikayla will be happy because she can use all the eggs she wants without having to sweet-talk Brown into fetching them."

Reuben rolls his eyes. Mikayla nods cheerfully.

Ben doesn't say anything. He just keeps watching his sister.

She smiles faintly. "I can't know, Benny. My anxiety attacks don't follow any rules, so I can't make any promises. But a bathing pool sounds like a pretty nice way to relax." She takes a deep breath and lets it out. "It feels nice here. My chest isn't all tight like it is at the den."

Every single den wolf winces.

Brandy scrunches up her face and starts the breathing exercise she uses to stay calm. "Shit. Sorry."

"Don't you dare apologize." Myrna's voice is low and fierce. "We needed to hear that, Brandy Dunn. We forget, those of us who live at the den, just what you lost, and just what you remember when you cross that perimeter and come visit."

Brandy swallows. "It's not so bad. Sometimes."

"That's not good enough." Myrna looks at Hayden, her eyes blazing. "If moving the den will help our wolves come home, then we move it. My wolf is going to need some help, because I was with my daddy the day he stood by that bend in the river and decided it was going to be the heart of our new pack, but I can bring my good memories with me and make more."

There are wolves moving before she's done speaking. Surrounding her. Comforting the animal inside her that's quivering even as she speaks.

She picks up Mellie and kisses the top of her head. "I couldn't see it. The den has always been the center for me, so I couldn't see it being anywhere else. But I'm not fighting for a place. Pack isn't a place. It's people. Hearts. Souls." She looks around at all of us, and there's a light in her eyes that my bird is ready to follow anywhere. "If some of those hearts and souls who can't live at the den can make it to Banner Rock, then I will go pack up our kitchen and be ready to move in an hour."

I feel myself swaying.

Ben's arms are around me in an instant. And Bailey's.

I look at her in shock. "When did you get here?"

She snorts. "In time to see the ravens leaving. They congratulated me on being an aunt. They said to tell you that they'll be back, and next time they promise to be extremely boring."

My fingers reach for the beads in my hair.

Kelsey touches hers and smiles.

The buzz starts low and dizzy in my belly, and rises up my ribs, warm and wild and free. *Belonging is simple.*

Bailey shoots a look at everyone else. "Are we really doing this?"

Lissa nods slowly. "Yes. We ask so much of everyone who isn't at the den. This feels like meeting you halfway. Or some of the way, at least." She doesn't take her eyes off Bailey. Off her best friend. Guardian, alpha, and protector of the ghosts.

Bailey sighs. "I don't know, Liss. It will take time. Lots of time, and I don't know if it will ever work."

Hoot clears her throat. "I don't know, either. But it will help. It will be better." She stops, her shoulders scrunching. "Mama is less angry when we're out here. I can feel it."

"Oh, sweetie." Myrna swoops her into a fierce hug. "I didn't know you could feel Ruby like that."

Judging from Bailey's fierce, whispered curses, nobody knew.

"Well, then." Myrna looks up, and no one in the universe would dare mess with the steel in her eyes. "We move. We move and we hope and we build a bathing pool and a den with warm floors and we get ourselves ready for a baby."

Kelsey's hand touches my belly, her eyes shining.

Hoot looks at me, and the soft joy in her tear-filled eyes makes my knees wobble. "You're making us a sister."

I sniffle so that I don't drip snot on poor Kelsey's head. "I'm making a small black fuzzball who is apparently going to screech at all of us and demand food every two minutes."

They beam at me like I just promised them unicorns and magic.

I close my eyes and rest my forehead on Ben's chest. That look in their eyes is the same one I saw in his when he first set eyes on newborn Kelsey. The moment when he chose, from the depths of his own pain, to love her.

This baby, I don't know if she'll prefer the shadows or the light, and I don't know if she'll have any idea how to be a proper raven, and I don't know if she'll eventually understand the difference between a cousin and a sister or not. But she'll have all the wooden blocks in the universe, and she'll know all about sedimentary layers, and she will be so very loved.

My mate holds me close. Holds us close. Croons quiet wolf song to the tiny being in my belly who might have feathers, but she will absolutely be a wolf.

A growling sound breaks into my reverie.

I raise my head.

My pack looks around, mystified.

Rio, looking sheepish, pulls his sat phone out of his pocket and scowls. He reads his screen, chuckles quietly, and holds it out to his alpha. "You might want to take this. It's Jules."

Hayden eyes him skeptically.

Lissa turns a little green. "We should talk to her. The den is almost ready to ship and I don't know if it will work here or not." She swallows hard. "We can't afford a lot of changes."

My stomach turns over. The new den is the most shiny thing I've ever seen. I never even thought about whether this might mess it up.

Rio and Hayden exchange a look that I saw plenty of on the street. Ride or die. Hayden runs his hand down Lissa's back. "It will work."

My raven makes quiet promises to steal from polar bears again if necessary.

I manage not to strangle her. She has a baby in her belly. No more risky business.

She chortles. Fine. She'll just ask the polar bears nicely. They like babies.

Hayden taps on Rio's phone screen. "Hey, Jules. You're on speakerphone."

"Good. Myrna, you need to take away my brother's cookies for not answering his phone."

Myrna chortles. "We were busy, dear. And we're about to make your life complicated."

"Oh, joy." Jules somehow manages to sound disgruntled and amused and entirely competent, all at the same time. "Let me guess. You want everything redone in hot pink and you want to move all the interior walls three inches to the left."

Kelsey looks intrigued by hot pink. The rest of us just look worried.

Rio walks over to Hayden's shoulder. "Three words, Jules. We have geothermal."

Wild, happy squealing. "Why didn't you say that first? Where?"

Hayden rolls his eyes. "At Banner Rock. We've decided to move our den there. So we'd like to rejigger the design, if you won't kill us and it can be done within our budget."

A long pause—and then deep, rolling laughter. "Let me get this straight. You want to build a den on the side of a mountain, which is basically an entire redesign, and you want it with geothermal baked in, which is a whole new engineering project, and you'd like it before winter. Without it costing you."

My bird wants to puke. I never considered any of that.

Hayden grins at the tiny phone screen. "Yup. Is that going to work?"

Jules's sigh is long and heartfelt and rumbly like a bear's. "Yes, actually."

Rio's eyebrows fly up. "It is?"

The CEO of HomeWild chuckles ruefully. "That's why I've been trying to call you. I might have sent your old den up to the Arctic."

Dead silence as a lot of very confused wolves stare at a phone.

It's Reilly who figures it out. He pops his head into view beside Hayden and waves. "That's where Ronan is."

"Hey, my favorite bear cub. I require a long and detailed

story about what the heck is going on up there, okay? But in the meantime, yes. Ronan is in the Arctic with a pack who had an emergency. Their existing den fell through the permafrost. They ended up with a lake where forest used to be, and that was pretty hard on their buildings."

Reilly nods solemnly. "He sent me pictures."

"Pretty bad, huh?" The brisk empathy in Jules's tone makes my bird proud to know her. "So anyhow, they need a new den, and winter comes early up there, and your den was almost ready to ship. Ronan and I had a chat, and it seemed to make sense to send them your den and then ask you very nicely to wait a little longer for a replacement."

Hayden's lips are quirking. "That would be acceptable."

A snicker from his sister. "Brat."

Rio takes the phone from his alpha. "So I can design what I want from scratch and you'll put a rush on it? Because it snows here, too. And we have a pregnant mama to keep warm."

More wild, happy squealing.

Ravi clears his throat. "Two, actually."

Cori offers me a shy, awkward smile as our pack erupts in loopy jubilation that somehow includes my belly just as much as hers. Brandy hugs me tight, and Mikayla, and a serious squeeze around all of us that can only be Brown while Wrinkles gazes at me with a look in her eyes that means some really nasty teas in my future. Even Reuben smiles quietly at Ben, and I somehow know that I'm not going to need to go track him down in the forest anymore.

Sometimes, belonging is simple.

Jade climbs her daddy's leg and sticks her nose right against Cori's belly. "My have a baby?"

Wrinkles pats her head. "Yes."

Jade beams beatifically. "My have a bear baby?"

Wrinkles chuckles. "Not likely, cutie. But you can help me brush Reilly's fur to make a nice, warm baby nest."

Jade grins. "Bear baby."

The wild giggles in my bird finally leak to the surface. The new den is going to have plenty of shadows—but I so don't live in them anymore.

26

HAYDEN

Bedlam. I look over at Rio, who dragged me up to the top of this rock, which has an excellent view of the chaos below. Eliza and Brandy and Brown are rebuilding the sleeping platforms that they relocated from Fallon's camp, racing against the impending dark to get them finished.

It will be a miracle if no pups get nailed to boards.

Dorie and her crew showed up with their tents an hour ago, Lissa and Ebony are constructing a new fire pit, Kennedy and Ghost and Hoot moved the den's sleeping bags and dared me to object, and Kelsey is singing pretty songs to the hardy flowers that grow in the crevices of our new den. Kenny and Kel are trying to maintain some semblance of a secure perimeter, and Reilly is in bear form, dragging stumps and boulders around to make our new temporary living room.

Yup. Bedlam.

Rio managed to convince everyone to leave the refrigerator and stove in place until he has actual electricity flowing up here, but it was a close thing, which is probably why I'm currently standing on a rock. "Please tell me we aren't sleeping in tents all winter."

He snorts, which isn't all that reassuring. "Depends on how fast I can get the equipment up here to bore into some rocks and build at least a basic heat exchange system."

I already got a text answering that. "Ronan will be here in six weeks with the new den. In the meantime, he's sending Indrani and Scotty up with most of his toys."

Rio chuckles. "In that case, we have six weeks to build a hot pool or three, hook up some rudimentary electricity, and design a new den."

We are so fucked. "Is that all?"

He wraps an arm around my shoulders and grins. "Yes."

I sigh. My phone had more than one text. "The ravens have a hand bore and some piping they'll be driving over in the morning, unless I yell at them loudly."

"Perfect." Rio grins. "We can rig some bathtubs with that until Danielle sorts out where she's putting the pools."

We need to rig so much more than that. And keep Danielle from hyperventilating. "We need warm floors. My wolf is not going to deal if we have pregnant mamas and elders shivering as they sleep." He flatly refuses to let this new den be haunted by ghosts from the old one.

"I know." Rio bumps against my shoulder, talking as much to my wolf as to me. He points toward a flat area off to our left and just in front of a craggy playground of boulders. "I talked to Jules about sending us the school while we wait for the den. It's ready to ship and Ronan didn't steal it and she'll toss a set of pipes for in-floor heating on the trucks because she loves me. We could put it over there, hook up some makeshift hot water lines and electrical until we have the permanent systems built. It would be squishy to sleep all of us in there, but we can fit the pups and elders and pregnant mamas for sure, and we can get the greenhouse garden under way, too."

My brain exhales. "That works." It's a pretty spot with good lines of sight from almost everywhere, and the pups will love the rocks out back. Other than an endless supply of lettuce, it's practically perfect.

I look down at the milling chaos of my pack. I need to get back down there, but I have a question for my sentinel, first. Moving a den is about as big as it gets for a wolf pack. "Did we do the right thing?"

He nods slowly. "Yes."

There's no doubt in his voice. None. Which is what my wolf thought he felt when his pack emerged from the woods and looked at the mountain where they first reclaimed their power, but I was a little afraid he was just being an arrogant asshat. I exhale into the setting sun. "What's my most important job?" I'm not asking about buildings and fire pits, but Rio will know that.

He chuckles quietly. "You stood on these rocks once

and used formal, important ritual to steady your pack. You might consider doing that again."

I side-eye him. His wolf is up to something.

He grins. "I hear mating ceremonies are good for that."

I groan. It's not going to be a boring fall.

FALLON

Brandy erases one corner of her drawing and quickly makes an altered sketch in the empty space. "Like this?"

Shelley beams. "Yes. That's just right. It will catch the afternoon sun and block the wind."

I think they're working on the outdoor garden design. One of them, anyhow. At last count, I think there were going to be three. One right next to the kitchen, one full of things that don't need much watering and probably can't be destroyed by helpful pups, and one that's going to be a quiet, meditative zone.

That was Moon Girl's idea. She showed up with Ghost a couple of hours ago. People are listening to her a lot.

My raven hasn't seen her shake once.

Wrinkles taps on the drawing. "If we stretch it out this way a little, these would make some great sunning rocks for those of us with elderly bones. That way we can laze around while you young ones do the actual work."

I snort. The kitchen garden is going to be full of all

kinds of healing plants, and so is the greenhouse. I keep trying to vote for more watermelon instead, but I'm rapidly discovering that pregnant mamas get zero votes about things like that. I look over at where Cori is leaning against another rock with blankets tucked around her legs, surrounded by mugs and bowls of snacks.

I managed to escape the blankets for now, but every time I land after a reconnaissance flight, it's a close thing. Then again, Ben has reasons. I nuzzle into him. This is all so big and so fast and my comforting shadows keep dodging away when I least expect it, but at least I don't have a piece of my heart growing in someone else's belly. I'm amazed he can let go of me at all. I'm not sure I'd be able to, in his shoes.

Wrinkles says I have six months to get over that.

My bird scrunches her eyes tightly shut. Hear no evil, see no evil.

Brandy looks at me. "Hey Fallon, those rocks by the meditation garden, will they block the winds over the ridge well enough, or should we put in some taller plantings?"

I had no idea Brandy wanted to grow things, but she's been at this for hours. She's stepped away from the planning a few times, but when she does, people just smile and let her be, and a couple of the den wolves have already tried heading out to a quiet rock themselves, and come back smiling.

Brown walks over and collects the hammer innocently sitting at Ben's side. "Let me move this, so you don't accidentally decide to use it."

My mate chuckles in my ear.

My raven nuzzles him. He found some soft owl down for her nest already. He builds the important things just fine.

Dorie snorts. "That's mine, you mean old bear. Give it back. Ben was just supervising it while I found some nails."

Brown looks at the older cat like she might accidentally put one through his paw. "If you want something built, that's what Mikayla and Eliza are for."

We all blink. Brown rarely deigns to let anyone else use his tools. My raven tilts her head, curious. "What are you doing?"

His cheeks turn pink. "I'm busy, that's all." He walks away, clutching Dorie's hammer like it's his favorite new limb, and muttering curses under his breath that would probably be scary if he wasn't such a wonderful old bear.

Lissa chuckles as she looks over Brandy's shoulder at her drawing. "Kelsey recruited him for her new singing group. The one that's going to learn some pretty songs to sing in the quiet places. Also, Cori and Reuben would like lavender and chamomile if we have room to grow them. To add to the pillow stuffing. Apparently it will help people sleep."

I eye her suspiciously so that I don't turn into a puddle of mush about quiet songs, or about Cori calmly deciding that Reuben needed a job and he could darn well help her with pillows.

Wrinkles cackles. "I do like those two. We can grow both in the greenhouse. When spring comes, we'll have plenty of chamomile planned in the kitchen patch, and we can put lavender out in the frisky garden. It's sturdy, and it will make the pups smell good if they roll in it."

Ebony's lips quirk as she walks by. "Frisky garden?"

I roll my eyes. "Don't ask."

She grins. "Noted. Need anything?"

I have no idea. "Did you figure out where the first bathing pool is going?" My raven is trying hard to be reasonable. She can wait until tomorrow. Maybe.

She points over at Danielle, who's staring up at the mountain and talking to Kenny and Kennedy, her arms gesticulating wildly. "That's their job."

I contemplate moving closer so that I can hear what they're saying—and then my raven zooms in on a ledge just above Danielle's head. It's one of the three I helped add to Reilly's site map. It's the coziest one, with lots of shade, big enough for a wolf or two, protected enough to be reasonably warm and dry, and it has a great view of the den.

It's also currently occupied.

I try not to react, but I feel Ben's body snap to attention behind me.

Ebony follows my gaze and then carefully averts her eyes. "Shit. I wasn't expecting arrivals this fast. What do we do?"

"Here." Myrna drops an armful of goods beside me. "A warm blanket for under his hip or over his bony shoulders if he wants to shift for a while, a flask of tea with a little of Brown's whiskey in it, and some peanut butter cookies."

I stare at her. "How long have you known he's up there?"

She snorts. "I've known Cleve since the day he was born. That ledge might be out of sight, but the path to get to it blows a nice little breeze straight down to our new fire pit."

Ben huffs out a quiet, shaky laugh. "He used to sit and drink whiskey with Brown. You remember."

"Of course I do." Myrna tries for brisk, but her voice quavers.

Ebony wraps a steadying arm around her shoulder.

A sniffle. "You tell him that. When you take him his blanket and his whiskey and his cookies, you tell him that I haven't forgotten his sorry ass. And that this baby needs a grandfather, so he'd better come back tomorrow afternoon when there will be stew, and tea for ailing hips."

Ben winces. "I think maybe Fallon should make the delivery."

I try to do the complicated math of shadows and scars and a baby coming in six months and give up barely after I start. Instead, I rub my cheek against his and go with my suddenly crowded gut. "I'll deliver this load and let him smell my belly like all the rest of you crazy wolves. And I'll tell him to expect you with the stew tomorrow."

He lays a careful hand over my belly. Sharing his love. Leaving his scent.

"Good." The woman who brought the cookies nods, her movements stiff and jerky.

Ebony cuddles Myrna in tighter. "New den rule. Everyone talks about how they're feeling, remember?"

I scowl. I wasn't around when that rule got made.

Myrna's smile trembles, but her eyes are full of gladness. "I've lived in our old den my whole life, so I thought this move would be hard. I was over there helping lay rocks for the new fire pit and struggling not to feel sorry for myself, and then I caught the scent of a very old friend. Turns out, it's not going to be hard at all."

That's not true. It will absolutely still be hard some days. But sometimes we add embellishments to a story to make them more true.

Myrna reaches out and pats my shoulder. "He came because you made it possible. He'll stay for that sweet baby you're growing, but he's here because you told us what we needed to do. I won't forget."

My raven flaps her wings. Too many feelings.

Ebony flashes me a sympathetic look. Then she snorts. "This is all a part of Fallon's big, evil plan to make sure she has enough willing hands for when that baby turns into a howling menace in the middle of the night."

Myrna chortles. "Raven babies don't howl. Martha says they turn into black balls of fuzz and hide. Wolf noses are going to be very useful, I think."

I groan. I'm beginning to think that stealing from polar bears was the easy part. I disentangle myself from Ben's arms and start collecting the bundle of things to fly up to Grandpa Cleve. Where I might add a few more words than I originally planned.

Six months.

I need all the wolf noses I can get.

KEL

I watch the old gray wolf slide a little deeper into the shadows and shake my head. Fallon is a fucking genius. The kind of genius that only gets earned the hard way, but she's somehow figuring out how to speak it in ways that people who haven't walked in her shoes can understand.

With a little help. I only caught a single glimpse of the polished orange stone in her fist, but that was enough. I was off in some hellhole when Hayden's father laid it on the palm of his young son, but Rio was there. On the days when teenage Hayden got far too quiet and his grief threatened to pierce him, Rio would go and find that damn rock.

That another hand now holds it speaks silent, thunderous volumes.

James Scott, a submissive wolf legend, even as a ghost. One who understood what I didn't. I spoke to Fallon of movement, of inches—her own, and the ones she could help others make. Which is truth, even if some of those inches can feel more like a fucking mile. The part I had wrong is who needed to do the moving.

We didn't need her to lead wounded, wary wolves out of the shadows. We needed her to lead the wolves of the den into them. To ask us to think, from very first principles, on what a den would look like if shadows were foundational.

I can see the impact already. Feel it. In Brandy, in Ravi, in Kenny, in me. In the faint smile on Rio's face every time his paws listen to the earth. In the thoughtful looks and quiet ideas coming from wolves who are looking at ledges and figuring out where to place tents and play areas and quiet spaces, and working through how to be a pack that makes room right at its core for the shadow dwellers.

I am one, and still, I missed it. I come from a pack with hundreds of shifters who live in the light. They had enough gravitational force to bring even Adrianna out of the dark after James died. But this pack isn't like Whistler. We have a lot more wolves who live in the shadows. Which means our balance needs to be different. Something I couldn't see until a raven held a fire-orange rock in her fist and spoke five bell-clear words.

We didn't need Fallon to come out of the shadows.

We needed her to speak for their inclusion.

IVAN

I pick up the small wooden box, simple in design and flawless in its craftsmanship. What lies inside is not Phil's creation, however. It is treasure made by his daughter Reina, human in her body, bear in her heart, and the finest worker of metal castings I have ever known.

She is likely still scowling at me over this commission.

My bear finds much to appreciate in the fine line

work, in the bold detail, in the prescient use of sheen and shadow that will only grow more majestic as the coin ages. It is not treasure for the likes of my bear. It is too new, too lacking in history for his Russian soul. And it is not for a raven who still works to find pride in her own tarnished places, the ones she acquired in service and in valor.

But it is a fine gift for a baby, I think.

I spare a glance for my computer screen, where young Reilly has shared with the world what my bear smelled on a dusty street in a human town some days ago. The raven with the warrior heart has new life in her belly.

I touch my finger to the fierce eyes Reina engraved on the front of the coin. They are surrounded by feathers, by a hint of beak. Just enough to see the spirit of the raven. But it is the eyes my bear remembers—the ones that met his on that dusty street.

Tonight, my bears will gather to toast the thief of Ghost Mountain. The coin will join us at the table, and begin its journey by listening to rousing tales of the fierce warrior who stole to feed her pack. We will speak of her bravery and cool daring, of her steadfast wings and loyal heart, of choices made without apology.

I will lift a glass and speak Reilly's contribution as well. The story inside the story on my computer, of the quiet wolf who caught the raven thief when she tumbled from the sky, who saw her tarnished soul and did not try to polish her.

I turn the coin over. I could find only a single photo

of Benjamin Dunn, but it was enough. Reina is still cursing my eternal soul, but she rendered truly. Kindness is not something bears truly understand, but looking at the eyes on this side of the coin, I believe that is perhaps to our detriment.

I nestle the coin back in its box and set it down on my table next to a pressed flower. I remember the day a small girl with a heart as old as the rocks of this land laid it in my hand.

She is kin to the raven baby who comes.

I touch a finger very gently to the flower's dry petals. Their likeness graces the edges of the new coin, a detail that Reina believes only an obsessed, deranged, unreasonable bear will notice.

She has an alarming fondness for insulting bears who could eat her in a single chomp. Much like a certain raven I know.

I set the lid on the box. I will deliver it soon. Once the snows come and the weather is more palatable. May its future be glorious.

Next up: The next few months need to be sensible and practical and steady. So says Shelley Martins, anyhow. Her wolf maybe has different ideas. Get Breath, book five in the Ghost Mountain Wolf Shifters series!

Made in the USA
Monee, IL
26 November 2023

47437284R00194